MURDER ON THE CANTERBURY PILGRIMAGE

A Geoffrey Chaucer Murder Mystery

Mary Devlin

Writers Club Press
San Jose New York Lincoln Shanghai

Murder on the Canterbury Pilgrimage
A Geoffrey Chaucer Murder Mystery

All Rights Reserved © 2000 by Mary Devlin

No part of this book may be reproduced or transmitted in any form or by any means, graphic, electronic, or mechanical, including photocopying, recording, taping, or by any information storage or retrieval system, without the permission in writing from the publisher.

Published by Writers Club Press
an imprint of iUniverse.com, Inc.

For information address:
iUniverse.com, Inc.
620 North 48th Street
Suite 201
Lincoln, NE 68504-3467
www.iuniverse.com

ISBN: 0-595-09878-9

Printed in the United States of America

In Memory of Shaun, Edward and Charlie

I loved you then and I love you now.

Prologue

Would it be wise to try to save the knife?

Shivering in the chill of a spring night, the cloaked figure glanced uneasily up at the full moon, then at the prone body beside him. The silver-handled Italian stiletto that protruded from the dead man's back had cost the assassin a small fortune, and he was unwilling to let it go.

He sighed. Why did he use it, anyway? Cheap daggers were readily available from any blacksmith in any village, and the purchase of one would have been all too easy. Well, it was too late to think of that now.

Tentatively the killer reached down and grasped the handle of the knife. God's bones, it was stuck tight in the man's body! To pull it out would undoubtedly release a gush of blood which would spatter all over the surrounding bushes, making it more obvious to any passerby that all was not as it should be.

There was no help for it. He would have to abandon the knife. He grasped his victim's ankles and dragged him into the brush, stopping momentarily to catch his breath. The spot was dangerously close to the road to Kent, but with a little luck anyone on his way from London to Kent would be too caught up in his own affairs to notice the few broken branches resulting from the concealment of the corpse. A man on horseback wouldn't notice it at all. A man on foot probably wouldn't—at least not until the body began to smell, and by that time the murderer would be safe in Canterbury.

He must report to the Archbishop: the messenger was dead. Their enemy would never know of their nefarious plans.

Carefully the killer pulled the branches of a nearby bush into such a position as to mask the presence of the dead man from anyone who might come that way. Then he recalled his error.

The Master's instructions had been very explicit: Let anyone who finds the body know what we think of heretics!

The murderer fumbled through his pockets until he found what he was looking for. He moved away from the trees so as to have better access to the moonlight and rifled through his pack of cards. *Ah! There's a good one. The Goddess Fortuna, blindfolded, turning the Wheel of Fortune, so that one man was on his way up, one at the pinnacle, and one crashing onto the ground.*

Pushing the branches aside, he dropped the card onto the body. It landed on the wound and stuck onto a puddle of blood. Good! It would not blow away.

He must reach Canterbury soon, but traveling alone, after leaving a dead body in his wake, was too dangerous. The Master had cautioned him that it would be best to travel to Canterbury from London, in the company of a large band of pilgrims. Frustration passed through his mind as he realized that such a band would probably pass close by here, and that returning to London to join one would only add a good fifty useless miles to his journey.

Nonetheless, caution was of the essence. Replacing the pack of cards in his pocket, the murderer turned his long nose toward London and literally ran down the road.

Perhaps returning to London was the wisest course, inconvenient though it might be. It would be wise to put as many miles as possible between him and his victim. The Master would not be pleased if anyone vaguely connected with him was implicated in murder.

He had to find his way to Canterbury as quickly as he possibly could.

One

Agatha Willard scrutinized her horse's bridle carefully as she removed it from the animal's head.

"There, there, Falala," she whispered, soothing the nervous gelding. He never seemed to function well in strange stables—even with Robert's placid, companionable gray mare in the stall next to him.

One of the silver studs from the side of the bridle was missing."Damn!" Agatha swore, then quickly crossed herself to ward off the Devil.

I'll flay Roger Grimsby alive, that I will. It's his carelessness that caused this to fall off.

But in her heart Agatha knew she wasn't being fair. Roger Grimsby, who ran a livery stable near Agatha's tavern at Aldgate, was something of a buffoon—everyone laughed at and made fun of him—but the boy loved horses and was meticulous in every way in his care of them and their trappings.

She sighed. The bridle was old, after all. She would simply to have another one made.

Agatha hung the bridle on a nearby nail, patted Falala one more time, then stepped from the stable out into the sun. It was a lovely April day, too pretty to still be stuck in Southwark. The sky was clear and bright, the air crisp and fragrant, and the people passing the Tabard Inn seemed to be in good spirits. Agatha and her husband, Robert, a retired Oxford mathematician, were taking time off from running Agatha's tavern, The Herb and Flower near the Aldgate. They had left it in the capable hands of Agatha's younger sister, and embarking on a pilgrimage to Canterbury, to the shrine of St. Thomas à Becket. They had arranged to accompany a group planning to leave the next day from the Tabard Inn in Southwark, the London area just south of the Thames. As far as Agatha knew, she and Robert, perhaps because they lived so close, were the first of the pilgrims to arrive.

She passed a broken fragment of mirror that a stableboy had propped up to use for shaving. Almost automatically she glanced at her reflection, then smiled complacently. Not bad for a great-grandmother! She was fifty-two, and had become a wife for the first time at fourteen, a mother at fifteen and a grandmother at thirty-two. Now her first great-grandchild was two years old. And she was still beautiful; her customers at the tavern still propositioned her. True, there were a few crow's feet around her eyes, and the furrows from nose to mouth grew deeper every year, but her sky-blue eyes were still bright, her skin still good and relatively unlined, her muscles still taut from hard work, and in spite of having borne six children her waist had thickened only slightly since she was a girl. Her hair had always been very pale, so the increasing number of silver strands that were creeping in among the gold only caused her lush tresses to look that much fairer.

"Isn't that cloak rather warm for this weather?" asked a voice behind her.

Agatha started. She turned from contemplation of her own reflection and found herself looking into the face of Harry Bailey, the owner of the Tabard, who would be accompanying the Canterbury pilgrims on their journey. He was tall, large-boned, muscular from years of lifting and hauling, bearded, with dark hair turning gray, nearing fifty but still handsome.

"I suppose it is," said Agatha, shrugging the offending garment from her shoulders and draping it over her arm. "It was cool this morning, though, when Robert and I crossed the river. Don't you feel uncomfortable, leaving the Tabard like this?"

"No. Do you feel that way about your place?"

"My sister is very competent."

"So is my son. I must confess, as much as I love London, I appreciate it more if I leave it once in awhile. We've had a rough winter, and now that spring is here I feel the need to get out into the country, away from the city and its filth, and all the dreadful smells."

"So you're going to Canterbury." Agatha walked with Bailey to the front door of the tavern, where a splendidly dressed knight and his squire were dismounting.

"Canterbury's as good a place as any," said Bailey, opening the door and allowing Agatha to enter. "Besides, I've never seen the shrine of St. Thomas."

In the main room of the tavern several guildsmen were sitting at the largest table in the room, drinking ale and laughing raucously. Their voices, combined with those of others enjoying the drink and the company, merged together into a loud but nonetheless soothing roar. The room was dark; it took a moment for Agatha's eyes to adjust. Her sensitive nose was immediately assaulted by the combined smells of ale, sweat, and smoke from the fire. A group of *religieux*—two nuns, three priests, a monk, and a country parson—sat uncomfortably in front of the hearth, clearly unsettled by the worldly and somewhat bawdy conversation that was going on at the table behind them. The elder of the two nuns, clearly someone of importance, sat straight in her chair, prim and dignified, holding one small black and brown hound in her lap and caressing the ears of two others.

The younger nun spotted Harry Bailey and hurried over to him. "Excuse me," she ventured. "but are you the landlord?"

"I am that, sister, and proud to be so," Bailey replied. He looked her over appreciatively. She was young, certainly not much more than twenty, very pretty, with wide blue eyes, a perfect nose, and creamy fair skin. Her hair was hidden beneath wimple and veil, but Harry would have taken a bet that it was golden in color. There was nothing of the sensual about her, however; her eyes projected that clear spirituality and dedication which marks one with a true calling to the religious life. Her companion, Harry Bailey could see through the corner of his eye, was much older—certainly well past sixty.

"I am Sister Cecily, one of the Canterbury pilgrims," the young nun continued. "My prioress, Dame Eglantine, asked that I speak with you. We've already got a bit of a problem," she added apologetically.

"God's bones! What kind of problem?"

"One of Dame Eglantine's stirrups, sir—it's missing."

"One stirrup? Surely it simply dropped off!"

"It was solid silver."

Agatha's head jerked around and she stared into the young nun's face. "When did Dame Eglantine last see it?" she demanded.

The pretty nun gazed at her curiously, as though wondering who this assertive woman was. "When we turned our horses over to the stable-boy," Sister Cecily replied politely. "One of our priests just went into the barn to check on the horses. He noticed that the stirrup was gone."

Agatha's eyes opened wide as she recalled her own missing silver stud. "Sister Cecily, would you please excuse us?" she asked. Without waiting for an answer, she took Bailey's arm and steered him into the small room behind the bar. She then told him about her loss.

Bailey clearly wasn't pleased to hear this. "Are you saying that one of my stablehands is a thief?" he demanded. "They've all been with me for years! I would trust them with my life."

"Yes, but how well do you know all their friends and relatives? I cannot be sure my stud was stolen, nor Dame Eglantine's stirrup, but it seems very strange that two items of tack made from solid silver both disappear on the same—"

Suddenly the sound of loud voices poured in from the taproom. "But father, she is a heavenly, beautiful creature! You always said—"

"Dammit, boy, she's a gypsy!"

"I'm not a boy anymore, I'm a man! At least I'm a man when you want me to polish your weapons and see to your horses and put away your armour, but when it comes to running my own life—"

Bailey, followed by Agatha, hurried into the taproom.

"Silence!" Bailey thundered.

The knight and the squire turned towards Agatha and Bailey, breaking off their argument abruptly at the sound of the landlord's voice. *They must have entered after we left the room,* Agatha realized. A wanton in her youth, Agatha still had an eye for a handsome man, and both of this particular pair were quite appealing. The knight, who appeared to be in his early forties, was tall and strong, with the ropy kind of muscles that come from years of practice with wielding weapons. His hair and mustache were like burnished gold; his eyes a piercing cobalt.

The squire was as tall as the knight was, though much slimmer, with paler eyes and hair, and features that stopped just short of being pretty. What saved him from too girlish an appearance was a slight arch to the bridge of his nose. His hair reached his collar, waving and curling, meticulously cared for—as were his clothes. Agatha estimated his age to be around twenty. She noticed with some amusement that Sister Cecily's eyes lit up with appreciation at the sight of him. Vowed to chastity the girl might be, Agatha reflected, but underneath veil and wimple she was still a woman!

The knight frowned disapprovingly, as if wondering who this upstart innkeeper was to think he had the right to raise his voice to one of a superior social standing.

"You're upsetting the sisters," Bailey said more reasonably.

The knight turned red as he caught sight of the two nuns, still huddling near the fire, both clearly ill at ease. He hurried over and bowed gallantly to both of them. "My apologies, dear ladies," he said courteously. "Sir Richard de Burgoyne, at your service. This is my son Simon. I apologize for quarreling in your blessed presence, but it seems that Simon has developed an infatuation for a pagan gypsy—"

"She is no pagan!" Simon cried. "She is a devout Christian! Is she not accompanying us to Canterbury?"

The two nuns exchanged a shocked glance. "A gypsy? Coming with us?" said Dame Eglantine, somewhat affronted.

The parson, who had hitherto been silent, suddenly stood. "My esteemed sisters, if you will recall the words of St. Paul, 'In Christ there is no Jew nor gentile, master nor slave, male nor female.' Surely Our Lord will not deny a gypsy access to the blessing of one of his saints? Rather, like the prodigal son, he would welcome her into our fold."

The nuns visibly relaxed, as though the parson's words had reassured them. But Sir Richard de Burgoyne plainly did not share their feelings.

"Simon," he said sternly, "if you would be a knight, then you should behave like one." With that, the knight turned abruptly to Harry Bailey. "Show me to my room!" he demanded imperiously.

Bailey returned his demand with a sweeping bow that stopped just short of mocking. "Yes, my lord!" He stood aside, politely showed the way to the stairs, then followed as Sir Richard climbed out of sight.

Simon, apparently overcome by anguish, glanced around the room, then, seeing no sympathetic face among his companions, dashed through the door and away from the inn.

Agatha hurried over to the window and watched as the squire strode toward the stables. She caught her breath. By the stable door, a fat, rather grimy friar was laughing merrily with a beautiful, highly sensuous young woman. Her hair, eyes and skin were all dark, her figure lush and shapely, her boots of fine leather, her clothes a colorful polyglot of smock, shawl, sash and jewelry.

This, then, must be the beautiful gypsy with whom Simon is so smitten, Agatha reflected as the poor boy stopped to talk with the distinctive duo.

The girl's eyes lit up when Simon spoke to her; if Agatha had believed in such things, she would have sworn the girl directed psychic arrows of desire towards the poor boy. The friar, unaware of such energy, merely looked annoyed and somewhat jealous.

Agatha's attention was then distracted by the arrival of three more apparent Canterbury pilgrims. Her curious eyes swept over them, thoughtfully appraising each one. A miller—huge, bearlike, muscular, with cropped hair and an extremely ugly face. A reeve—skinny, sallow, with the corners of his mouth permanently turned down. A pardoner, smooth-faced and beardless—equally unattractive, with thin, dirty yellow hair hanging down his back and a long pointed nose. Each of them obviously distrusted his companions and, though arriving together, still managed to keep their distance from each other.

They dismounted, casting furtive looks on everyone nearby, each clearly seeking to keep his moneybag hidden from any of the others. A groom took the reins of their three horses and led the animals away to the stables.

"Cover your belt buckle!" a voice hissed behind Agatha.

Curiously she turned. It was one of the guildsmen—the haberdasher, she believed. He was whispering conspiratorially—yet still loud enough to be overheard—to his fellow tradesmen.

"Don't let anyone see it!" the haberdasher continued. "It's silver, isn't it? Well, I had a silver pin on my cloak—an award from my guild, you see—and I had the cloak draped over the back of my saddle, and now the pin is gone!"

Suddenly a thrill of excitement passed through Agatha. Perhaps this journey to Canterbury would prove more entertaining than she had even imagined.

"So what do you think of Harry's idea?" asked Robert Willard.

It was later on that evening, after supper. The entire party of Canterbury pilgrims had finally arrived, and they were all gathered in the main taproom, relaxing after a hearty meal of thick soup, meat pasties, bread, and cheese, enjoying the warmth. Robert and Agatha shared a table by the fire with William Richemont, a physician from Yorkshire, and Alisoun, a widow from Bath about Agatha's age, still sensual and attractive, but with a coarseness Agatha thankfully lacked. Alisoun, in spite of her age still brimming with lust, was trying to catch Richemont's eye while at the same time casting jealous glances at Sophia, the gypsy, who was sitting on the hearth between the adoring

Simon and the jovial friar, drawing the surreptitious attention of nearly every man in the room.

But Richemont paid no attention to Alisoun's flirtations, nor did he appear to notice Sophia except to remark that she had a fine set of teeth. He seemed to have eyes only for the sick; his sole contribution to their conversation had been the possible ailments suffered by their companions on the pilgrimage. Agatha noted that he appeared less concerned for their suffering than for the intellectual problems their illnesses posed for his own brilliant and logical mind.

Agatha herself was skilled enough in the healing arts to surmise that many of their fellow travelers probably nourished secret hopes that St. Thomas would cure whatever was afflicting them. Alisoun was a bit deaf, the miller had a dreadful wart on his nose, the reeve appeared choleric, a summoner who had joined them right before supper had boils, pimples and other disfiguring skin problems. The gallant knight, Sir Richard, and Dame Eglantine both moved stiffly, somewhat stooped, as though age and years of endless activity had brought them near-crippling back pain. Even the lovely Sophia, Agatha's quick eyes had noticed, tended to limp when she tried to move quickly. What had happened to her?

Agatha's thoughts inevitably turned to Robert's rheumatism. It had never been severe, but Robert was nearly sixty now, and when the weather turned damp—as it often did in London—his joints pained him dreadfully. Was there really something to the claims she had heard of miracles occurring at the shrine of St. Thomas à Becket? And if there were, would the blessed martyr take pity on her husband?

The guildsmen were arguing again, Agatha noticed. The haberdasher was still lamenting the loss of his silver brooch, and the dyer and the weaver were accusing him of being too jumpy. Yet there were uneasy tones in their voices despite the apparent bravado of their words. *And well should those puffed-up clowns be uneasy,* Agatha told herself tartly. *There is someone among us who has a knack for stealing silver—and their daggers all, without exception, are decked with hilts made of nothing less than solid silver!*

"Agatha!"

Agatha jerked her head around. What had Robert been saying? She had been too lost in her own thoughts and observations to pay any attention.

"I'm sorry, Robert," she said guiltily. "I didn't hear you. What were you saying?"

"I asked, what do you think of Harry's idea?"

In an attempt to settle a quarrel between the miller and the friar, each of whom had a story he was dying to tell, Harry Bailey had proposed that in the course of the journey every pilgrim would be allowed to tell a story. Each would tell two tales on the way to Canterbury and two on the way back. Bailey also proposed that in order to avoid quarrels and other problems on the journey, he should be governor of the group. Everyone had agreed. Since Harry had made the proposal, however, the miller had fallen asleep, and the friar had become too caught up in Sophia to worry about his story, and so no tales would be told that night.

"I think it's a fine idea," said Agatha. "Do you have a story that you might want to tell?"

"My darling, I am nearly sixty years old. Do you think that one could live for nigh on sixty years and never hear a good tale? I have several! And what about you?"

"I've had five husbands," said Agatha shortly. "That should say it all."

Suddenly a scuffle broke out near the bar. The guildsmen's cook, a mountain of a man named Roger, was raising his hand as though threatening the thin, sharp-faced young man who stood before him. A small hound, clearly frightened, cowered between the two men. Agatha recognized the hound; it was one of the ones that the prioress had brought with her. Although the prioress and her entourage had long since retired to their rooms, the dog apparently had managed to sneak back down to the warmth of the main tavern.

The thin young man, a pleasant-looking clerk from Oxford whom Robert and Agatha had met earlier, stood calmly, unabashed by the cook's size or his threatening gesture. He trembled—but more from anger than from fear, Agatha surmised. "How dare you!" the youth cried. "Striking a poor dumb animal like that! You should be ashamed!"

"If the bastard gets underfoot, then he should expect to be struck!" Roger the cook hissed. "Get him out of here, or I'll—I'll roast him, I swear it!"

"Over my dead body!" shouted the clerk.

"Perhaps I can manage that," said the cook, advancing menacingly.

"What's this?" demanded an angry voice.

All eyes in the room turned to Harry Bailey, who had stepped between the two men.

The clerk was the first to speak. "This poor little dog belongs to Dame Eglantine," he said. "She is an abbess, no less, but this man here took a stick and hit the poor thing. And now see how scared the creature is!"

Harry bent down and picked the dog up in his arms, then swept the room with his eyes. "John!" he shouted. From the back room came a young man of twenty-five, a younger mirror of Harry, clearly his son. Harry handed the dog to John. "Take this animal upstairs and return him to Madame Eglantine!" John nodded, plucked the hound from his father's hands, then disappeared up the stairs. Harry then turned to the cook. "You! I'll have no violence of any kind in my tavern, including beating dogs! You're drunk, and so I'll serve you no more ale tonight! An early start tomorrow, remember? Get upstairs and sleep it off!" The cook, visibly shrinking before Bailey's angry gaze like a child before a father, trembled, but seemed frozen and unable to move.

The physician then stepped forward. "Perhaps I should come upstairs with you," he said. "I could give you something to calm you down, and perhaps put a poultice on that running sore of yours. I am sure it is painful and itchy. Would you like that?" He bent down and touched the sore roughly with a pointed finger, causing the cook to wince in pain.

The cook then pivoted on his heel and headed toward the stairs, with the physician following.

Why would he poke at an injury like that, Agatha wondered. *Does he feel nothing for his patients?*

Bailey then turned to the clerk. "What's your name, lad?"

"Walter."

"Well, Walter, I certainly admire your championing of the weak. But if I were you I'd temper my ideals with a touch of caution. A man like that could turn literally turn you into mincemeat!"

A loud raucous laugh filled the room at Harry's little joke. Walter's thin face turned bright crimson. He returned to his chair, burning with embarrassment.

Robert chuckled. "How well he reminds me of my days at Oxford. The place is literally full of Walters!"

"I'm sure you weren't all that different from him yourself," Agatha responded affectionately. She turned and leaned on her elbow, facing Robert. "Do you know who would really enjoy being here? Telling stories—observing this motley collection of human creatures? Geoffrey!"

Robert frowned. "Geoffrey is a busy man, Agatha. His time is valuable. He has much work to do in King Richard's customs office."

"But he has a number of lieutenants he could rely on to keep his business going," Agatha persisted. "And Philippa is visiting Katherine again. What better time for Geoffrey to get away and travel for a while? He used to travel often in his youth, Robert. He hasn't traveled far from the Aldgate for quite some time. I am sure he must be longing for parts unknown."

"I'm sure he's been to Canterbury," said Robert. "But never mind. Very well, I would enjoy Geoffrey's company on this journey. He would make a boon companion. And since you say he'd want to come I will take your word for it, and send a message to the Aldgate asking him to join us. But don't be surprised if he says no!"

"That would be his choice," said Agatha. She leaned back and closed her eyes, taking in the sounds and smells of the tavern. It wasn't like hers; hers was larger, brighter, merrier.

But she had an uncomfortable feeling that this group of pilgrims were not ordinary ones—that they were high-strung, volatile people, each suffering from anguishes all his own—and that before the pilgrimage was over, she would have received a thorough education in the darker side of human nature.

Two

Geoffrey Chaucer blinked his eyes frantically in an effort to stay awake. Beneath him, his horse Remile moved swiftly but confidently, as though he were familiar with the pressure of every part of his master's body and knew just what to do to keep his master comfortable and secure in his seat.

Chaucer gazed out into the east; the first faint rays of sunlight were appearing over the waters of the Thames, and if he didn't hurry, the pilgrims would leave him behind. The night before, when he had received Robert's elegantly-crafted missive inviting him to join them, he had felt a rush both of excitement and of foreboding, as though the proposed journey would provide adventure the likes of which Geoffrey, as Agatha had so astutely observed, hadn't known for years.

Chaucer's wife Philippa was away, visiting her sister Katherine. Katherine was the beautiful mistress of Chaucer's own dear friend John of Gaunt, a brilliant though ruthlessly ambitious man of Chaucer's own age. Gaunt, third son of the late King Edward III, was now serving as Regent to the young king, Richard II, and striving to make himself King of Castile. But Gaunt's ambitions had in recent years interfered with his relationship with Katherine, and thus the Lady Katherine was restless and unhappy. So Philippa, ever the devoted sister, spent a great deal of time away from home, minding Katherine as a nurse minds a child. Geoffrey loved Phillipa and was proud of her, but her tendency to run whenever Katherine beckoned rankled him somewhat.

Chaucer had met Philippa when she was in the service of her namesake, Queen Philippa of Hainault, the now-dead wife of the late King Edward III. Chaucer himself had been an up-and-coming young soldier, fluent in several languages, who later served King Edward as ambassador to France and later to Italy. There had been times when he had also served as a spy, executing his duties commendably, but in the process learning much about his fellow human beings that he would rather not have known. Now, under King Edward's grandson, Richard II, Geoffrey, a skilled accountant, was serving the young king as Controller of the King's Petty Custom.

Both the king and Chaucer knew, however, that the purpose of that position was less to use Geoffrey's accounting abilities than to provide him with an income so that he could indulge his penchant for writing poetry, composing music, and reading astrological charts. Even at so young an age, King Richard was a devout worshipper of the arts, both creative and occult. The latter was an interest Chaucer shared with only a few—in fact, Robert Willard and the King himself were the only ones still living with whom Chaucer felt comfortable discussing such matters.

Chaucer sighed as his mind was suddenly engulfed in painful memories of the late King Edward's second son, Prince Lionel, whom Chaucer had dearly loved and who had also toyed with astrology. Lionel, a powerful man, whose six feet, seven inches of height had made him exactly one foot taller than Chaucer himself, full of life and the picture of health, had died suddenly and unexpectedly from some strange fever when he was only twenty-nine years old. That had been fifteen years ago, and Chaucer still wasn't quite used to the loss.

Nine years later, another whom Chaucer had loved, respected and admired had died: Guillaume de Machaut, perhaps the greatest French composer of his time, from whom Chaucer had learned much about the arts of both poetry and music. Guillaume, though a churchman, had secretly been an impassioned *aficianado* of alchemy, astrology and other forbidden realms of knowledge, and he and young Geoffrey had spent many fascinating hours together discussing and experimenting with them. Though, unlike Lionel, Guillaume had lived to the ripe old age of seventy-seven, Chaucer felt nonetheless that it was a pity that such talent and genius could not remain in the world forever. Oh, Guillaume had had his faults. He had a monstrous ego, well aware of his brilliance and not above constantly reminding others of his superiority. He had had an explosive temper as well, and was impatient with ignorant young students such as Chaucer had been. Yet he was kind and sensitive as well, and Chaucer had been in awe of him—perhaps too much so. And now he too was gone.

The rattle of a wagon loaded with kegs of ale driving past him startled Chaucer back to the present. His horse had already crossed London Bridge to Southwark. Chaucer shook his head in amazement. Horses were incredible; it was as if the creature had known instinctively what direction to take, without any guidance at all from his rider.

But Remile's abilities seemed to falter at being able to sense how to find the Tabard Inn. He passed the correct turn, and Chaucer was forced to jerk at the reins and steer the handsome roan gelding down the street that led to the Tabard. The street was like most other London streets of the time: filthy, noisy, crowded with people in dress of all modes, yet intriguing, lined with street vendors hawking their wares, some of which, like flowers and ribbons, added a welcome touch of color to the gray and brown of the stones that made up the buildings and streets. Others, mainly the fresh pies and pastries, put forth enticing aromas that for a moment at least blotted out the stench of the gutters. The cries of the vendors—called out in a singsong almost like plainchant—sometimes clashed, sometimes harmonized with the songs of a group of minstrels—a recorder player, a lutenist, a fiddle player and a tired-looking young girl singer who also played the tambourine—that stood on the corner and performed merry *estampies* and plaintive songs of the people.

London was a wonderful place. But Agatha had been right. It was time for Chaucer to leave the city for awhile—to explore the countryside and its inhabitants, to widen his horizons and give him more material for his ever-increasing volumes of poetry.

Chaucer reached into his right pocket and drew out the astrological chart he had drawn up for the pilgrimage as soon as he had received Robert's letter. Strange goings-on indeed there would be on this journey! The Sun and Mercury conjunct Mars and Jupiter in Aries, all squaring Saturn in Cancer! Nefarious doings, plottings—more than simply the plotting of stories! The Moon in Gemini—a good time for initiating the telling of tales, but also a period when people tended to talk out of both sides of their mouths, a time when lies flowed as readily as the truth. Anyone with any sense would stay away from a journey beginning with such aspects. But Geoffrey Chaucer had never been known for having any sense. When common sense battled with curiosity, curiosity almost always won. It had this time.

The Tabard Inn was easily visible from the corner where Chaucer had turned. Ah! He wasn't too late after all! The front yard was crammed with travelers, some sitting astride their horses and waiting patiently while the others continued to tie up their saddlebags and load their packhorses. Robert Willard's russet hood and Agatha's blue kerchief—she always wore a kerchief in some shade of blue so as to set off the arresting sky-blue of her eyes—were easily visible; both, as usual, had been up well before dawn and had undoubtedly been ready when many of their fellow pilgrims were still snoring.

Chaucer kicked Remile gently; the gelding obligingly picked up his pace. He must have caught the scent of Agatha's Falala—they shared adjacent stalls at Roger Grimsby's livery stable—for it was only a moment before Chaucer found himself being greeted enthusiastically by his friends.

"Robert didn't really think you'd come!" said Agatha, reaching across and squeezing Chaucer's hand.

"I only thought you'd be concerned about your job!" Robert protested.

"Robert, you know King Richard has structured that job so that I can take time off almost whenever I want," Geoffrey chided. "I have an army of capable lieutenants who will enjoy the opportunity to prove themselves!"

A merry laugh caught Chaucer's ear; instinctively he turned his head in the direction of the sound. It was Sophia the gypsy, flirting outrageously with Robyn the miller. But the girl was so beautiful! Why was she bothering with an ugly, redheaded lump of a man with a wart on his nose?

"That young woman does that with every man who isn't maimed or dead," said Robert, sensing the question in Geoffrey's mind. "She's even cast her eyes on the priests, and on an old relic like me. She'd best watch herself and be a bit more careful. Robyn the miller's not a bad sort, in spite of the fact that he resembles a gargoyle, but one of these days little Sophia is going to cross the wrong man."

Robyn, a lusty man already in his cups, guffawed loudly at something Sophia had said, then reached out, grabbed her arm and pulled her towards him, making motions as if trying to kiss her. Angrily the girl pulled back, raised her hand and slapped him hard across the face, then strode away, highly indignant.

Robert shook his head. "The girl has much to learn of the ways of the world," he remarked.

"Master Chaucer?" came a voice behind them. "Master Geoffrey Chaucer?"

"Yes."

Chaucer found himself looking into the adoring grey eyes of a very thin young man, dressed in shabby clothes and sporting a thick shock of pale brown hair that had obviously been cut with a dagger.

"Mistress Willard told me you were coming," he said breathlessly. "I'm Walter Locksley. I'm a clerk, from Oxford. I read your poems—*Parlement of Fowles* and *The Book of the Duchess*. I think they're wonderful!"

Chaucer smiled congenially. "Thank you. It's always good to know one's work is appreciated. Are you a poet?"

"Well," said Walter modestly, "I have been known to try my hand. But I'll never have any hope of surpassing you!"

"And I wouldn't want to, if I were you," said Chaucer."You need strive only to surpass yourself. Comparing poets is like comparing red to blue."

"I—I didn't bring any samples of my work with me." Walter spoke regretfully, but inwardly Chaucer breathed a sigh of relief."If I'd known you were going to be here, I'd have brought some. I'd like to know if—if you think I'll ever be any good."

Chaucer leaned down from his horse and slapped the boy on the shoulders."Never mind, my dear Locksley. I understand from Master Willard here that our host, Harry, has decreed that each of us will tell two tales. I shall simply listen to your tales and let you know what I think of them. How does that sound?"

"Thank you, Master Chaucer!" His gratitude was so overwhelming as to be embarrassing. Chaucer hoped no one was watching."Thank you!"

"You're very welcome," said Chaucer. He turned pointedly to Robert."Who's that hideous creature there with all the boils?"

"A summoner, I believe," said Robert. Chaucer watched out of the corner of his eye as Walter slinked away into the crowd."His name's Jack. My impression is that he is as evil and corrupt as anyone in that profession. The church is fairly well represented in this little band. We have two nuns, four priests, a monk, a friar, a pardoner and now this summoner."

"Ugh!" said Chaucer, whose contempt for most churchmen was well known among his friends."If I'd known that I might not have come."

"On the contrary, you'd have come that much faster," Robert returned dryly."You welcome any excuse to harass and pester churchmen."

Chaucer grinned. His head popped up with a jerk. The nuns, surrounded by their entourage, swept out of the tavern. All eyes immediately went to Dame Eglantine, who mounted her horse with all the dignity of a queen. Chaucer's eyes softened at the sight of Sister Cecily; he had often met young girls with a true spiritual calling. They were inspiring creatures, guaranteed to uplift the spirits.

Simon de Burgoyne hurried out of the stable, leading his horse, burning with anger. Chaucer cocked an eyebrow. "Who is that gorgeous young Apollo, and why is he so angry?" he asked.

"I suspect he's had another quarrel with his father," Agatha replied. "Simon is madly, passionately in love with Sophia the gypsy, and, needless to say, his aristocratic father, Sir Richard, disapproves."

As she spoke, Sir Richard, a dark frown on his handsome face, emerged from the stable. His yeoman, a muscular fellow with close-cropped hair dressed in green trousers and cloak, followed, leading three horses.

"Is that Sir Richard?" asked Chaucer. In his head his poetic instincts were already working, almost against his will: "A KNYGHT there was, and that a worthy man…"

Agatha nodded. "And Simon is not only his son, but his squire as well. I expect their continuous proximity to each other does their relationship no good."

Sir Richard stopped to greet the nuns, and called his son over to introduce him to them. Undoubtedly the knight was swearing that he and his son would die fighting rather than allow any harm to come to the holy women, Chaucer mused. Simon bowed very low before Sister Cecily; he too had been moved by the girl's beauty, even though it and everything else about her was consecrated to the service of God. Sister Cecily held on to the squire's hand a bit longer than propriety dictated, and when she did let go, Chaucer sensed it was with some reluctance. Yet as soon as Simon turned his back on the nuns his eyes darted around the noisy, milling crowd, doubtlessly searching for Sophia.

A cloud passed over their heads; from behind it came the morning sun, bright and showing promise of warmth later on in the day. Remile snorted and struck the ground with his hoof impatiently. A wave of exhilaration passed through Chaucer. "What a fascinating cross-section of humanity we have here!" he cried. "The men range from the lowest dregs of society—like that disgusting summoner—to a group of obnoxious guildsmen to a learned professor like yourself, Robert, all the way to our handsome knight and squire! And the women! We have spring, or the dawn, in that lovely little nun and in the gypsy with whom young Simon is so infatuated! We have summer, or the day, in you, my dear Agatha, and for autumn, or evening, Madame Eglantine! No winters of course—women that old rarely venture out into their gardens, much less on pilgrimage—but a fine group, nonetheless! How interesting this is all going to be! Thank you so much, dear friends, for inviting me!"

Agatha was blushing, flattered that Chaucer classified her as summer or day when she was closer to Madame Eglantine's age than she cared to admit. "Well, I knew you'd enjoy such an excursion! Interesting people, all with tales to tell! The shrine of the blessed martyr! It all sounded like the perfect place for our Geoffrey to be!"

"Well, I plan to enjoy myself thoroughly!" cried Chaucer. He waved to Harry Bailey, who was an old friend, as the latter called loudly for the party to start out, and to line their horses up two by two. Hastily Robert and Agatha kicked their mounts up ahead, so that they rode together in front of Chaucer. Geoffrey was somewhat unsettled to find himself riding next to the worshipful young clerk, Walter.

Oh well, Chaucer told himself. *Admiring fool or none, I'm still going to enjoy this.*

When the sun was approaching noon, the little party stopped for a meal at a meadow outside a small village called St. Thomas-a-Watering. All had brought provisions for the journey, and so they dismounted and began unpacking their food and spreading cloths on the grass, forming a rough circle. While they were eating, Harry Bailey called for everyone to draw straws to see who would tell the first tale. The knight won—and obligingly stepped into the circle and announced that he would recite a long narrative poem telling of two knights who love and fought over the same fair lady.

Was Sir Richard thinking of three members of their own party? Chaucer wondered. Simon was still hovering around Sophia, while she flirted with him outrageously, teasing him with light caresses and brief kisses. Wandering along behind them was the friar, fat and greasy from the consumption of an entire chicken, glowering with jealousy and anger. Chaucer remembered the ominous astrological chart he had drawn up for the journey and shuddered.

"Long ago," Sir Richard began in a rich, sonorous voice, "in Athens, in faraway Greece, there lived a king named Theseus, married to Hippolyta, the powerful and beautiful queen of the Amazons. Hippolyta had a younger sister named Emelye, whose loveliness and sweetness were legend among all who adored women. Once, when King Theseus had been riding out with Hippolyta and Emelye, on their way home they met a band of women, dressed in black, weeping and wailing. The women told the royal party that they were queens or duchesses who had lost their husbands during a siege of the city of Thebes. The conqueror, the tyrant Creon, was now planning to despoil the dead bodies of their beloved men…"

Chaucer leaned back against a tree, took out a fresh new manuscript book and a quill, and began to write, taking notes of both the knight's story and Chaucer's own observations of the man himself. While he was doing this, Sophia and Simon walked by. Sophia took one look at Chaucer and stopped short. She gazed at him appreciatively, honoring him with a broad, beautiful smile. Simon looked bereft; the friar glowered that much more. Chaucer smiled back.

Geoffrey had never been able to understand women's attraction to him. He was comely enough, with large soulful blue eyes and arresting features, but he certainly could hold no candle to Sir Richard or Simon, or even Harry Bailey. Chaucer, large-boned and muscular and therefore never thin, had, since abandoning the military life, acquired an irritating tendency to put on weight. In spite of efforts to fight corpulence by walking instead of standing or sitting whenever he could, he almost always sported a considerable paunch—which was hardly in keeping with the current standard for male beauty.

Agatha had once told him that women were attracted to him because they sensed that he, unlike most men of their time, genuinely liked, respected and understood the female of the species. Philippa—and other lovers he had had in his youth—had told him that he was a skilled and sensitive lover, and if Agatha's logic was correct, women probably sensed that as well. But still, Chaucer had no direct experience of what the women divined of him. His direct experience was only that which he saw in his mirror.

"You're wasting your time, Sophia," said a voice behind the three. "Master Chaucer is a married man, and has never strayed from his wedding vows yet."

It was Robert. Simon and the friar were clearly disgruntled, but Sophia seemed utterly nonplused. She tossed her wild dark locks and gazed knowledgeably at Robert.

"I can always try!" she said defiantly, yet still smiling.

Chaucer coughed. "Come, we must be quiet. I want to hear the rest of Sir Richard's story!"

"After defeating and killing King Creon, and restoring the bodies of the dead to their women," Sir Richard was continuing, "King Theseus took prisoner two gallant young knights named Arcite and Palamon. He swore that he would never release them, but would hold them in his dungeons for the rest of their lives. In the course of the many years that followed, the only pleasure the two knights ever had was peering through the dungeon windows as Emelye passed, admiring her beauty and grace. Both Palamon and Arcite eventually fell madly, passionately, in love with the fair Emelye."

Obligingly Sophia, Simon and the friar sat down beside Chaucer, while Robert winked, waved and went to find Agatha. Geoffrey gazed down at what he had written:

> A KNYGHT there was, and that a worthy man,
> That fro the tyme that he first bigan

To riden out, he loved chivalrie,
Trouthe and honour, fredom and curteisie.
Ful worthy was he in his lordes werre,
And therto hadde he riden, no man ferre,
As well in cristendom as in hethenesse,
And evere honoured for his worthynesse.

How appropriate a picture that was of Sir Richard...And Chaucer, though writing a poem of his own, had never missed a word of the story. That he would write down later.

"Eventually, Arcite was ransomed. But a requisite of his ransom was that he never return to Athens. And so Arcite spent the next two years grieving for the loss of Emelye, while Palamon remained in prison, watching her pass by every day."

"One night, Palamon escaped. By sheer chance, while hiding in a field, he encountered Arcite, who had been so anguished over his loss of Emelye that he had dared to violate the terms of his ransom and return to Athens."

"In anger, Arcite challenged Palamon to a duel. They were fighting fiercely, in a bloody debacle, when King Theseus and his entourage happened upon the gory scene. Upon learning who they were, King Theseus agreed to pardon them both and give them their freedom, if they would return to Thebes in a year and fight a proper joust for the entertainment of King Theseus and his court. The prize would be the hand of the fair Emelye.

"The two knights spent the next year sharpening their strength and skills for the sake of winning both the joust and the woman the two of them loved..."

At this point in the story one of the guildsmen—the dyer, Chaucer believed it was—came striding angrily into the circle, waving his arms frantically.

"My silver dagger!" he cried. "It's been stolen! And someone here has it!"

"I told you to take care of it!" chided the haberdasher. "Someone in this group is a thief. I'm still missing my silver pin."

"And I my stirrup!" said Dame Eglantine. "I had to have it replaced with a brass one. See?" She walked over to her horse and held out the offending stirrup,

Chaucer caught Agatha's eye across the circle. While they were on their way out of London she had told him of the missing stud from her bridle.

"Someone here, it appears, has a great love of silver," said Harry Bailey. "When was the last time you saw the dagger?"

"What does that matter?" the dyer demanded.

Chaucer stood and walked over to stand by Bailey's side. "I think that what our host is trying to determine is if you saw it after we left the Tabard Inn," he said reasonably. "If not, you may have left it there, or it could have been stolen by anyone in Southwark. But if you have seen it since, then someone among us indeed is a thief."

"I last saw it after we stopped!" said the dyer triumphantly. "I used it to cut my bread. So there!"

Simon then spoke up. "But why steal such strange things?" he queried, perplexed. "A pin, a dagger, a stirrup. One stirrup, I ask you! What good is one stirrup, for the love of Our Lady?"

"And one stud from a bridle," added Agatha. "One stud, when there were a whole row of them."

"All these objects could easily have been lost," protested Harry Bailey. "This could all be no more than mere happenstance."

"Happenstance? When all that was stolen was made of precious silver?" snarled the dyer. "No! Somewhere among us there is a thief!"

"I believe," said Chaucer carefully, "that Master Dyer is probably correct. It seems unlikely that four objects would be lost in so short a period of time—all made of the same valuable metal. But I do believe that our host is right on one point. They could all have been lost. Mistress Willard's bridle stud could have dropped off anywhere between Aldgate and the Tabard Inn. The leather surrounding Dame Eglantine's stirrup could have loosened and the stirrup tumbled into the hay of the stables. Brooches fall off cloaks all the time. If the thief had taken both stirrups, or more than one of Mistress Willard's studs, then it would be an obvious theft. I believe the thief was hoping that, when and if the objects were missed, whoever had owned them would simply assume that he or she had lost them and say nothing to anyone else. Unfortunately for him, that didn't happen."

"Well," said Harry Bailey, "now that we know there is a thief among us, it would be very unwise for any more thefts to take place. Whoever is doing the stealing, I advise that you find a way to secretly return the objects to their owners. Now! Let Sir Richard finish his tale! We have a long way to go, and we need to start soon. Sir Richard?"

The knight nodded, then continued: "During the year of training, Arcite prayed and constantly made offerings to Mars, god of war, while Palamon entreated Venus, the goddess of love, that he be awarded the hand of the fair Emelye, for if he could not have her, he would rather die by Arcite's spear. Emelye, on the other hand, prayed to the virgin goddess Diana, asking that she be allowed to remain virgin as the goddess had, but if she must marry, let it be to the one who loved her the most."

Chaucer stopped taking notes, entranced. He was a devoted student of the classics, a lover of the Greek pantheon of gods and goddesses, and thus this was the type of story that never failed to fascinate him.

"Mars promised Arcite victory, and Venus assured Palamon that he would win his ladylove. Diana informed the lovely Emelye that it was destined that she marry one of the young knights, but that the goddess was not free to tell her which one. The three prayers and promises caused a great quandary on Mt. Olympus, and finally the problem was placed in the hands of Saturn, god of destiny, who promised that each prayer would be granted."

Sir Richard paused for breath. Everyone leaned towards him, their eyes alight with anticipation. The knight smiled, and then deliberately took a bite of his apple and chewed it slowly, as though to draw out the suspense.

Finally he swallowed and went on. "The day of the tournament dawned, clear, bright, and beautiful. All the people of Athens crowded into the amphitheater. The two knights, their palfreys snorting and pawing the ground in excitement, gathered at the ends of the arena, facing each other, nervous but determined. King Theseus declared that this would not be a fight to the death, but would be considered finished as soon as one was badly wounded. And so the battle began.

"Finally, Arcite struck Palamon a blow that was so severe that King Theseus's marshals were called to remove him from the field. Arcite was declared the winner—but as he was parading triumphantly around the arena something startled his horse. The frightened steed reared, and the victorious warrior plunged to the earth.

"Mortally wounded, Arcite died. But as he was dying, he promised that he would love Emelye forever, and declared that no man was worthier than Palamon for the lady they both loved best. And so Palamon married Emelye, and the god of destiny, Saturn, had managed to work it so that both knights received their due. And Palamon and Emelye lived happily ever after."

A hush fell over the crowd. Sir Richard had clearly finished his tale, but his audience was still caught up in awareness of the capriciousness of the gods, and the tragedy of Arcite.

Harry Bailey looked up at the sky. The sun had already passed its peak, and the little party needed to move on. "Well told, Sir Richard! A fine tale indeed! But it is now time to go. Robyn the Miller has offered to tell the next tale. He can tell it while we ride—and make the miles disappear under us that much more quickly."

Offered, indeed, thought Chaucer. Robyn had brought with him a jug full of cheap ale, most of which he had quaffed during lunch. He had not merely consented to tell his story, he had made a drunken demand—probably with ulterior motives! Well, if that were the case, the story would probably be that much more interesting!

Chaucer heaved his pack back up on his saddle, then climbed back upon Remile, who had been patiently waiting for the break to end. Chaucer suddenly felt sorry for his horse. Merry tales or no, it was going to be a long ride.

That night Chaucer tumbled onto his bed at the Catford Inn, roughly twenty miles from their starting point. They had arrived late, as the days were starting to grow longer, and had ridden and talked on into the night. Five tales had been told, and Chaucer had made careful notes of all of them, along with sketches of the tellers.

He chuckled as he recalled the undisguised antagonism between the miller and the reeve. The miller had told a story which made a carpenter—which the reeve was by trade—look ridiculous, then the reeve had countered with a tale that poked open fun at a miller. Chaucer reached over and opened his manuscript book, reading what he had written about Robyn the Miller:

> The MILLERE was a stout carl for the nones,
> Ful byg he was of brawn, and eke of bones.
> That proved wel, for over al ther he cam
> At wrastlynge he wolde have alwey the ram.

He had written similar poetic descriptions of the others who had told tales. He wasn't thoroughly happy with all of them; he would revise them later. Thoughtfully Chaucer closed the book and set it on his bedside table. It had been quite a day indeed! The tales had been fascinating, both for their own sake and for what they revealed about the tellers. And there was still the baffling problem of the thefts. Ruefully Chaucer wondered exactly how well he would sleep tonight, with so much to occupy his mind.

Geoffrey enjoyed the company of his fellow travelers, but was glad that he had chosen to pay the extra money involved for a room of his own. He was tired and wanted to sleep, and had enough challenge to that need coming from his own mind without help from other quarters.

He could still hear the raucous laughter and heated quarrels that usually took place in a common sleeping-room. The noise promised to continue on into the night. Geoffrey thought he recognized the harsh voice of the dyer, who was still angry over the loss of his silver dagger.

Chaucer blew out his candle and sank into the straw mattress. What exactly had happened to the missing silver? Why had so few items been taken when there were obviously many more valuable objects in the possession of the Canterbury pilgrims? Dame Eglantine's gold crucifix; the belts and scabbards of Sir Richard and Simon; the physician William Richemont's gold rings; the Man of Law's golden chain belt, decorated with a carved amethyst—all had cost a pretty penny and would be worth a small fortune to a merchant sailing for France.

Either the thief is frightened and consumed by poverty, Chaucer reasoned, or he is very clever. Or both. Such insignificant trinkets are just valuable enough to bring a very poor man a sum of money far beyond any he had ever hoped to see, yet most of the time their absence would be noted by the owners only as a frustrating inconvenience, not as a major disaster. In most cases the person suffering the loss would hardly bother to take the time and effort to seek out the thief—if in fact they suspected theft at all. Yes! The thief had to be a person unaccustomed to possessing money or valuables, yet well acquainted with the hearts and minds of the wealthy! Whatever else the thief was, he was not stupid.

But who among the pilgrims fit that description? Few, Chaucer had wryly noted, could be described as poor. They were either wealthy members of the aristocracy, like Sir Richard, Simon, and Dame Eglantine, or successful tradespeople, such as the physician, the franklin, the merchant, or Agatha and Harry Bailey. But there were a few whose ragged clothing and haggard countenances clearly bespoke of poverty.

There was, of course, Walter Locksley. As a student at Oxford, he was constantly in the company of students from higher social circles than himself. Undoubtedly he was familiar with churchmen. What wealth Walter possessed clearly lay in the intellectual rather than the material plane, and even so small a piece of silver as Agatha's bridle stud would probably have fed him for a month. But would an idealistic youth, willing risk the wrath of a much stronger man than himself to champion a dog, actually stoop to thievery?

Chaucer shook his head. Perhaps. The human psyche was far more complex than even the wisest could fathom.

There were others who were poor, and certainly would welcome a sum of money such as that which the sale of the silver could bring. The churchmen, the plowman, the yeoman who traveled with Sir Richard and Simon—few of them probably ever enjoyed any luxuries and had known few comforts. The churchmen had taken vows of poverty, but Chaucer knew all too well that taking such vows didn't always wipe out earthly desires. The plowman seemed honest enough, but to work hard from dawn to dusk for as many years as he had—and still barely manage to survive—often fanned resentment and vulnerability to temptation, even in the most honest of men. And Chaucer sensed that if the yeoman ever needed anything, Sir Richard would be all too glad to provide it for him.

There was still one other person whom Geoffrey knew he must consider—though he was reluctant to do so. That was Sophia, the gypsy. He wondered why, so far, suspicion had yet to fall upon her. Gypsies had a bad reputation; many people automatically assumed that they were all thieves.

Certainly their fingers were deft; Chaucer had encountered a number of young Romany pickpockets in the streets near the Aldgate, where he lived. It was easy to picture Sophia, flirting outrageously with the haberdasher or the dyer, batting her beautiful dark eyes and thus capturing their attention while clever fingers lifted the brooch or the dagger.

Somehow Chaucer did not like that picture. Feminine beauty often masked amorality—but that was not the way it was supposed to be.

But he was too tired to ponder on this enigma any further. Still resonating to the discomfort projected by the idea of Sophia as a thief, Chaucer sank into a deep, dreamless sleep.

Three

There was a bit of a nip in the air, but the sun was already high over the distant hills, and Chaucer was in a grand mood. Ahead of him stretched the road, on a slight downgrade so that he could easily see the backs of his fellow travelers. Harry Bailey, flanked by Sir Richard and the four guildsmen, led the procession. Between the leaders and Chaucer was a colorful array of brown, black, grey, and white horses, and the more common traveling clothes of off-white and tan were punctuated with brighter costume such as that worn by the wealthier members of the party.

The pilgrims had set off early that morning, after a grand breakfast of porridge, bread, cheese and sausages. Alisoun, the flirtatious widow from Bath, had already told her tale—a clear adaptation of the ancient legend of Sir Gawain's marriage, prefaced with a rather matter-of-fact account of Alisoun's own vast experience in romantic matters. The tale concerned Sir Gawain, King Arthur's most-loved knight and one of his most famous—though in Alisoun's version of the story she had not named him, calling him only "the knight". As punishment for rape, the knight had been forced by Queen Guinevere to go on a quest to find the answer to the question, "What one thing, in all the world, does a woman most desire of a man?" In the course of that quest, Sir Gawain had encountered a hideously ugly woman, who had offered to give him the answer to his question in exchange for a promise of marriage. Desperate, the knight agreed. The answer was "mastery over her man."

After the marriage was celebrated, the hag revealed that she was actually a young and beautiful woman who had been transformed into a crone by an evil magician. She asked if the knight would prefer to have her beautiful by day and ugly by night, or ugly by day and beautiful by night. The knight said, "The choice must be yours."

Before his eyes his wife was changed into the loveliest of young girls. She announced that she would always be so, because by leaving the choice to her he had given her what all women desire: mastery over her man. And thus the spell had been broken.

Chaucer had enjoyed Alisoun's story, but he was intrigued by the fact that the version she knew was so different from his. The story he had heard—in the form of an old epic romance—had made Sir Gawain seem much more heroic. Alisoun's version, he reflected, made the knight seem considerably less valiant and the women far more clever.

The friar, whose name was Hubert, was to tell his tale after they had stopped for lunch. Chaucer was quite curious as to what kind of story a man like Brother Hubert would choose to tell. Now they were searching for a promising place to rest and to eat, riding down the narrow road in a rather impressive procession.

Sophia the gypsy, who had laughed merrily at Alisoun's tale, broke the pattern. Instead of riding two by two like the other pilgrims, she chose to ride off to one side, away from the main body, sometimes cantering up to the front of the line, then merrily turning her horse and cantering back to the end, her purple scarf blowing in the breeze. Unlike the other women, she wore neither veil nor kerchief, but went bareheaded, her thick, curling black hair streaming out behind her as she rode.

Occasionally she would stop and ride along beside Simon, teasing and flirting with him, but she would never stay there. Eventually she would abruptly break away from him, leaving him stricken with lovesickness. She would then ride like the wind, sometimes even vanishing over a hill or into the trees, but she would always return—though not always to Simon. She had managed to enthrall half the men on the journey, including some of the more wealthy ones. Against his will Chaucer found himself wondering if any of them would find themselves short of silver.

Friar Hubert, riding next to Master Richemont, caught at Sophia's scarf as she rode by his horse. She stopped and pulled her mount over close to his, smiled appealingly at both the friar and the physician, then turned suddenly angry. Chaucer shaded his eyes with his hand, and frowned when he saw what was going on. *My God—the friar had actually reached over and tried to cup her breast!* She lashed out at him with her riding-crop, much to the dismay of Master Richemont, then laughed mockingly and turned her horse to gallop back to the end of the line.

A true free spirit, Chaucer decided. Ah, that all of us could be like Sophia!

The scarlet-and-gold kerchief of Alisoun of Bath was clearly visible a horse or two up from where Chaucer was riding. On a sudden impulse, Chaucer kicked up his horse and rode up next to her. She turned and gazed provocatively at him, revealing an appealingly crooked, gap-toothed smile.

She must be at least forty-five, Chaucer told himself. Still, she could easily pass for ten years younger than that.

Alisoun was more flamboyant than beautiful; she had the doughy, indistinct features associated with a long history of peasant ancestry. Though plump, her body was shapeless rather than curvaceous. But she had nice eyes, brown and kind, rather like those of a cow. *Not very flattering, perhaps,* Geoffrey realized, *but then the Greek poets had often referred to the beautiful Queen of the Gods as "ox-eyed Hera."* Alisoun's skin was still smooth and creamy, though somewhat sunburned, and her crooked gap-toothed mouth was endearing. Above all, she projected a sensuality only slightly less obvious than Sophia's. *Yes, my dear,* Chaucer reflected, *I believe you when you say you've had several husbands and scores of lovers.*

"That was a rather interesting story you told this morning," Chaucer said. "It was the story of Sir Gawain, wasn't it?"

"Sir who?"

Chaucer raised his voice, remembering she was a bit deaf. "Gawain. The most gallant of King Arthur's knights. Arthur's beloved nephew, whose strength waxed in the morning and waned in the evening. Who battled and overcome the challenges of the Green Knight. He who was forced to wed the loathly lady."

Alisoun waved her hand in a gesture of dismissal. "I never heard of him. I only know that that story was told to me when I was a child, by my grandmother."

"Told? It wasn't a song? You know, there is an old poem about Sir Gawain's marriage." He sang a few lines of it. Politely Alisoun cocked her head and listened, but no light of recognition dawned in her eyes. "Never mind," said Chaucer. "I just wanted to let you know that I enjoyed your tale. I hope the next one you tell is just as inspired."

"Ah!" Alisoun turned modestly away. "Our host—handsome Harry—is right. Telling tales does make time pass more quickly. And when you grow up trained for hard work, you learn many stories to help you make it through the day. I'm a weaver by trade, and nothing can be more tedious than hours and hours and hours spent on the loom. A good story actually makes it bearable."

"How true that is," Chaucer agreed. "That, I suppose, is why I devote my life to songs and poetry. They make life much more interesting."

"I hear you write verses, and are rather famous," said Alisoun. "Though as I can't read, I don't know much about anyone who writes."

"Well," Chaucer said humbly. "I have been fortunate enough to attract the support of two kings. That's as important as talent if one is to become a renowned poet!"

Suddenly Geoffrey became aware of a powerful presence near him. The robust, musky aroma of a sensual body stirred him uncomfortably. He turned to his right. Sophia was riding beside him, her head cocked attractively, her black hair tousled around her exquisite countenance, a slight smile on her full lips. Chaucer, somewhat disconcerted, could only nod politely to her.

"Good day, Mistress Sophia," he said cordially, his heartbeat quickening in spite of himself. "And how are you feeling this fine morning?"

"I can feel anything you want me to feel," said the gypsy pointedly. "Whenever you want to see if the young is as eager as the old, let me know!"

A wave of anger passed through Chaucer. How cheeky of the girl to insult Alisoun to her face! "My dear Sophia," said Chaucer sternly, "when you've lived a few more years you will find that the wisest of men like women of all ages. Each age has its own particular charm, and each individual woman can be appealing despite the number of years she has lived. As long as a woman is bright and healthy, her age is irrelevant!"

Realizing her banter had backfired on her, Sophia looked chagrined for a moment, and then she smiled sweetly at Alisoun. "I didn't mean to offend, Mistress," she said politely, with an aristocratic polish Chaucer didn't know gypsies possessed. "I want you to know I enjoyed your tale. I will certainly remember it when I return to my family. They enjoy a good story." Without waiting for a reply Sophia kicked up her horse and galloped up to the front of the line, into the secure retreat of Simon's adoration.

Chaucer turned once more to Alisoun. "I'm sorry," was all he could think of to say.

Alisoun laughed—a loud, resounding bark, though it was not unattractive. "None of the young girls in my village understand why their husbands and lovers still turn their heads to look at me when I pass. Perhaps someday they'll learn!"

Chaucer agreed. The appeal of a certain type of woman remained constant whether she was eighteen or eighty.

A loud cry of "Halt!" echoed from the front of the line. Chaucer glanced up; Harry Bailey was drawing the pilgrims into the circle for their luncheon stop. Gallantly Chaucer held his horse back so that Alisoun could circle ahead of him, then, when all were assembled, he stopped his horse and dismounted.

"Master Chaucer."

Geoffrey turned, and immediately suppressed a sigh of irritation. It was Walter, the hero-worshipping student. Chaucer found such worship embarrassing, which was why he often tried to avoid Roger Grimsby, the stableman whose establishment was down the street from Chaucer's apartment over the Aldgate. Roger, though quite a competent horse-keeper, aspired to be a poet and was constantly badgering Geoffrey to read his works.

"Good day, Walter," said Chaucer courteously, trying desperately to be distant without seeming unfriendly. "And why haven't you unpacked your saddlebags? I believe Master Bailey intends this to be our midday meal."

"I don't eat in the middle of the day," said Walter with some bravado. "I find it unsettles my stomach."

Chaucer sighed. Such a statement could be roughly translated: *I am so poor I have no food.* "Nonsense, boy," he said. "You must eat. We have a long ride ahead, and you need to keep your strength up. I have here with me a fine cheese and onion pie that I bought freshly baked only yesterday, and some apples. I brought far too much food to eat myself; if I try to keep it more than a day or so it goes bad and thus is wasted. Could I prevail upon you to share it with me?"

Walter's face flushed with excitement. "Well—" he said, trying hard not to sound too eager. "If you really think you have enough."

"I have more than enough," Chaucer assured him. His heart sank; he had been looking forward to that cheese and onion pie all morning. Oh, well—if he didn't eat the whole thing, perhaps he would lose an inch or two off his middle. Resolutely he took the carefully wrapped pie out of his pack, broke it into two pieces and handed one to Walter. "I can also share my ale with you, and the apples are in that bag over there. Help yourself whenever you want."

"Thank you, Master Chaucer," said Walter, biting into the pie with relish.

A commotion was taking place in the middle of the circle. Friar Hubert, who was to tell the next tale, was speaking loudly to Alisoun, complimenting her on her performance.

"You have lived an interesting life," he said. "But tell me: How have you managed to escape the notice of your local summoner?" He was speaking of the official duties of the summoner: to nose out sinners and bring their names before the church courts.

"The same way everyone escapes the summoner," said Alisoun simply. "I bribed him."

Jack, the summoner in their party, immediately rose to the bait and jumped up, his arms stiff at his sides. Chaucer then understood that the friar had spoken loudly not for the purpose of circumventing Alisoun's deafness, but so that his words would reach the ears of the summoner.

Not that I disapprove, Chaucer told himself. *Quite the contrary, in fact. But I doubt if the friar's ethics are any more upright than the summoner's.*

"Hah!" the friar chortled. "I have a story to tell about a summoner that will show you just how moral and decent such individuals are!"

Harry Bailey then stepped in. "No!" he said firmly. "This tale-telling contest is not to be a general forum for venting quarrels! Leave the summoner alone and find another story to tell!" He was obviously still smarting from the bout of insults exchanged the night before by Robyn the miller and Osewold the reeve.

"No, don't stop him," said Jack. "I want to hear what he has to say about summoners! And then I myself will tell a story about friars, so as to remind him of Our Lord's words on the mote and the beam! For though I may have a mote or two in my eye, he certainly bears a beam—seeing as he, a supposed man of God, dares to openly pursue the attentions of a pagan gypsy witch!"

A gasp spread through the crowd; all eyes suddenly went to Sophia, who was sitting close to Simon, holding his hand. Simon was shaking with rage. But Sophia calmly stood and walked over to where the summoner stood.

"If I am a witch," she said steadily, "then, if I were you, I would take care not to offend me. I might put a spell on you that would cause boils and pimples to break out in other places besides your face!"

The nuns and priests gasped, scandalized; the rest of the crowd chuckled. But Sophia took no notice. She merely drew a silver cross out of the top of her boot and handed it to the summoner. "I believe this belongs to you," she went on, speaking clearly enough that the entire crowd could hear her. "I think I saw you taking it from someone nearby whom you were threatening with a summons." She turned and faced the entire company. "I am not the thief whom you seek!" she cried. "But I could be—if I so wanted! And I believe this summoner here knows who the thief really is!" With that she stalked back to her place in the circle.

On the way back she passed too close to Dame Eglantine, and brushed the prioress's left arm. Dame Eglantine gave a cry of alarm and pulled her habit aside. Sophia swept the nun with a haughty, contemptuous gaze, while Sister Cecily stepped forward to protect her abbess from any possible verbal onslaught. But Sophia said nothing; she merely raised her chin high and returned to Simon's side. Simon glanced apologetically at Sister Cecily, who seemed rather disconcerted by his gaze. Ah, what chaos lay in the wake of the lovely Sophia!

But if Sophia saw the thief, Chaucer suddenly realized, then the summoner is not the only one who knows the true identity of the culprit. She does!

Suddenly Geoffrey's attention was drawn away from the gypsy and back to the group in the middle of the circle. "That's mine!" cried one of the priests. He broke out of the circle and hurried over to the summoner, yanking the cross out of his hand. "You were bribed with stolen property!"

The circle of pilgrims suddenly started all shouting at once. Harry Bailey spoke to both the summoner and the priest, but Chaucer could not hear what was being said.

"I believe I had better pay a little more attention to what is going on around here," said a voice beside him.

Chaucer looked up. It was Henry de Coverly, an attorney from London who had been introduced to Chaucer by Harry as "a man of law." De Coverly was apparently a rather well known attorney among

London tradesmen, having successfully represented many in the course of his career. He was a stocky, heavy man in his forties, gray-haired and bearded, with a bigger paunch than Chaucer's. He dressed well and expensively, obviously with the intent to impress.

"It certainly seems as if there has been a great deal of circumventing of the law," Chaucer agreed.

"I often pause to wonder why people are not more discreet about their little sins," De Coverly ventured. "To openly boast of larcenous talents such as that gypsy woman just did—why, such a practice could well be dangerous."

"Not to mention that she admitted being witness to a crime," added Chaucer. "But I suppose you, as an attorney, see this sort of thing every day."

"I do indeed. Theft! Bribery! It is indeed a lawyer's field ripe for harvest," said De Coverly. "Of course nothing has taken place yet that would be worth my time and effort to defend, but if this little band continues on the path it is on now it seems that there might be, very soon."

Bailey seemed to have calmed everyone down; the friar was telling his tale. "There was once a summoner for a certain bishop who was renowned for his skill at his profession. He made use of a vast crew of spies, including cutpurses and harlots, who would seek out gossip and name names as to who was sinning with whom, and how. The summoner rapidly grew rich by squeezing tribute from his victims, threatening to turn them in to the bishop..."

Chaucer tried hard to pay attention to the story, so that he could write it down later, and at the same time converse with the man of law.

"Tell me, Master de Coverly, what would you consider worth your time and effort to defend?" asked Chaucer curiously.

"Theft on a grander scale than a few mere toys," De Coverly answered promptly. "Bribery of a more important official than a corrupt summoner—for aren't all summoners corrupt? Fraud. Treason. Murder."

A wave of uneasiness passed over Chaucer as he recalled the astrological chart he had drawn up for the pilgrimage. Fervently he hoped that his calculations had been wrong. "Well, you may well hope for the worst, but I pray to Christ or Our Lady or any saint who may be listening that the scene we just witnessed is the most unsettling thing that happens, from here all the way to Canterbury and back!"

De Coverly turned bright red. "Well, I didn't mean to imply that—I mean, I don't hope for dreadful things to happen—"

"Shhh!" Chaucer hissed.

"One day," Friar Hubert was continuing, "as he proceeded with his insidious blackmail, the summoner met a handsome young yeoman who confessed first that he was as evil as the summoner, and then declared that he was a demon from Hell."

Chaucer was beginning to feel stifled, there in the crowd. In spite of his desire to hear the friar's tale, he broke away from the oppressive company of De Coverly and the ever-adoring Walter and strode over to a copse of trees. He stepped inside and took a deep breath. The air did seem sweeter, clearer. What a churning morass of contradictions was the human race!

Between the spreading roots of an old ash was a patch of grass marbled with soft moss; Geoffrey nodded approvingly at this inviting perch and sat down, leaning comfortably against the tree trunk. From his pocket he drew his manuscript book and immediately began to write:

> A SERGEANT OF THE LAWE, war and wys
> That often hadde been at the Parvys,
> Ther was also, ful riche of excellence.
> Discreet he was, and of greet reverence

There he got stuck. He put the book away. He would have to devote more thought to his portrait of the odious sergeant of the law. Instead, he began writing his verse portrait of Alisoun of Bath. He sat for several minutes, pondering how best to portray the aging and yet still fascinating wanton. Then, suddenly inspired, he began to write.

"Master Chaucer?" said a hesitant voice beside him.

Damn! Walter again! He would have to have a talk with that boy.

"What is it?" Chaucer asked shortly.

"Well, I wouldn't have disturbed you, but Mistress Willard asked that I find you—"

"Shh!" Geoffrey grabbed the clerk's wrist.

A few feet before them a clearing opened, revealing a colorful little vale inside the circle of trees. Wildflowers were starting to peep out beneath rocks and in clumps among the grass; a few bushes were starting to bloom, permeating the air with the faintest hint of their perfume. Birds were singing; here and there a small animal dashed beneath the bushes or from tree to tree. The sound of merry laughter permeated the air as Simon and Sophia, hand in hand, emerged from between two gigantic pines. Simon seemed somewhat ill at ease.

"Sophia, hadn't we better go back? They may be leaving at any time—"

"Don't be ridiculous! They won't leave without us! Your father is among them, after all! Besides, they're listening to the friar." She threw her arms around his neck and pulled him down on the ground beside her, laughing gaily. Wrapped in each other's arms they rolled over several times, till Simon could stand it no more and pressed his mouth hungrily to hers. She responded in kind, running her slender fingers through his curly golden hair.

A moment later they parted. "Oh, Sophia!" Simon groaned. "Sophia, I adore you! Why do you torture me so?"

"What do you mean, I torture you?"

"Those other men. Why do you pay so much attention to them!"

"They are all asses!" Sophia cried contemptuously. "So full of their own importance, when they are ugly and disgusting! I only make fun of them."

Chaucer's face began to redden. Did her words imply her opinion of him?

Sophia was continuing. "It is only you, my beloved one, only you that I truly desire. Now relax and behave like a young man in spring should!" She put both her hands on either side of his face and pulled his mouth to hers again. For a moment the two of them, pressed so close it would be difficult to get a pry-bar between them, actually seemed to sink into the earth, the grass almost stretching up to protect them from curious, prying eyes.

Embarrassed, Chaucer turned to leave, but something caught his eye. A flicker of movement, on the other side of the clearing, to the left of them. What was it? An animal? No—too tall. It had to be human. Was that a gray robe? Who could it possibly be?

But the shadow—for Chaucer had really seen no more than that—was gone as quickly as it had appeared. Geoffrey stood staring at the spot for several moments. He knew he had seen something—or someone—and he couldn't shake the idea that it would someday prove important.

Walter was clearly very ill at ease. "Master Chaucer, do you not think that we should leave?"

"Quite," Chaucer agreed, casting one last look at the young lovers, who were oblivious to the presence even of the twittering birds. He began to walk back up towards the road, Walter following close behind. "Did you say that Mistress Willard wanted to speak to me?"

"She only wanted me to tell you that the friar has finished his tale and Jack the summoner is about to tell his, and she knew you wanted to keep records of all the tales."

"Yes, yes, I do indeed. Thank you for coming to fetch me, Walter. How did the friar's tale end?"

"The summoner—that is, the character in the story, not our Jack—and the demon met a farmer on the road whose hay cart was stuck in the mud, and the horses were unable to pull it out. The farmer was so angry he shouted that the devil could take it all—horses, cart, hay, and all. The summoner then asked the demon if he was going to take the horses and everything, but the demon said he couldn't because the farmer didn't really mean it.

"Then they came to a house where a rich widow lived who had constantly refused to pay the summoner bribes. The summoner demanded that she give him twelve pence. When she refused, he threatened to take her frying pan. She said, 'The devil take you and the frying pan!' And this time she meant it, so the demon took the summoner down with him to Hell."

Chaucer let out with a loud guffaw, then clapped his hand over his mouth. Could Simon and Sophia have heard him?

"Master Chaucer?" Walter ventured.

"Yes?"

"If you need any help with note-taking, if your hand gets tired perhaps—well, sir, I write a fair hand, and I would be very glad to—"

"Thank you, Walter. I may indeed need you."

If Jack was only now beginning to tell his tale, Chaucer reflected as they emerged from the trees and the band of pilgrims once more came into view, then Simon and Sophia will have plenty of time to continue with whatever mischief they had in mind.

Oh, well. 'tis none of my affair, he reminded himself as he and Walter approached the circle surrounding Jack the summoner. Jack was in the middle of a funny and yet chilling tale of a friar who had had a vision of Hell. An angel had guided him through that horrible realm, and the friar had noticed that he saw no friars there, and so made that observation to the angel. The angel had asked him to lift up Satan's tail, and suddenly the friar viewed millions like himself swarming around Satan's arse-hole. He had awakened in a chill, quaking with fear over this vision of his own future.

The pilgrims laughed heartily, though Friar Hubert was incensed, and several of the réligieux crossed themselves fearfully. Jack then hastened to assure his audience that this was not his tale, only a prologue.

Ah! Then I haven't missed anything, Chaucer told himself with some relief. *And I am certain that Agatha will fill me in on whatever I haven't heard.*

He and Walter took seats on the same fallen log with Agatha and Robert and in a moment were caught up in the story of a greedy and unwise friar.

Four

The gypsy's dark eyes actually turned green in the firelight as she held her audience spellbound. "So Queen Isis bathed the little prince every night in a blazing fire, so as to burn away every trace of his mortality," she was saying. "But one night his mother walked in while he was bathing. She screamed and pulled the little boy out of the fire—and thus deprived him of the gift of immortality." She paused for breath—and for effect. A concerned buzz spread through the room at the fate of the unfortunate baby prince.

"Heathenism! Blasphemy!" said one of Dame Eglantine's priests, who was sitting in the back of the crowd. "When Master Bailey proposed this story-telling contest, I didn't anticipate having to listen to devilish stories about pagan gods and goddesses! First there was the knight's tale—and now this!"

Chaucer chuckled and slapped the priest on the back. "Relax, Father Matthew, it's just a story. I doubt if these pilgrims are going to abandon their journey to the shrine of St. Thomas and rush out to build a temple to the goddess Isis."

They had stopped for the night at an inn near St. Mary Cray, a tiny village about twenty-five miles out of London. The friar and the summoner had told their stories at noon; the merchant and Walter the clerk on the road throughout the afternoon. Now, after a fine meal of roast beef, pudding and pottage, it was Sophia's turn. She had chosen to highlight her ancestry, telling an ancient story from Egypt.

Chaucer was barely aware of Master Richemont and Don John the monk sitting in front of him, whispering and laughing softly. Geoffrey felt uncomfortably full; he had thoroughly enjoyed the dinner and was now relaxing in the peaceful atmosphere of the room. He patted his stomach affectionately. Some day soon he would have to do something about his growing stoutness. Philippa was always insisting that he cut down on honeycakes and ale. But honeycakes and ale were two of the few commodities that made life worth living!

Honeycakes, ale, poetry, music, history, astrology, women, cats. His mind inevitably turned to a recently acquired prized possession, which he had forgotten he'd brought with him. "Look," he said to the priest in a sudden fit of inspiration. "Let me show you something. I brought them back with me on my last trip to France." He fished through his pack until he found a rectangular wooden box. Opening the box revealed a bright blue silk cloth wrapped around what appeared to be a rather large stack of small pictures.

Father Matthew's eyes fairly goggled. "What are they?"

"Tarot cards."

"Cards!" The priest stared at Chaucer, uneasy. "But hasn't the Church forbidden card games?"

"No. Some monastic sects have condemned them, but as far as I know the Holy Father has not yet forbidden them. Besides, I don't play. I study them."

Like Adam tasting the forbidden fruit, the priest was gingerly thumbing through the cards. "But these are beautiful! What's this?"

He drew a card from the front of the pack. It showed a seated nun crowned with the coronet of St. Peter.

"La papessa," Chaucer replied. Then, seeing a blank look on the priest's face, he realized the man probably spoke no Italian. "The Popess. The female pope."

Father Matthew gasped. "Apostasy! No woman could ever be head of the Church!"

Chaucer gave up and sighed. He spotted Agatha sitting across the room, listening avidly to Sophia's story. Agatha...Now there was a woman for you! Chaucer had no doubt that she could run the Church just as well if not better than some of the bishops and archbishops he had met.

And that gypsy wench! After having had two days to think about it, Chaucer still couldn't fathom Sophia, or her feelings, or her motives for anything. She was still a mystery to him, which perhaps was part of her mystique. It was easy for Chaucer to imagine her as high priestess of an ancient Egyptian temple—perhaps the temple of Isis herself.

Sophia continued with her story. "Isis's brother-in-law, Set, had hated Osiris, and had taken his revenge upon the great god, tearing his body into little pieces, and scattering the pieces throughout the land of Egypt. The sarcophagus of Osiris had been hidden in a tree which had been cut down and made into a pillar that held up the royal palace where Isis acted as nursemaid to the little prince. But Set had thrown Osiris's manhood into the Nile, where it had been swallowed by a fish."

A titter spread around the room. The two nuns present hid their heads in shame, while Agatha and Alisoun of Bath laughed heartily.

"God's bones!" The priest crossed himself breathlessly. "What evil!"

"Good God, Father Matthew, mentioning a man's cock doesn't require absolution!" said Chaucer, annoyed, jerking his attention back to the priest.

"No, I'm looking at this!"

Chaucer had quite forgotten the Tarot cards. He grinned when he saw the priest contemplating a card depicting the Devil. "It's only a picture!" Chaucer exclaimed. "A symbolic representation of the evil side of man, just as this card—" He pulled out a card showing two lovers holding hands while an angel hovered above them. "—represents the good!"

Sophia was continuing: "Isis informed the boy's mother that she was the great goddess, and that the body of her husband Osiris was concealed in the pillar that held up the palace roof. She asked that it be given to her. When the pillar was cut open and the coffin of Osiris revealed, Isis threw herself upon it and wailed. It was then that her son Horus was conceived, immaculately, by Osiris's very spirit."

Chaucer took the Devil card and the wooden box from the priest, replaced the two cards, rewrapped the pack in its silk covering and closed the box. "I didn't mean to touch off a spiritual crisis, Father. These cards were hand-painted by the famous French artist, Jacquemin Gringonneur, and I thought you might enjoy seeing his work."

"And so Isis managed to regather the lost parts of Osiris's body and bring him back to life with the power of her love," Sophia was saying. "So the sky-goddess Nut banished Set forever to the underworld for the foul murder of his brother. And Isis and Osiris were married, and reigned forever over all the people of Egypt." She paused expectantly; the story was clearly at an end. The listeners hesitated, then applauded.

"What a ridiculous tale!" said Father Matthew. "A god who dies and then comes back to life! A god conceived without any carnal contact! Sheer nonsense!

"Sheer nonsense," agreed Chaucer, grinning sardonically.

The fire was starting to die; the crowd was yawning. Agatha, accompanied by Robert, came towards Chaucer and tapped him on the shoulder.

"That's all the stories for tonight, Geoffrey," she said. "It's nearly midnight. Coming to bed?"

Chaucer nodded and scrambled to his feet. Father Matthew's company was wearing on him.

Sophia passed them, wearing a haughty, sultry expression until she saw Chaucer. Her face lit up with a radiant smile; she winked lecherously at Chaucer, then hurried on up the stairs to the bedrooms. Chaucer nodded appreciatively.

"She's too young for you, Geoffrey; besides, Philippa would be furious."

It was Agatha's voice. Chaucer looked back at her, smiling. "Relax, Agatha. I have no designs on Sophia. But that doesn't mean I can't look!"

"She's a vampire, that one," said Robert. "The kind of woman who will suck a man's very soul from his body."

After witnessing the scene in the woods between Sophia and Simon, Chaucer tended to agree. He fell into step with Agatha and Robert; together the three of them wearily climbed the stairs and said good night.

Once more Chaucer was glad he had chosen to pay the extra money required for a room to himself rather than sharing the communal sleeping quarters with the rest of the Canterbury pilgrims. Not only did he wish to distance himself from the snoring and farting of the other travelers—my God, he had told himself, that summoner snored like a herd of braying asses!—but Sophia the gypsy had inspired him to make an addition to the poetic diary he was keeping of his pilgrimage to Canterbury.

His room sported a rickety table, which he pulled over to the bed to use for a desk. From his pack he took a candle, which he lit from a torch in the hallway, then he sat down with his manuscript book and began to write.

> Apart from the reste rode a fayre GIPSIE
> Dark and loveli shee was, like a leppard
> (An animal to whome she was aften compared.
> Blakke were hir eyen, and eke hir copious herr
> (A bit too abundant, if swich a thing be likeli)
> Wylde and exotic, shee tempted all men
> But whan they approached, hir fyr turned to is
> Small shee was, but ample where a mayde sholde ample be
> Yonge she was, but in hire eyen shone the wisdom of a thousand yeren.
> Those yen wolde gaze upon your hand and than into your soul
> Burnyng, it semed, thro skin, muscle, blude.

As he penned this last line Chaucer stopped writing, thoughtfully chewing the end of his quill. There was surely more to be said about Sophia, but his fount of inspiration seemed for the moment to have dried up.

No matter! He could add the rest later. He skipped to the next page and wrote at the top of it: THE GIPSY'S TALE. Then he continued:

In that ancient lande where my fathers once walked
There lived twa gods, twynne brothers, in truth
Set was ane, Osiris the ither; twixt tham there was no trust.
Secretly Set despised Osiris, an planned to se hym dust.
He called a gathering for all gods of the Nile, forsooth,
An ordered the building of a fayre casket, bilt to Osiris's measure
Claiming its purpose were a game, to gyve the gods pleasure

Chaucer sighed. How could he, through mere words on a page, possibly capture the quality by which Sophia had kept her audience rapt, spellbound, benumbed to all consideration but the anguish of Queen Isis?

His head fell down upon his hands. *I shall rest but a moment,* he told himself, *then perhaps I can try again...*

He awoke with a start, some time later. He wasn't sure of the hour; it was still dark. His candle, however, had guttered, and it had been a new one. Many hours, then, must have passed.

Chaucer cursed when he saw that candle wax had splashed onto his new manuscript book, smearing some of the words of his poem. Why couldn't he have awakened before that happened? For that matter, what had awakened him? Gradually Chaucer shook the remnants of sleep from his brain. The sound of voices—some in a panic—was drifting in from the hallway. Soon there came a deafening pounding on the door to Chaucer's room.

"Geoffrey! It's Agatha! Open up!"

Chaucer struggled to his feet and rushed over to open the door. Agatha, her kerchief askew, stood before him.

"Agatha? What's happening?"

"Oh, Geoffrey, there's been a murder!"

"A murder? For God's sake, who?"

"The gypsy, Sophia."

"Oh, no!" A wave of grief passed over Chaucer. He had not known Sophia for very long—nay, he had not really known her at all—but he had been all too aware of her beauty and youth, her vitality, her love of life, her gifts for telling stories. What a waste!

Agatha sighed. "I know, love, it's hard to accept that the young can go as quickly as the old. But I think you had better come. There's something you should see."

Mindlessly Chaucer followed as Agatha led the way into the ladies' common sleeping-room. The two nuns were sobbing; Alisoun of Bath stood by the girl's body, straightening its limbs. Beside her stood Harry Bailey, apparently at a loss for what to do.

"Alisoun! Don't touch her!" Chaucer barked out.

The wife of Bath stood stock still, shocked. "But why not?"

Chaucer ignored her. "Harry, put her back the way she was when she was found!"

Automatically the innkeeper obeyed, tilting Sophia's head to one side, rearranging her limbs slightly.

"I'm sorry, Alisoun; I didn't mean to frighten you, but I have to see her as she was if I'm going to have any clue as to how she died."

"But she hasn't been shriven!" Alisoun protested.

"Nay, and she won't be!" spoke up Sister Cecily. "A heathen worshiper of pagan idols!"

Chaucer's face flushed with anger. "She will be shriven!" he thundered. "Get that sniveling priest, Father Matthew—or the parson, it doesn't matter—in here at once!

Intimidated, Sister Cecily ran for the door. Chaucer then returned his attention to the body of the girl.

Her eyes were closed, her expression peaceful, her body in an attitude which suggested she had been asleep when she was killed. *Well, that was a blessing, anyway,* Chaucer reflected as he knelt beside her. A thin dagger protruded from her side and had apparently penetrated directly into her heart. Death had been instantaneous.

A sudden thought popped into Chaucer's head. "Harry, get the dyer in here. I think we've found his stolen dagger. And while you're at it, fetch Master Richemont, the physician, and the sergeant of the law. I think we're going to need their help." In the days of old King Edward III, Richard II's grandfather, before Chaucer was made ambassador to France he had been a soldier, and had fought at several decisive battles. His powers of observation had been just as keen then as they were now, and he had learned about death in all its forms; what made it come quickly, what made it slow and tortuous, what hastened it, what staved it off, how long a body had been dead, what had caused the death. Sometimes he had even been able to discern, from boot prints and the marks left by weapons, if the killer had been English or French.

And now he was using that knowledge to study the body of a young woman—not a soldier, not a knight, but merely a girl, who apparently had had at least one enemy.

Chaucer looked up and studied the faces of Alisoun and the nuns. "What happened?" he demanded. "You were all sleeping here. One of you at least must have heard something! My God, she's not even near the door!"

Madame Eglantine spoke up. "We all stayed away from her, Master Chaucer. She—she didn't bathe, you know, and—well, her smell was a little strong. So she slept by that wall and the three of us slept over here. The men's common room is on the other side of our wall, you seen, and we have grown use to hearing their noises throughout the night. So I am afraid it is all too reasonable to believe that someone could come in while we were asleep. If we heard anything, we'd think it was coming from next door."

"Oh." Chaucer's mood turned blacker. "Well, what do you know about her?"

"Not much," said Sister Cecily. "In fact, I am sure you know more about her than we do. She didn't talk much about herself, but she asked a lot of questions about us."

"She read palms," Alisoun spoke up. "The sisters wouldn't allow her to read theirs, of course, but I let her read mine. She laughed and said

I'd be married one more time and would die in my bed, an old woman surrounded by children, grandchildren and great-grandchildren,"

"I wonder what she saw in her own," Chaucer mused.

"I asked her once," said Alisoun.

"What did she say?"

"Death," Alisoun replied simply. "I laughed it off—told her that was no great prophecy, for Death awaits us all. But she said, 'Not like mine.' And that was the end of it."

Harry Bailey then returned, with the physician, the dyer, and the man of law. Richemont immediately knelt beside the body. "She's been dead for about an hour," he announced. "It's obvious what happened. She probably died immediately." Chaucer turned to the dyer. "Is that your dagger?" he demanded.

The dyer's eyes bulged. "My god, it is!" Instinctively he reached for it; Chaucer put out a hand and stopped him. "Don't," he warned.

"But why? It's mine!"

"It is evidence in a murder," said De Coverly. "I am sure it will be returned to you once the murderer has been found and hanged."

Harry Bailey glanced up at Chaucer. "Do you think the same person who stole the dagger and everything else killed her?"

"It's possible," said Chaucer. "She knew who the thief was."

"But how do you know that?" demanded De Coverly.

Chaucer reminded him of the exchange between Sophia and Jack the summoner.

"Do you think she was killed because she knew the thief?" asked Harry Bailey.

"If that is the case," said Chaucer, "then we'd better find some strong bodyguards to guard Jack. For he is in danger too."

"But why didn't they go for him first?" asked Alisoun curiously. "He, after all, was the one who threatened the thief."

"Well, if Sister Cecily is correct in saying that there was always noise coming from the men's common sleeping-room, but that the three of you slept pretty soundly and far away from Sophia, then it would have been easier to kill Sophia than the summoner. The summoner was in a room full of people, all wide awake."

"But I don't understand!" Harry protested. "Why commit murder over a few stinking baubles? It doesn't make sense!"

"Because," De Coverly said calmly, "under the law, theft of even a few baubles is a hanging offense. And no sane person wants to die."

"I am sure Sophia didn't either, in spite of her prophecy," Chaucer remarked. "She was young and full of life, and deserved to live at least another fifty years. This is a heinous crime, Master de Coverly—very heinous indeed!"

"Of course," said Agatha. "But Geoffrey, you'd better look at this." She held something out to him. "It was found beside her body."

In a daze Chaucer took what she held out to him. A Tarot card: The Sun.

"Is it yours?" Agatha asked.

"Yes—yes, of course, at least I'm sure it is," said Chaucer finally. "But would you help me some and go to my room and bring the cards? We really should make certain." Agatha nodded and left the room.

Chaucer studied the card closely. Yes, he was sure it was his. Any sort of Tarot cards was rare in England. Hand-painted decks like his were expensive, and there was no mistaking Jacquemin Gringonneur's work. The chances of there being two identical Gringonneur decks in the same inn—yea, in England!—were infinitesimal.

Suddenly Chaucer felt himself overcome by sadness. Blood covered the gilt Sun at the top of the card and smeared over the face of the naked boy riding the white horse. He tried to wipe it off on his sleeve, but the effects were minimal. If this card was in fact his—and he was sure it was—his pack was spoiled until he could send to France for a replacement card.

He shook his head. Good God! Where were his values? A young girl lay before him murdered and he was mourning a card!

But why The Sun? he wondered. The Sun was the most fortunate card in the entire deck. Why not Death, or The Devil, or the House of God?

And then a thought occurred to him: *Perhaps the good fortune was the murderer's.*

Agatha then returned. Chaucer snatched the card box, opened it and rifled through the cards. Yes—The Sun was missing. It was his card.

"Geoffrey, the landlord has sent for the local deputy sheriff," said Agatha gently.

The landlord…Chaucer had met him earlier in the evening. Aleyn Atte Wood, his name was: a tall, lean man in his late thirties, concerned, hardworking and conscientious. Of course his first thought would have been to notify the proper authorities.

"You know the deputy is going to think you did it," Agatha continued.

Chaucer's head jerked up; he stared at her, thunderstruck. "Me!"

"It's your card, Geoffrey."

"But why would I be such an ass as to commit murder and then leave my own card?"

"I don't think the deputy sheriff is going to care about the logic of it, Geoffrey," Harry Bailey put in. "This isn't London, after all. People around here are too simple to realize that all may not be as it seems. They will firmly believe that since your card was found beside her, therefore you must have killed her."

"But what about the thief?" asked Alisoun, wide-eyed. "The dyer's stolen dagger was used to kill her!"

Henry de Coverly spoke up. "The local louts would assume that Master Chaucer was the thief, as well. Believe me, my lady, Master Bailey is right. I know the type of ignorant peasant that runs these small villages. They don't care about the truth. All they want is to avoid anything that would take them away from their work and thus interfere with an already-inadequate income. And investigating Sophia's murder would involve a considerable amount of time."

Chaucer's mind was racing. "I think it's time for me to call in some favors," he finally said. "Harry! Is there someone in this company whom you believe trustworthy enough to take a message to London for me?"

"Sir Richard's yeoman," said Harry promptly. "He seems dependable enough, and I seriously doubt if he was the killer. He spent the night in the stables, and I am certain he was there all night. He could not have re-entered the inn without being seen. I'll send him."

Chaucer glanced quickly around the room. His sharp eyes spotted a piece of paper in Sister Cecily's saddlebag. Politely he asked for it, and the young nun took it out and handed it to him. Borrowing her quill, he scrawled out a note, then folded it and sealed it with his signet ring. He then handed the note to Harry Bailey, who nodded and left the room.

"Who did you write to, Geoffrey?" asked Agatha curiously.

"Who else? My old friend John of Gaunt, Duke of Lancaster. Even a rude country sheriff such as we would find here would hesitate to pass judgment too quickly on a friend of John of Gaunt. We can now breathe a little more easily. The time we have between now and the time we receive a reply from the Duke can be used to find the true murderer."

At that point Father Matthew entered, accompanied by Dame Eglantine. He gasped when he saw the gypsy's body and crossed himself quickly. He hesitated, then caught the ferocious expression on Chaucer's face and hurried over to give her the last rites. Respectfully Chaucer and the others withdrew to another part of the room.

Geoffrey sighed with frustration, then turned to the women. "You say she told you little about herself," he ventured. Alisoun and the two nuns nodded vigorously.

"Well, someone must know something more about her than what you've told me. What about that foppish young squire? Surely he must know something! She was practically never out of his sight!" Chaucer leaned against the wall, closing his eyes as if in deep thought. "Friar Hubert knew her, too. And that arse-hole of a summoner as well! Get him up! Somebody must know something!" He headed for the door. "I'll see them in my room!

When he arrived at the door to his chamber, he noticed that he had left it open. Or had he? In some concern he pushed his way inside, then stamped his foot in anger, accompanying that gesture with a loud curse. His silver candleholder was missing,

Someone is very brave, he told himself. *Or is this the murderer's way of mocking me?*

Fumbling through his pack, he drew out a second candleholder, this one made of brass, and another new candle. He set them down beside his manuscript book. His eyes fell upon the poem he had written about Sophia, and a sudden wave of grief passed through him. When he had penned those lines, Sophia had been alive.

Wearily he collapsed into his chair. Who besides the thief would have wanted Sophia dead? Agatha's admonishment about the local law enforcers had started him thinking. Was it too easy a solution to assume that the person who had been stealing the silver had also murdered Sophia?

There was, of course, Sir Richard. He was a knight, accustomed to killing; he had disapproved highly of Simon's infatuation with Sophia. It was Chaucer's experience that knights were trained to think of anyone other than Christians as less than human—and the Christianity of gypsies was often suspect, even though many of them attended mass faithfully. Yet Sir Richard was a devout believer in the code of chivalry, which held that women were always to be protected and cherished—and Sophia had not only been a woman, but a young and beautiful one, in spite of Sir Richard's reservations about her. Could a man sworn to uphold the rules of chivalry even to the death actually bring himself to kill a mere girl?

And there was the friar—Brother Hubert. He made no secret of the fact that in spite of his religious calling he enjoyed the pleasures of the flesh, and he had certainly lusted after Sophia. Yet she—understandably—had preferred the beautiful Simon to the fat and aging Hubert. Was this a crime of passion, rooted in jealousy?

Jealousy…An uncomfortable possibility popped into Chaucer's head. He had witnessed Sophia's callous insinuation about Alisoun, needling the older woman because of her age. Women, as wonderful as they were, could resemble she-bears when threatened in any way. And Alisoun had been lying only a few feet from Sophia. How easy it would have been for her to sneak over and plunge the dagger into that fiery young heart.

But no! Chaucer chided himself. You're letting your poet's imagination run away with you, Geoffrey. Surely the killer must be the thief.

His weariness began to take over his body. His eyes closed in spite of himself; he was tempted once more to lay his head on the table.

"Master Chaucer?"

Geoffrey looked up with a start. Walter, clearly very nervous, stood in his doorway.

"Master Bailey sent me," said Walter timidly. "Ill tidings, Master Chaucer, very ill tidings!"

Suddenly Chaucer was wide-awake and alert. "What is it, Walter?"

"It's Jack the summoner, Master Chaucer! He's gone!"

Five

"Gone!" exclaimed Chaucer, half rising from his seat. "What do you mean?"

"I mean he's gone. Scarpered. Run away, it seems. His pack is gone, and Master Bailey went to the stables himself to try to catch him. But his horse's stall is empty, and there's no sign of his saddle or bridle."

Chaucer breathed a sigh of relief as he sank back into his chair. He had thought Walter had meant the summoner was dead. "When was this discovered?" he finally asked.

"When Master Bailey went into the men's common sleeping-room to fetch him."

Chaucer eyed Walter carefully. "When was the last time he was seen?"

"When we heard that Sophia had been stabbed. I saw him myself, right at that moment."

"And how did he appear?"

"Terrified, Master Chaucer. As if he'd just had a vision of the devil himself."

Chaucer's mind began to work faster than he believed possible. The summoner had jumped to the conclusion that the thief—a man whose identity he was as aware of as Sophia—had murdered Sophia. Realizing that his own life was in danger, he had run.

A wise man, indeed, Chaucer reflected. *But without him how are we to determine the identity of the thief?*

"Well, no matter. He can't get far. As soon as the deputy sheriff and his men arrive we'll send some out after him."

"Master Chaucer," said Walter, suddenly eager. "Is there anything I can do to help you?"

Chaucer was rather taken aback. He had been embarrassed by Walter's undisguised admiration, but it was good to know there was one person other than Robert, Agatha and Harry Bailey who would stand solidly in his corner should the deputy sheriff accuse him of the murder.

"Yes," he finally said. "I want you to take notes for me. I'm going to be talking to some members of our party, and I won't be able to talk and write at the same time. Could you do this for me?"

Walter's face fairly glowed. "Of course!"

At that moment a tentative knock sounded at the door, and it opened a crack. A young girl of about sixteen, with fair hair, a slender but ripening body, and an unassuming yet winsome countenance, stood in the crack carrying a pitcher and tankard on a tray.

"Master Chaucer?"

"Yes?"

"I am Jenifred Atte Wood, the landlord's daughter. Master Bailey told us you'd be awake for awhile. My father thought you might want some ale?"

"Yes, of course. Thank Master Atte Wood for me. You can set it down on the table."

Jenifred did so, bending just enough to offer an enticing glimpse of appealing young cleavage. Chaucer's face registered his appreciation, then his heart sank as he noticed the enchantment which had suddenly appeared on Walter's face.

Oh, no, he thought, not another lovesick young fool. Yet I can't say that I blame him. She's lovely.

Jenifred noticed Walter's expression, then smiled rather nervously, as though she had never before been confronted with a young man who liked her. "Call me if you need anything more. I'll be downstairs," she mumbled, then, plainly flustered, she dashed out the door, closing it behind her,

Walter, bereft, turned his face to Chaucer, his mouth open ridiculously.

Geoffrey rose and offered his chair to the clerk in an attempt to set him at ease. He glanced down at his new manuscript book, unwilling to sacrifice it to the cause of taking notes on a murder. He thought for a moment, then went to his pack and took out an old manuscript book, used for his astrological studies, and handed it to Walter. "Use this," he said. "I believe there are some empty pages in the back." He then walked over to the door, opened it and called out, "Harry! Can you send young Simon in here?" A few moments later Simon entered the room, his face streaked with tears, shaking with both grief and fear.

Chaucer gestured for Simon to sit on his bed. "Calm down, young man! I only want to know everything you know about Sophia."

"Only that this afternoon she was alive, I loved her, and now she's dead!" He broke into loud, racking sobs, burying his face in his hands.

"It's terrible, and a sad day for all of us. But we can't change it. All we can do now is try to find the one who killed her. And perhaps you can help. Tell me: You witnessed the scene at noon today between her and Jack the summoner. Did she say anything to you at all about who the person was that the summoner had threatened?" Though Chaucer hoped he was wrong, secretly he doubted that Sophia had had anything in mind other than spiriting the youth away to the woods.

Simon shook his head wildly. "No! She never did! And I didn't like to ask her—didn't want to pry, you understand."

I do, thought Chaucer. *You didn't want to be rude. But how much better off we'd be now if you had been!* "Well, then," said Chaucer. "perhaps we should learn something about her past. Did she say anything about where she was from, or who her family was, or anything like that?"

"She acted strangely, Master Chaucer. She only spoke of how her grandfather had come from Egypt and was trained in all the mysteries of that country."

Chaucer sighed. "The gypsies are no more Egyptian than you or I," he said. "I was informed of that fact by the writings of no less a great mind than Dante Alighieri himself. The gypsies are probably from Arabia somewhere. But they love to play on that lie. It makes them sound more mysterious."

"Well, that's all she told me," said the squire defensively.

"In short, you know nothing."

"Well—" The squire hesitated, then shook his head. "No. Nothing."

Chaucer's ears pricked up. "You were going to tell me something. What was it?"

"Well—it sounds rather foolish."

"So does this murder. Tell me. If it's foolish no one ever need know you said anything."

The squire breathed a sigh of relief. "It was her horse. Its name was Nicholas. She said it was named for her brother."

"Nicholas, eh?" said Chaucer thoughtfully. "Well, it's not much of a start, but it certainly isn't foolish. Thank you, my lord. I may want to speak to you later."

The young man nodded his thanks and hurried through the door. Obviously, Chaucer told himself, the boy was worried about something. But did it relate to Sophia?

"Harry!" he called. "Send Hubert in."

Friar Hubert, annoyed at being kept from his sleep, lumbered in unwillingly, and plopped heavily onto the bed when Geoffrey gestured for him to do so.

"May I ask, Master Chaucer," Hubert said. "by what authority you've taken control of things? I wasn't aware that you had any such standing!"

"I am Controller of the King's Petty Custom," said Chaucer patiently. "That makes me a direct employee of the King himself, and thus the one person here with any royal authority at all. And I am only taking charge of this investigation until the local deputy sheriff arrives."

"As an employee of the King, you have no jurisdiction over me," said Friar Hubert, starting to rise. "I answer only to the Holy Father, or to any of his bishops or priests. Therefore, if it is all the same to you, I shall return to my bed."

"Sit down!" Chaucer shouted. Friar Hubert, startled by the outburst, sank back onto the bed. "Brother Hubert, a murder has been committed here. You as a churchman know that it violates one of God's primary commandments, and is regarded as perhaps the most heinous of sins. Now unless you want to be instrumental in allowing a murderer to escape—which would be almost as unspeakable as the murder itself—you had best cooperate with me and answer my questions!"

"Well, I don't know what questions you might have," said Hubert defensively. "It's pretty obvious who killed the girl."

"Who?" Chaucer demanded.

"Why, that blasted summoner, of course."

"Oh, really?" said Chaucer cynically, remembering the antagonism between Friar Hubert and Jack the summoner. "Why do you say that?"

"Good Lord, man, didn't you hear what she said to him yesterday, at noon, before I told my tale? She humiliated him before the entire company! And now he's gone—escaped! Surely it doesn't take any great mind to see the truth here!"

Chaucer turned to Walter. "You said you saw the summoner in the men's common sleeping-room as soon as the news was given out about Sophia. Did you see him any time before that?"

"Yes, Master Chaucer," Walter replied. "Most of the men in there were still wide awake, talking, laughing, trading insults. But Jack the summoner, I think, was too drunk to take part. I didn't participate, either—I was too weary. It would have been impossible for me to sleep, with all the noise. Yet that cursed summoner was so drunk he passed out immediately after we all came upstairs. I remember wondering how he could possibly do so, the other men were so loud. And he snores like a nagging virago—it would have been impossible to ignore him. It wasn't until Madame Eglantine raised the cry about Sophia's murder that he awoke—and as I told you then, he looked terrified, like the devil himself had appeared in the room."

"Then from the time we all came upstairs, to the time we all knew that Sophia had been killed, you were totally aware of the summoner's presence?"

"Yes, Master Chaucer."

"So much for your theory," said Chaucer to Friar Hubert.

"How do you know this insolent puppy isn't in league with that rogue?" Hubert demanded.

"I shall verify his story by asking some of the other men," said Chaucer. "But now I'm talking to you. You were constantly seen in the company of Sophia, so you must have known something about her. Tell me all you know about her."

"I know that she was a cruel little tease!" Friar Hubert shouted. "She flaunted herself to every man in the party—including you, Master Chaucer! I saw it! But once she had captured their interest, her interest went out like a candle flame! A Jezebel, she was—a pagan gypsy Jezebel! Surely she got no more than was coming to her!"

Chaucer's deep-seeded dislike of friars caused his anger to flare dangerously. He remembered Sophia on the journey—laughing merrily, riding her horse up and down the line of pilgrims—and in the hall below, holding her audience rapt with her story of Isis and Osiris.

"There are those who would say the same thing about murdered friars," said Geoffrey, trying hard to control his temper. "I think when you are more rational, Brother Hubert, you will agree that no one deserves to be murdered! No man has the right to terminate the life of another before God calls him, no matter how evil that person is. But I am not here to collect opinions, friend friar—only facts. Now tell me: when you were in Sophia's company, did she tell you anything at all about herself? About her family, about her home, about anything that could help us learn more about her? Think, man!"

Friar Hubert thought, his face and the crown of his tonsured head growing red with rage and humiliation. Suddenly it seemed as if he had made a decision to talk. Probably, Chaucer reflected, because he knew that if he didn't he would never get back to his bed.

"She spoke of Canterbury," Friar Hubert finally said. "She spoke of how eager she was to see the cathedral. She said that she had come from the north, that as a child she had often visited York Minster, and had loved it. She expressed the opinion that the cathedral at Canterbury could not possibly be more beautiful than that of York. She also asked a great deal of questions about the church—about priests, monks, friars."

"And did you answer them?" asked Chaucer.

"Why should I? Women are not bright enough to know such things. I only sought her company to—to—" he floundered.

"Never mind," said Chaucer. The air in the room suddenly began to suffocate him. "You may go now, Brother Hubert. And as you go, please ask Master Bailey to send in Sir Richard de Burgoyne."

A moment later Hubert was out the door. Chaucer immediately hurried over to the window and opened the shutters, wide. The night air was cold, but fresh. He turned to the clerk, who was busy scribbling away at his notes of Hubert's account.

"Walter," said Chaucer. "tell me where the friar was tonight—during the same period of time you told me about the summoner."

"He was one of those making all the noise," said Walter, pausing for a moment and setting down his quill. "He was right in the thick of the crowd. I must admit I wasn't watching them every moment, but I don't see how Friar Hubert could have left and returned without attracting attention."

"Well, then, I shall have to ask some of the others. Who was it that was so involved with that conversation, Walter? Tell me, as much as you can remember."

"Well," Walter screwed up his forehead thoughtfully. "The knight and the squire weren't there. I assume they had their own room. Neither were the doctor or the man at law, or the franklin or the merchant. But the miller was there, and the monk, and the pardoner, and the reeve and the plowman, and the guildsmen and their cook. Master Bailey, of course. The three priests that came with Dame Eglantine huddled together, in the back of the room, and the country parson was sleeping near the summoner."

"Take all that down, please," said Chaucer. "We may need to refer to it later."

Conscientiously Walter again began to write, just as Sir Richard de Burgoyne entered. He was bareheaded, his golden hair tousled boyishly, dressed in hose and an unbelted tunic. Nonetheless he appeared naked without his sword. His face, Chaucer noted, was white with shock.

Sir Richard sat on the edge of Chaucer's bed, hands on his knees, looking every bit as noble as a knight should be. He didn't wait for Chaucer to speak.

"I know what you're thinking," he said. "You know how much I disapproved of my son's involvement with the gypsy girl, and are wondering if that would constitute a good reason to kill her. But I assure you, Master Chaucer, I did not."

"I don't believe you did," said Chaucer kindly. "However, you may have observed something important that others missed. How long had young Simon known Sophia?"

"We met her at a fair, on the road here from York," said Sir Richard. "She was dancing, playing a tambourine, while another gypsy musician played the symphony. Simon was captivated. As soon as the dance was finished, she noticed him right away. He is—well, a rather handsome youth, and quite noticeable in a crowd. Sophia managed to engage Simon in conversation and gleaned from him the information that we were traveling to Canterbury. She was thrilled at the idea and decided to come with us. Simon, of course, welcomed her heartily."

"And you allowed it?" Chaucer asked curiously.

"I protested, of course. And I pointed out to Simon that it was highly unseemly that a lone girl travel with a company of three men. But the girl was determined to come, and His Majesty's roads are open to everyone. How could I stop her? She would ride along beside Simon for awhile, then she would dash off and do God knows what, then reappear after an hour or so."

"How long did she travel with you?"

"Two days, no more."

"Where did she sleep at night?"

"The first night she wanted to sleep in the forest, some distance away from our camp. As much as I disliked the girl, I couldn't in all good conscience allow her to sleep alone in the woods, at the mercy of robbers and wild beasts. I sent my yeoman to ask her to come sleep closer to the fire, near us, for warmth and safety. At first she declined, stating that she was used to sleeping alone on the ground, but my yeoman finally persuaded her to come nearer the fire. Needless to say, she spread her bedroll near Simon's. I don't think he slept at all that night."

Chaucer's ears pricked up. "What do you mean?"

"Oh, they didn't do anything," Sir Richard hastened to add. "I just mean he was extremely bothered by her nearness. Can you blame him? He was young and vulnerable; she was beautiful and passionate. But he has been carefully instructed in the rules of chivalry, which do not include compromising a woman, even a pagan gypsy. Still, I am certain his body was quite—well, shall we say ill at ease? The second night we stopped at an inn, and she slept in the stables. I must confess, that was a much more comfortable arrangement for all."

Chaucer frowned, then spoke up. "How involved was Simon with Sophia? Do you think he'd have wanted to marry her?"

"God forbid!" exclaimed Sir Richard. "I don't think he ever thought that far ahead. And I believe that once the initial flame of his desire for her had died down a little, he had enough sense not to even consider such an idea. Yet I've lived among the tail end of the nobility for many years, Master Chaucer. I know what it's like to straddle two worlds—the world of the aristocrats to which we all aspire, and the world of the common man with which we feel more comfortable. I have seen the results of arrangements where a young man of Simon's status marries a young noblewoman for the sake of rising in the hierarchy—and then keeps a lusty peasant girl for a mistress. It's always a disaster, Master Chaucer. Such an arrangement, though touted as practical by certain insensitive men, can only hurt the parties involved."

Geoffrey was reminded uncomfortably of the painful involvement of his beautiful sister-in-law, Katherine, with his friend John of Gaunt, Duke of Lancaster. He could only agree—overwhelmingly.

"I want my son to marry well, Master Chaucer," Sir Richard was continuing. "But I want there to be love in that marriage. I don't want any daughter-in-law I might have to lose sleep at night, alone and heartsick, because her husband lies in the arms of a gypsy mistress!"

Chaucer nodded, approvingly. He liked Sir Richard more and more every moment.

"Still, as much as I disapproved of Simon's involvement with Sophia, because, at this moment in time, my son loved her, I would have given my life to protect her," Sir Richard continued softly, gazing at the wall, a faraway look in his eyes. "I know what it's like to lose a girl you love, Master Chaucer. It happened to me when I was sixteen—a cousin, Marian, whom I grew up with, whom I thought of as a sweetheart—the plague—" Here he choked. Chaucer thought he could see tears glistening in the man's eyes. The expression then turned to anger. "I would never have wished that on my son, not for the world and all its riches! If there is anything, anything at all, Master Chaucer, that I can do to help you bring this cursed killer to justice, tell me!"

"I will," Chaucer promised. "Sir Richard, in the course of your travels with Sophia, did she say anything at all that might tell us anything about her background?"

Sir Richard shook his head. "If she did, Master Chaucer, I was not present," he said. "I avoided her company whenever possible."

"Tonight, after everyone went to bed, did you see or hear anything?"

"Nothing, Master Chaucer. I sleep rather soundly, I fear, and would be unlikely to hear anything short of the house falling down around me."

"Thank you, Sir Richard," said Chaucer. "That will be all for now. I will keep you informed at all times. Would you please tell Harry to send in Master Richemont?"

Sir Richard nodded, then left. Chaucer sat for a moment pondering what Sir Richard had told him, ignoring Walter's quizzical look. There was no doubt in Geoffrey's mind that Sir Richard had meant every word he said. But there would be those more cynical than Chaucer—John of Gaunt, for one—who would suspect the man of being a skilled and consummate actor. A quick dagger through the heart would to some seem an easy way to dispose of a promising son's unwanted ladylove.

Chaucer sighed. How he wished he had Sir Richard's astrological chart! That would tell him in a moment whether the man was a proficient liar or not!

At that moment Master Richemont walked through the door.

"Good evening, Master Chaucer," said the physician. "How can I help you?"

"You can provide me with information," replied Chaucer. "First of all, I know you examined Sophia's body pretty closely. I need to know what you found."

"Well, as you know, she died of a stab wound in the side, right to the heart," said Master Richemont, clearly pleased with his own importance. "She had been dead for about an hour when I examined her. The dagger was angled in such a way as to imply that the killer was facing the back wall and that he was right-handed."

"You say he," Chaucer interrupted. "Is there anything to indicate that the murderer might not have been a woman?"

Master Richemont shrugged. "No, nothing at all," he replied. "The girl was asleep, and to stab her like that would not have taken extraordinary strength."

"What did you know about her?" Chaucer asked.

"Not much," said Master Richemont. "She appears to have been young, about eighteen or twenty. She hadn't yet started to lose her teeth, and her skin was still taut and firm. Although I didn't examine her closely enough to know for certain, I don't think she'd ever had a child. She had strong, firm muscles, probably from dancing, as gypsies often do."

"When she was alive, did you ever have occasion to speak to her?"

"Only once. She flirted with me, the way she flirted with everybody. I made it clear I wasn't interested."

"What exactly did she say?"

"What difference does that make?" Richemont asked curiously, somewhat affronted at this invasion of his privacy.

"Perhaps none. But it might provide us with a piece of valuable information, no matter how insignificant it may seem to you now."

Richemont sighed. "She asked if I was married. I told her I had never wanted to do so, that I had long aspired to the priesthood and to joining an order of hospitallers. She pointedly hinted that perhaps celibacy was weighing on my loins. I told her that was my concern, not hers. She replied that if I ever decided to make it her concern, I was to let her know. That's all."

"And you know nothing else about the girl?"

"No."

Chaucer leaned against the wall and folded his arms. Something told him that "no" did not comprise the whole truth. "Now tell me," he said. "what, if anything, you heard tonight, between the time we all came upstairs and the time Madame Eglantine raised the cry about Sophia's murder."

Richemont frowned. "Well, I don't sleep in common sleeping-rooms. I share a room with the attorney, down at the end of the hall, as far from the common sleeping-rooms as I can get. I came upstairs with everyone else, climbed into bed and fell asleep as soon as I hit my pillow. The next thing I knew Mistress Willard was pounding on my door, saying that Sophia had been murdered and I was needed to examine the body."

"And you heard nothing throughout all that time?"

"No."

"And was the man of law there all the time as well?"

"I think so, though I couldn't swear to it. I was too deeply asleep to say honestly I would have noticed it."

"Thank you, Master Richemont," said Chaucer. "You may go now. And please send Master de Coverly in."

Richemont nodded and left. Chaucer then turned to Walter. "Write this down on another page," he directed. "Head it: Facts about Sophia."

Walter wrote furiously.

"One: She has a brother named Nicholas. Two: She was from the north, claimed familiarity with York Minster and was curious about the Church. Three: She was eighteen or twenty, an outrageous flirt, but apparently had never had a child."

Walter looked up with a start. "That does seem strange, doesn't it?"

"One would think so. Of course there is always the chance that she could be barren, but for a young girl so obviously healthy that would seem unlikely." His head jerked up as Henry de Coverly entered and without invitation seated himself on Chaucer's bed.

"You have already stepped on a few toes tonight, Master Chaucer," said De Coverly pompously. "If I were you I would take care to make no enemies. You are in a very precarious position legally, as we discussed earlier."

"Well, by the time I finished talking to everyone here, perhaps my position will be stronger," said Chaucer. "I am not accusing anyone, Master de Coverly. I am merely trying to learn as much about Sophia and about what happened tonight as I can. Now tell me what you know. Do not worry if it seems too little to tell. Sometimes the smallest bit of information causes a puzzle to all come together. What did you know about Sophia?"

"Aside from the fact that she was one of the ripest little morsels I've seen in a long time, practically nothing. But she must have been a skilled and clever thief—she did managed to steal that cross from the summoner."

"Do you think she was the thief who has been stealing silver from this group?"

De Coverly shook his head. "No, I don't. I have dealt with criminals for nigh on thirty years, Master Chaucer, and I have never before seen any guilty person reveal himself the way she did. I think she was only trying to put the summoner in his place. And perhaps the friar, too. I don't know."

Chaucer nodded. He had only asked out of curiosity. He knew that Sophia had not been the thief—his silver candleholder had disappeared only after she was dead.

Unless someone else stole it, because he wished to clear her name. But why would anyone do that? Perhaps Simon?

Chaucer shook his head, as though trying to shake the fragments of information it contained into some kind of coherency. "Tell us what you heard tonight—if anything," he then said.

"Well, as you probably already know, I was in my room, with the physician," the attorney answered. "I don't sleep well on straw pallets, Master Chaucer. I fell asleep soon after we came upstairs, but noises kept awakening me. I thought they were rats in the walls, but now I wonder."

Chaucer's ears pricked up. "What did you hear?" he demanded.

"About midnight, I suppose, I heard some scratching sounds. At first I thought it was someone at the door, but then when I awoke I realized I'd been dreaming. Then I heard some rustling. It sounded as if it were coming from the walls, and so I decided it had to be rats and went back to sleep. The next thing I knew, Mistress Willard was rousing me. That's all I can tell you."

"Thank you, Master de Coverly. You can go now." As De Coverly walked out the door, Chaucer turned to Walter. "Add to our list of facts about Sophia: She was a skilled thief, but probably not the thief who's been stealing from us." He sighed. "And now I'm weary of questioning people. Let's get out of this room for awhile," he said.

Walter nodded. His wide gray eyes, ringed with lashes a girl would envy, fairly radiated dedication. "Shall I bring the book?" he asked.

"Yes, by all means. Let's go to the men's common sleeping-room! We can try to learn if anyone there saw or heard anything!"

As soon as they stepped out of the room, the sound of angry shouts, derisive laughs, breaking crockery and loud thumps assailed their ears.

Chaucer's shocked gaze met Walter's, then, after only a moment's hesitation, they headed for the men's sleeping-room.

Chaucer threw open the door. The combined odors of spilled ale, unwashed bodies, smelly feet, and urine-filled chamberpots suddenly assaulted his nostrils; for a moment he felt nauseous. His eyes immediately were drawn to a spot in the middle of the floor, where a crowd of eager spectators, chortling drunkenly, were goading two scuffling bodies. Harry Bailey gazed helplessly at Chaucer; he had been trying to break up the fight, but all in vain.

"Stop this!" shouted Chaucer. "Stop in the name of the King! I demand it!"

As he drew closer he could see that the two antagonists were Simon and Friar Hubert. Simon's face was bleeding from a cut at his hairline, and one of his eyes showed promise of turning bright purple by morning. The friar had lost a tooth, and his robe was torn.

Deftly Chaucer stepped between them, defying them to strike. "Now what's going on?" he demanded.

Simon's wild eyes met his in an almost desperate plea for help. "He called Sophia a whore!"

"Ay, I did, and that she was!" rasped Friar Hubert. "Flaunting her body at every man in the party—even priests—and then turning them down flat if they showed signs of accepting her offer—

"You only say that because she rejected you!" cried Simon. "How can you blame her, you fat, drunken old hypocrite!"

The friar lunged for Simon once more; Chaucer stretched out his arms and held them apart. Sir Richard stepped forward and gripped his son's shoulder.

Harry Bailey then reached out and held the friar firmly by both arms.

"Calm down, Simon," Chaucer commanded. "And you, Brother Hubert, I'm surprised at you. You're supposed to be a man of God, and I am sure you are aware of our Lord's admonishment that only he who is without sin should cast the first stone. Besides, it's bad luck to speak ill of the dead. And under any circumstances a true man of God would think twice before calling anyone a whore!"

"If you're speaking of the late Sophia, it's a term that is totally unwarranted," said a voice from the door. All eyes turned toward Master Richemont.

"I can say on the best authority that Sophia was no whore," he reaffirmed confidently. "Master Chaucer, could I speak with you alone?"

Noting the perplexed expressions on the faces in the room—and certain that an identical look appeared on his own face—Chaucer stepped away from the fray, leaving the two scufflers in the capable hands of Harry Bailey. Together he and Master Richemont walked out of the door and closed it.

"After speaking with you, I went back to the body," said Master Richemont. "I discerned that there was more to learn from it, and so I performed a rather intimate examination. And distasteful though it was, I did learn something important."

"What was that?"

"Not only had Mistress Sophia never had a child," Richemont answered, "she was a virgin."

Chaucer caught his breath. "Are you sure?"

"As sure as King Richard is the second of that name since the Conquest," said Master Richemont. "And come with me! There is something else I noticed about the body. You must see!"

With some trepidation—for he had no desire to view the private parts of a corpse—Chaucer followed Master Richemont into the women's common sleeping-room. Someone—probably Alisoun—had laid Sophia out properly, with her eyes closed and her hands folded over a wooden crucifix, undoubtedly a gift of the prioress. Candles burned all around her; the two nuns, Alisoun, and Agatha all sat around keeping a solemn vigil, as was considered proper after a death.

Inwardly Chaucer relaxed when Richemont showed no inclination to lift Sophia's skirt, but knelt beside her head.

"Mistress Alisoun?" said Richemont. "Would you mind letting down your hair?"

Alisoun grinned; apparently she was proud of her hair. "Not at all, my lord doctor," she said. She removed her veil and coif and released from its knot her mane of auburn hair—undoubtedly her best feature, Chaucer surmised—and then came over and sat beside the doctor.

Master Richemont took a hank of Alisoun's hair in his hand. "Mistress Alisoun, have you ever in your life cut your hair?" he asked.

"Never!" Alisoun declared. "The same hair you have in your hand is that which grew on my head when I was a babe!"

Richemont nodded. "I thought probably so. Now, Master Chaucer, I know the light in here is poor, but I want you to take a close look at the ends of Mistress Alisoun's hair."

Chaucer tried, but he couldn't; the very effort gave him a headache. The dim light was only part of the reason; his eyesight wasn't what it used to be. "Wait a moment," he said. From one of his pockets he drew a small circular lens. "This is something I picked up in Italy, years ago. The Italian explorers brought it from the Far East. It makes things appear larger than they are." He held the lens over the lock of Alisoun's hair that Richemont held in his hand. It suddenly appeared ten times its size. Chaucer studied it carefully, but saw nothing worthy of note. He looked questioningly at Master Richemont.

The physician removed his cap and coif, revealing a thick head of graying brown hair surrounding a bald spot at the back. "Now look at mine," he directed. "I cut my hair about a month ago. Take your glass and look at the ends of my hair."

Chaucer obeyed, then light dawned on his face. "The ends of your hair are blunt. Alisoun's are tapering."

"Exactly!" said Richemont. "Now study Sophia's, and tell me what you see." He held up a lock of the dead girl's thick mane.

Geoffrey took it from him, gazed at it through his glass, then looked up at Richemont, his brow puckered. "Hers are blunt, like yours."

His mind began buzzing like a bee, moving quickly from point to point, assembling all the facts about Sophia that he had learned that night. She was a gypsy, whom many assumed to be pagan, but was on a pilgrimage to a Christian shrine. She had shown a strong interest in learning about Canterbury Cathedral and in the workings of the Church. She was a virgin. And at one time she had cut her hair.

Something Robert Willard had said of her suddenly rang in Chaucer's ears: "That girl knows little of the ways of this world."

Chaucer's eyes widened as they met Richemont's. "You don't mean to tell me—"

"Yes, I do. At one time, Sophia was probably a nun."

Six

"Of course, if she had applied for a novitiate at my convent, I would never have even considered admitting her!" said Dame Eglantine, nervously twisting her scapular. "I still have a hard time believing it. That outrageously wanton girl—coquetting with all the men—and now you tell me she was once a nun?"

"We don't know for sure, Madame Eglantine," said Chaucer. "But all the evidence seems to point to it. And you are the only person in our party who would be totally familiar with the ways of convents. You must tell us what you can."

They were once more sitting in Chaucer's room, with Master Richemont observing, Henry de Coverly listening and occasionally adding sage comments with regard to the law, Walter conscientiously taking notes, and Sister Cecily acting as chaperon.

"Well, all the orders with which I am familiar," said Dame Eglantine, obviously still very uneasy. "would not take a gypsy into their convents. Oh, I am not saying they are not as worthy as anyone else to serve Our Lord," she said, waving aside Chaucer's protest before he could verbalize it. "but most nunneries only take girls from the wealthier, more highly-born families, who can provide the order with a substantial dowry. However, there are in England a few scattered chapters of the Poor Clares, the spiritual descendants of St. Clare. They make no distinction between rich and poor—in fact, they live in such reduced circumstances that few highborn girls wish to join them. They also do not discriminate according to a girl's—ancestry. If Sophia was indeed a nun, I suspect that the only order she could have joined would have been that of the Poor Clares."

"Is there a chapter of the Poor Clares in York, Madame Eglantine? Do you know?"

"I suppose so. I think that most of the English chapters of the Poor Clares—and there aren't that many, I assure you—are centered in the north. The south is dominated by the wealthier orders." There was a touch of pride in her voice as she said that.

"Well, now we're getting somewhere," Chaucer mused, pacing the floor. "A young gypsy, a devout Christian, with a brother called Nicholas, joins a convent in York, then for some reason leaves it and comes south to go on a pilgrimage."

"But I don't understand!" protested Walter. "If she was so devout as to become a nun, then why did she act the wanton?"

"She didn't, really," said Chaucer. "She only flirted with the men. I suppose if she had been shut up in a convent for a few years, seeing no one but women most of the time, she would enjoy again being with members of the opposite sex. You will recall that one of the complaints Friar Hubert had about her was that she led men on, but didn't follow through. The only man she really encouraged was Simon, who is too chivalrous even to think of compromising the virtue of his ladylove. And she might have had other reasons as well. Perhaps we'll learn more."

There was a sudden knock at the door. "Come in!" Chaucer barked.

Harry Bailey opened the door and stepped into the chamber. "I have spoken to every man in the men's common sleeping-room," he said. "None of them saw Jack the summoner leave the room from the time we all came upstairs to the time we heard about Sophia's murder. In fact, Robyn the miller and Roger the cook, who were sitting in such a place as to be able to see where Jack was sleeping, state that he was there sleeping all that time, like young Walter here claims. I'm afraid we'll have to eliminate the summoner as Sophia's killer."

"Well, he was too easy a target, anyway," said Chaucer. He turned pointedly to Dame Eglantine. "Thank you very much for your help, my lady. I believe that Master Atte Wood, our good landlord, has arranged new sleeping quarters for you ladies, so that you won't have to spend the night in the same room as a corpse. I suggest that you and Sister Cecily fetch Mistress Alisoun and go to the new chamber. You need your sleep. We men will take turns sitting up with Sophia."

With a relieved nod, Dame Eglantine stood and, summoning all her dignity, literally swept out of the door. Sister Cecily followed her.

"Harry, close the door," Chaucer directed. Bailey obeyed, then sat down on Chaucer's bed beside Henry de Coverly. "I can't get my mind off that damned friar," Chaucer confessed. "Aren't the Franciscan friars a male counterpart to the Poor Clares? In view of what we have just learned, I can't help wondering if our good friend Brother Hubert knew Sophia before he met her on this pilgrimage!"

"It could be. It could also be that Sophia knew Don John the monk, any of the four priests, or even our pardoner friend," said Harry Bailey. "But why kill her? And how does all this connect with the thief?"

"I'm as confused as you," Chaucer confessed. "We've learned much about Sophia, but it's raised more questions than it's given answers!"

Henry de Coverly then spoke up. "This is all very interesting, Master Chaucer, but legally I don't know if it's going to do you any good."

"What do you mean?" asked Chaucer.

"No matter who Sophia was or where she came from, that was still your card found beside her."

Jack the summoner swatted his horse again and again with his crop. They had found him—one of them was among that damned crowd of pilgrims! Jack knew who it was—and by letting the person know it, all for the sake of a damned silver cross, the summoner had signed his own death warrant. Not for the first time did Jack the summoner repent his greed. How ironic that his sins would catch up with him while he was on his way to the shrine of a holy saint, to seek forgiveness!

He wondered if they had noticed that he was gone. His horse, frightened nearly to death, was now foaming at the mouth, running at the fastest gallop the summoner had ever known. They passed under a low-lying branch; Jack cursed as it swept his hat off his head. His bald spot would now grow unbearably cold—but he didn't dare go back for the hat; every moment counted. He had to put as much distance as he could between himself and whoever had killed the gypsy wench.

Why had they killed her? Didn't they know she was a total innocent, thinking only that the person she saw with the summoner was no more than a thief? But the people he was dealing with took no chances. Too much was at stake.

Where would he go? Not to Canterbury—that would be the first place they would look for him. Not to York—there were too many of them in the far north.

Norfolk. Or perhaps Suffolk. Or maybe Cornwall.

Cornwall. Yes! That would be an unlikely place for someone like him to go. He would head for the far west, for Land's End. There he would grow his hair and beard long, to hide his boils, and he would take up some other occupation. All the bribes and the resulting high living that went with being a summoner wasn't worth his life.

He turned his horse towards the west and rode for dear life.

It was still well before dawn when John of Gaunt, Duke of Lancaster, was roused from his bed by his aide, Sir Oliver Radley.

"Good God, Oliver, do you know what hour it is?" snapped the Duke, slowly sitting up and rubbing his eyes.

"I do, my lord, but I think you would want to receive this message," said Sir Oliver. He handed it over. Gaunt snatched it from his hand and opened it. He perused it quickly, then jumped out of bed.

"Geoffrey's in trouble," he said, climbing out of the warm cocoon of his quilts. His wife, the princess Costanza of Castile, a thin, pale, nondescript girl more interested in piety than politics, opened her eyes and moaned briefly.

"*Juanito, por qué eres-tu revellado a este hora?*" she asked sleepily.

"Nothing to concern you, *mi cara*. An old friend needs me. Go back to sleep," said Gaunt. "Fetch my valet!" he barked at Radley. Radley nodded and disappeared.

Gaunt steered his magnificent, battle-scarred naked body over to his washing bowl and pitcher. The water in the pitcher was icy cold, but it served to awaken as well as to wash. He poured it over his head, shook his short grey-gold hair, then wiped his face and beard with a towel just as his valet arrived with his everyday riding clothes. They were of the best quality, but dyed a dark brown color, so as not to show the grime of the road. Gaunt, however, unable to avoid indulging his vanity, always dressed this outfit up with a richly embroidered belt of red, green or blue. Today, his valet had chosen the blue.

It took the Duke only a few moments to dress. While doing so, he ordered Sir Oliver to summon four soldiers, get their horses and meet him outside. Sir Oliver fairly goggled at him.

"This man certainly must be very important to you," Oliver remarked.

"Yes, he is," said Gaunt shortly. "Don't stand there gawking! Do as I say!"

Sir Oliver nodded, bowed, and disappeared through the door.

John of Gaunt had been friends with Geoffrey Chaucer ever since they were both in their teens, when Geoffrey had been a page in the household of Gaunt's father, King Edward III. In those early days, both had aspired to be soldiers, and so they were often thrown into each other's presence in spite of the vast difference in their social status. They enjoyed each other's company, as both were brighter than their peers were, and thus they shared a common bond: that of being different.

Chaucer had been present at the wedding of John of Gaunt and his first wife, Blanche, the beautiful, kind, and well-loved young woman who had captured the hearts of everyone in England, including young Chaucer. Geoffrey had become a devoted satellite of the Lancaster household, bestowing the gifts of his intelligence on John and his love on Blanche. But only three years later Blanche had fallen victim to the plague, and the entire realm had grieved. The friendship shared between John of Gaunt and Geoffrey Chaucer had comforted them in their grief, and had further cemented the bond between them. One of Chaucer's finest poems, *The Book of the Duchess,* had been written in Blanche's honor.

A few years later, Chaucer had married Philippa, and John of Gaunt took for his mistress Philippa's younger sister, Katherine Swynford. The two households—the royal household of the Duke of Lancaster and the humbler one of the poet/accountant Chaucer—thus became closely involved with each other. Geoffrey Chaucer loved John of Gaunt like a brother, but the Duke was too ambitious to let himself get very close to anyone, and he didn't share Geoffrey's interest in the hidden and mysterious. Yet Gaunt's bond of loyalty towards his old friend was strong enough to drive him out into a foggy, misty morning before dawn, ordering four soldiers and the long-suffering Sir Oliver Radley to ride with him to St. Mary Cray.

What good were power and influence, Gaunt told himself as his little party galloped through the cold, miserable weather, if one could not use it to help one's friends?

Geoffrey Chaucer guilty of murder indeed! Why, even in Geoffrey's soldiering days the man couldn't stand killing! As soon as a battle was over the young Chaucer would hie himself over to the nearest bush and throw up everything he had eaten within the past twenty-four hours! Geoffrey had never even gone hunting, though it was highly fashionable to do so, because he couldn't stand the idea of killing animals!

John of Gaunt had little respect for the peasantry. To him, they were of little more account than the beasts of the field, to be used and exploited and otherwise ignored. Geoffrey's letter, outlining the suspicion of a respected attorney that a local sheriff might think him responsible for the killing of a worthless girl, served only to reinforce Gaunt's contempt for such people. It was up to Gaunt to use his name and position to stop any such nonsense until he and Chaucer could discover the truth of the situation.

At midmorning Robert and Agatha Willard were sitting in the main room of the tavern, toying with the remains of their breakfast, while the other pilgrims sat around glumly, paralyzed by shock over the death of Sophia, wondering if they would ever manage to reach the shrine of St. Thomas.

"I don't believe I actually slept through it all!" Robert was saying angrily. "Why didn't you awaken me? I might have been of some help to Geoffrey!"

"And so you still might," Agatha returned. "But last night there was so much confusion—so many people to talk to, so much to learn—that you probably would have been only one more cook to spoil the stew. It would have done you no good to lose a night's sleep. Why, I didn't manage to get Geoffrey into his bed before the hour of four! And even then he was so excited that the physician had to give him a dose of valerian! I looked in on him before we came down here. He's still sleeping like a baby."

"But what about the pilgrimage? Are we not going to be able to go to Canterbury afterwards?" asked Robert.

"Harry Bailey says that they all agreed—he, Geoffrey, and the sergeant of the law—that all should stay here until Sophia's murderer is found or it appears impossible to find him. Of course, the latter case would only be if the summoner turned out to be the killer, and I learned from the physician that it seems unlikely that he was. And you well know what that means!" she whispered conspiratorially.

"What's that?"

"That one of the pilgrims has to be the murderer!"

Hurriedly Robert crossed himself. "God forbid that such a demon be disguised as a supplicant to a holy shrine! But Agatha, how long will this take?"

"Master de Coverly—the man of law—says that if the matter is investigated thoroughly and efficiently, we should all be back on the road to Canterbury by tomorrow—or the next day at the latest. All but one!" she added with relish.

Robert shuddered.

Walter sat at the table next to theirs, half-listening to their conversation, half toying with his food. He was miserable. Jenifred Atte Wood had not waited on the pilgrims that morning, and Walter had hoped to see her again. While in Oxford he had come into contact with very few girls, and those whom he did see he hardly noticed. He was too deeply involved with his studies. But now the University was quickly fading into a memory. He was out on the road, in constant contact with nature; it was spring, he was a young man, and perhaps he had been more primally touched by the scene he had witnessed between Simon and Sophia than he would care to admit.

The primary reason he had decided to go on pilgrimage to Canterbury was that in recent weeks he had been in agony over whether or not to seek a career in the church. He had hoped to ask the holy martyr for guidance: should he or should he not take holy orders?

It seemed that St. Thomas had answered his prayer before he had even offered it. First there had been Walter's exposure to such charlatans as the friar, the summoner, and the pardoner, and such self-important hypocrites as the prioress and her three priests. Did he really want to spend his life in the company of people like them?

And now there was Jenifred. If the strangely pleasant stirring in his loins at the sight of her lovely little face were any yardstick by which to measure, then Walter was clearly not meant for a career in the church.

The door to the kitchen opened, and Walter's face lit up. Jenifred! She was carrying a basket of fresh bread, offering it to everyone at all the tables. She caught sight of him, and smiled shyly, then made her way to his table and held out the basket.

"More bread?" she asked. Walter took a piece, brushing her hand in the process, and opened his mouth to speak.

At that moment the door to the inn swung open and a band of rough-shed, coarse-looking men pushed their way inside. A tall, wiry but strong person stepped to the front of the party, his thumbs hooked into his belt, an air of authority about him. His hair was long, falling in a dirty yellow tangle below his shoulders. A rakish-looking scar puckered one eyebrow.

"I am Wulfstan Canty, the local deputy sheriff," he declared loudly. "What's all this about a murder?"

Harry Bailey, who had been sitting a table with Sir Richard and Simon, immediately rose and stepped forward. "I am Harry Bailey," he responded. "I am governor of this group of holy pilgrims. It is one of our number that has been killed. She lies upstairs, in what was the women's common sleeping-room."

"And who is—was she?"

"We know little about her, Master Canty. Her name was Sophia, she was young, she was a gypsy, and at one time she may have been a nun. Last night, as the women slept, she was stabbed to death."

William Richemont stepped up and stood beside Bailey. "I examined the body, my lord deputy. She died at about eleven o'clock last night. She was apparently killed in her sleep."

Canty's scarred eyebrow rose. "A gypsy, eh? Did she steal anything?"

Bailey exchanged a significant look with Agatha and Robert, then turned once more to Canty. "There have been thefts, Master Canty, but we doubt that Sophia was responsible."

"What do you mean? Of course she was responsible! All gypsies steal anything they can get their hands on! Someone whom she robbed simply took his revenge! Why take me away from my other pressing duties for this?"

Harry Bailey closed his eyes, counted to ten, then took a deep breath and faced the deputy again. "My lord deputy, a young girl is dead, murdered, long before her time. We doubt that she was the thief because Master Geoffrey Chaucer—" here Harry placed a very slight but notable emphasis on the name—"had something stolen after she was dead. There is something far more sinister happening here than revenge upon a thief, Master Canty."

Chaucer's name meant little if anything to Canty. "And who is this Geoffrey Chaucer?"

Agatha held her breath, hoping that Harry wouldn't feel honor-bound to mention the suspect Tarot card.

"Master Chaucer is Controller of the King's Petty Custom, and one of England's most famous poets," said Harry Bailey. "We were fortunate enough to have him accompanying us on our pilgrimage. He has gone far beyond the call of duty in helping us learn what we can about the girl, and about what happened last night."

"I have notes of Master Chaucer's investigation right here," Walter Locksley put in helpfully, holding his notebook up for Canty to see.

Father Matthew then stood up, wide-eyed and hysterical. "Geoffrey Chaucer is a magician, Master Canty, in league with the devil and possibly with that girl! I know for a fact that he carries cards around with him—cards which the Church has forbidden! And one of them was found next to the body!"

Agatha's heart sank. Obviously Dame Eglantine had been to confession.

Friar Hubert then contributed. "Chaucer has been nosing around, harassing everyone here, prying into our private lives, wanting to know how we were connected with that girl and how much we knew about her. He says he's trying to find out who killed her. However, I think that he is actually trying to find out how much we know. After all, those of us who were in the common sleeping-room can vouch for each other. Master Chaucer has his own room—and is free to come and go unseen by anyone!"

The dyer then spoke up. "He claims that he had a candleholder stolen after Sophia was killed. But none of us ever saw that candleholder. Perhaps he is also the thief and is only trying to cover his tracks!"

"And it was his card!" insisted Father Matthew.

"It was, eh?" said Canty, his rakish eyebrow rising again. "Then let us go find this Chaucer, and ask him to account for himself! Where is his room?"

Robert Willard stood up. "Master Canty, this is an outrage! Geoffrey Chaucer is one of the most respected royal officials in the kingdom! You have no right—"

"Stand aside, old man!" Canty snarled, pushing Robert aside. The mathematician stumbled and fell backwards into the arms of Walter Locksley. Jenifred dropped her basket and rushed to help Walter support him. Agatha hurried to her husband's side, practically spitting at Canty. "You beast!" she cried angrily.

Canty ignored her, pushed past Harry Bailey and led his soldiers up the stairs.

Geoffrey woke with a start at the sound of their heavy footsteps thundering up the stairs. Uneasiness suddenly permeated his heart, and he forced his weary body to sit up just as Canty burst into his room. "Take him!" Canty shouted.

Before Chaucer knew what was happening, he was pinioned on both sides by Canty's underlings.

"Geoffrey Chaucer!" Canty shouted. "I arrest you in the name of the king for the murder of—of—of whoever was killed here last night!"

"What farce is this?" came a harsh voice behind Canty. "Unhand that man, you rascals!"

Wulfstan Canty turned, his eyes blazing sheer fury, to the person who had countermanded his orders. "And just who do you think you are?" he demanded.

"John of Gaunt, Duke of Lancaster, Regent to King Richard, second of that name since the Conquest," said the intruder. "Who do you think you are?"

Canty's thugs stood staring, their mouths wide open. Their grip on Chaucer's arms loosened, and he collapsed gratefully onto his bed. Geoffrey had never before been attacked like that—and prayed he would never be so again. He was trembling with fright; his hands were shaking and his head was beginning to throb painfully. His eyes focused on those of his rescuer, still standing tall and strong on the other side of the room.

"Johnny, my old friend," he said, forgetting protocol. "Thank God you came!"

Seven

"Thank God you came," Chaucer said again.

Chaucer, Agatha, Robert, Harry Bailey, and Walter were closeted in the back room of the tavern with John of Gaunt and Sir Oliver Radley, drinking ale kindly provided by Master Atte Wood. Wulfstan Canty and his band of rowdy sergeants had been banished to the front yard of the inn, though not dismissed. Gaunt's four soldiers had been ordered to keep a close eye on them.

"You've all proven to be the most loyal of friends," Chaucer went on. "For that I thank Our Lady for her beneficence."

Walter beamed. Chaucer must be including him in that company—"the most loyal of friends." The clerk was in heaven, lighter than air. It had been honor enough not only to meet the great Geoffrey Chaucer, but to be asked to work for him! And now he was sitting across the room from the famed Duke of Lancaster! What had he possibly done to earn such status?

If he could impress them all favorably, then perhaps he would be able to acquire a secure and prestigious position. And then, he fantasized, he would have a living of substance to offer Jenifred.

"Well, we have to find the real murderer, or else both you and I will be forever under the shadow of this ridiculous accusation," John of Gaunt was saying. "If we do not learn who killed the girl, my enemies—and yours, if you have any—will spread the word that I used my influence to free my old friend from a just charge of murder. Not that I think for a moment that you are guilty, Geoffrey. The very idea of your doing it is laughable. But we have to find out who did."

Chaucer nodded to Walter. "Walter, give the duke the book," he directed. "Everything we have learned so far is written right there, my lord," he informed Gaunt. "I think we have learned all we can about Sophia. I believe it is now important for us to find the thief—and to learn what sort of connection, if any, he had with her."

Gaunt frowned. "You say he only stole trinkets, all made of silver—and left other pieces of silver alone? That's unusual, isn't it?" Chaucer explained his theory about the thief's motivation, "But I don't understand," said John of Gaunt. "If he took such pains to avoid being caught, why would he risk his neck further by committing murder?"

"Because Sophia had seen him," said Chaucer.

"But any of the women could have awakened at any time," said Gaunt, shaking his head. "It seems terribly risky. No, there's something else going on that we don't know about. The idea that a thief who was that clever would first allow himself to be seen by both the summoner and the gypsy girl, and then commit murder in a room full of people, no matter how soundly they were sleeping, simply doesn't make sense."

"I agree," said Chaucer. "But, my lord, we do have to explore all possibilities."

Gaunt's eyes scanned Walter's notes. "What about this young rogue, Simon de Burgoyne? According to what's written here, he was extremely upset and nervous when you questioned him."

"He was overcome with grief, my lord," said Chaucer. "He was in love with Sophia."

"Ah, but it also says here that she would leave his side to pay her respects to other men. You would be surprised to know how many men have killed the woman they loved out of sheer frustration," Gaunt said sagely. "It seems to me that the key to this mystery lies with that rogue whom you call Jack the summoner," he said. "Oliver! Who is the ranking officer in the party we brought?"

"Peter Adams, my lord."

"Well, then, I want you to go downstairs, tell Peter Adams to take one other of our guardsmen and all of that moronic deputy's sergeants, ride as quickly as they can to Bromley and commandeer whatever guards or soldiers they can find there. I'll give you my royal seal on the order." He tore a page from the book in his hand, scribbled an order, dropped candle wax on the page and sealed it with his signet ring. "As Geoffrey has pointed out, the man can't have gone far. Granted, he's had nearly twelve hours on the road, but he would have to stop sometime, or else he'd kill his horse. And from what everyone tells me he's fairly easy to recognize. Tell the soldiers to comb the countryside within a ten-mile radius of St. Mary Cray until they find this man. Then arrest him and bring him back here!"

Sir Oliver nodded, then disappeared. Gaunt then turned back to Geoffrey. "I want all of you to tell me all you know about everyone on this pilgrimage!"

Jack the summoner stood beside the dead body of his horse, overcome with grief, remorse, and fear. He should have stopped hours ago. He knew his horse should be rested! But he had been in far too much of a panic to think rationally.

Where was he? He had lost track of time and distance long ago. All he knew was he was in the middle of a small wood, a short distance away from the main road, which he had been scrupulously avoiding, and that he had been traveling in a westerly direction. What was he to do? How was he to get to Cornwall without a horse? For of course he had no money. In his haste to escape the party of pilgrims, he had left his purse at the inn.

He could find a local village, knock on some doors, accuse the people of sins and hope they'd be frightened enough to bribe him. But he would be intruding upon the territory of another summoner, no doubt—and that might draw attention to him. And then they might find him.

His stomach growled; he had had nothing to eat since supper the night before. The last time he'd eaten, Sophia had still been alive, and he had been totally unaware of his troubles. But what was he to do now?

There was only one thing he could possibly do. He searched the corpse of his mount and removed anything that he could possibly sell. Then he trudged back to the main road, hoping against hope that a wagon going west would pass and give him a lift. He turned his back on the still-rising sun and wearily headed towards Cornwall.

He had been walking for an hour, weighed down by the burden of his saddle, bridle and saddlebags, when a peasant driving an oxcart stopped and peered at him,

"What in God's name are you doing, hauling all that stuff by yourself?" demanded the ox-driver.

Jack raised his weary head. He was out of breath, gasping. "My horse died," he finally answered. "I had no choice."

"Where are you going?" The peasant was an older man, thin and stooped, with glittering dark eyes and a face so wrinkled it was difficult to discern his features.

"Cornwall."

"Cornwall! And you're planning to travel all that way like that?"

"Not if I have a choice. Where are you going? I'll be glad to trade you for a lift."

"Well, I'm certainly not planning to go all the way to Cornwall. But I can take you as far as Bromley. There perhaps you can buy another horse, or else ride with a freight wagon."

Bromley. There would certainly be dangers in going to such a place. But perhaps he could manage to get in and out of there quickly, without attracting attention from the local inhabitants. Anything was preferable to the painfully slow progress he had been making.

"Fine." Jack groped in his pack and pulled something out of it. "I have here a fine tooled leather wallet, for which I paid tenpence. I'll gladly give it to you if you'll take me to Bromley with you."

"Climb aboard," the peasant invited, taking the wallet from him.

Jack slung his saddle and bridle into the back of the wagon, then hefted himself into the seat beside the driver. "I thank you. You have saved my life."

The peasant's eyes glittered, casting a greedy glance back at the summoner's saddle and bridle. "It is always my pleasure to help my fellow man," he responded.

The summoner, soft and unaccustomed to hard labor, had been more wearied than he realized by the hour he had spent walking, heavily weighed down by the burden of his possessions. Only a few moments after he sat down, he began to nod off. He shook himself awake long enough to speak to his host.

"If I fall asleep, be sure to wake me when we reach Bromley," he directed.

"I surely will," said the peasant.

A minute or two later Jack's eyes closed; his head lolled on the back of the seat.

Then he was shocked wide awake. The driver of the cart was hitting him savagely with some kind of club. He cried out in protest, but the peasant paid no attention.

Jack tried to fight back, but he was still groggy from sleep, still too tired from his journey. He took several hard blows, to his chest, to his shoulders, and finally to his head. A scream of pain escaped his throat as he tumbled off the seat and into the mud beside the road.

"Why should I settle for a mere wallet when I can take all you have?" the ox-driver said callously, still wielding the club. "I'm sorry, friend traveler, but I'm a poor man." He tossed the club into the back of his wagon, then took the reins of his ox and started the animal going again.

Jack tried to rise, but he was simply too badly beaten. Exhausted, racked with pain, he allowed himself to collapse onto the mud and give way to unconsciousness as the wagon disappeared over a rise and out of sight.

Peter Adams listened contemptuously to the loud, raucous laughter going on behind him; one of the deputy sheriff's sergeants had just told a lewd anecdote. Adams was a bit irritated that he, a royal guardsman, had been saddled with the likes of such rude, uncouth commoners as Wulfstan Canty and his minions. Hopefully, after they arrived at Bromley, he could send them off to search another part of the area outlined by the Duke of Lancaster so he wouldn't have to listen to them anymore.

They were still a few miles from Bromley; hopefully, however, they would arrive there and embark upon their search within the hour. Adams, however, privately didn't understand why his Lord the Duke felt it was so important to find one repulsive summoner and haul him back to the inn at St. Mary Cray.

Adams understood that a murder had been committed and that a young girl was dead. But he also had been informed that it was unlikely that the man they were pursuing was the killer; the Duke had specifically instructed him not to hurt the man, to bring him back alive and in good health. Still, if the summoner was not the killer, then why bother to bring him back at all?

Adams shrugged. He was a soldier, not a magistrate. He knew nothing whatever of the procedures for tracking down and arresting murderers.

"What's that?" suddenly came the rough voice of one of Wulfstan Canty's sergeants.

Adams, startled, abandoned his musings and followed the man's pointing finger.

What appeared to be a bundle of old, dirty clothes lay on the side of the road a short distance ahead of them. Frowning, Adams kicked his horse up and trotted down the road until he could see it clearly. His heart leaped in jubilation; now he wouldn't have to ride all the way to Bromley and launch a massive manhunt. Middle height, somewhat fat and soft, black hair with a bald spot in back, a reddened complexion marred by vast numbers of boils and pimples, a moth-eaten beard. There couldn't be two such repulsive individuals in the countryside surrounding St. Mary Cray at this time; thus Adams nourished no doubt that this was the man they had been sent out to find.

"You!" he said authoritatively, pointing to Wulfstan Canty. "Take one of your men and find a nearby farmhouse where we can buy or borrow a wagon. We've found our man!"

Geoffrey Chaucer studied closely the astrological chart he had spread on the table before him. He and Robert Willard had worked over it for nearly an hour. To the best of their abilities, they had calculated the chart for the exact moment of the finding of Sophia's body. Chaucer had hoped that by studying the chart he could learn something about the killer that he didn't already know.

Sophia's body had been found at nearly midnight. That put Capricorn on the Ascendant and Cancer on the Descendant, and the sign on the cusp of the Descendant would, in a chart like this, rule the killer. The sign was Cancer, ruled by the changeable, moody, restless Moon. The Moon was in Leo, in the eighth house, a house associated with money and power—and so Chaucer knew that, to some degree, money or power (or both) had motivated the killing. In the seventh house was Saturn, squared by the Sun, Mars and Jupiter, implying frustration, restlessness, and fear.

According to the rules of astrology, Cancer and the Moon signified a person who should be warm, caring, and affectionate. But the presence of Saturn in that sign implied repression or total absence of those qualities. And Cancer and the Moon also implied moodiness and a love of luxury and comfort. There were certainly a great deal of people on this pilgrimage who fit that description, Geoffrey told himself ruefully, thinking of the *religieux* and the wealthy middle-class professionals. But at least this seemed to eliminate Walter, Father Harold the parson and Alfric the plowman from Chaucer's list of suspects. That was something, at least.

His mind jumped to Simon. John of Lancaster had been somewhat skeptical about the depth of his love for Sophia. Simon was certainly moody, and he had grown up accustomed to luxury and comfort. But many who were used to taking such advantages for granted were often among the first to renounce them.

Simon had certainly been frustrated in his courtship of Sophia, and probably deathly afraid of losing her. But would he kill? Chaucer shook his head. No matter what Gaunt's opinion of Simon was, Geoffrey couldn't possibly see him as anything but a devoted student of chivalry, choosing to fixate his idealistic view of women on the charming and beautiful gypsy.

But the description certainly seemed to fit Friar Hubert almost to perfection...Chaucer shook his head, as though to force awareness from its cracks and crevices. There was something wrong with this chart, something it was saying about the murderer that didn't fit the picture Chaucer had formed of him already. What was it?

Chaucer resolved to consult Robert Willard at the first opportunity.

The door to Geoffrey's room flew open. John of Gaunt, flanked by Sir Oliver Radley and—somewhat to Chaucer's shock—Sir Richard de Burgoyne, stalked in. Behind them Walter followed like a faithful dog, quill and notebook in hand.

"No one knows bloody anything!" shouted Gaunt, his frustration all too apparent. "I can't stay here in some Godforsaken little village, indefinitely seeking a common murderer, not even for you, Geoffrey! Someone bloody has to know something, and if anyone's lying to me, by St. George, I'll—"

"Calm down, my lord," said Chaucer. "You may have learned more than you think. What have you been doing, and what have you found out?"

"Nothing bloody nothing!"

Walter then stepped forward. "The Duke has been talking to everyone, Master Chaucer. Everyone's frightened of him, so I think they were more silent than they would have been with you or me. However, I did take some notes. Perhaps they may tell you something new." The clerk shoved the open book into Geoffrey's hand.

A name leaped up at Chaucer. "Brother Nicholas!" he exclaimed. "Who mentioned a brother named Nicholas? Was it Simon?"

Walter looked askance at John of Gaunt, then, when the latter showed no sign of speaking, went on. "No, Master Chaucer, this was not anyone's brother named Nicholas. The story was related to us by Alfric the plowman. This Brother Nicholas is a monk—apparently of the same order as Don John, who as you know is accompanying us. He was the one who informed Father Harold and Alfric that this little band would be gathering at the Tabard to go on pilgrimage, and that if they wanted to go to Canterbury perhaps it would be best if they joined with them, for safety's sake."

"Safety!" Chaucer snorted. "Hah! First a thief, then a murderer appears among us! Perhaps Father Harold and Alfric would have been better off going to Canterbury alone! Walter, send for Simon! And Don John the monk! I need to speak to both of them."

Walter nodded, then streaked out of the door, unruly brown locks bouncing.

John of Gaunt looked over from where he was leaning against the wall. "So you gleaned something from all that twaddle they were feeding me."

"It's like a puzzle, my lord. It all seems like twaddle until you have one valuable piece. Then it all falls together. There may be more than one valuable piece of information contained in here that seems useless until it is linked up with other pieces of information that could seem equally useless."

Gaunt shook his head. "You have far more patience with this sort of activity than I do. You always were more a man of contemplation than of action."

"Contemplation is but another form of action, my lord," said Chaucer.

The door opened a crack; Simon the squire peered through, then nearly shut the door when he saw his father standing next to John of Gaunt. Hastily Chaucer stepped forward, jerked the door open, then stood aside to allow Simon to enter. "Come on in, Simon! I desperately need your help! Please!"

Somewhat reluctantly Simon stepped in, then turned defiantly to Chaucer when his father glared at him. "How can I help you?" he asked graciously.

"You said last night that Sophia named her horse Nicholas because she had a brother named Nicholas. Did she ever say anything more about this Nicholas?"

"Why?" asked Simon suspiciously.

"Think, man! It's very important that we know this!"

Simon screwed his brow up as though he were trying to remember. "She mentioned that he was very thin, like her horse, even though he ate more than her horse would ever think of. She also mentioned that he could read and write, while she could not."

Chaucer's heart leaped with joy. "Did she ever say, definitely, that Nicholas actually was her flesh-and-blood brother?"

Simon looked over at Chaucer with a start. "No, she didn't. In fact, she only referred to him as 'brother Nicholas.' She never actually said, 'my brother Nicholas.'"

"Could he have been a monk?" Chaucer asked quietly.

A strange expression came over Simon's face. "Now that you mention it, he could have been. I remember once she said something about visiting Nicholas at Kirksdell."

"Kirksdell! Kirksdell Abbey? But that's up north!" Still, it made sense, Chaucer reflected. By all accounts, that was where Sophia had hailed from.

Without saying anything more, he thumbed through the manuscript book until he found the notes of John of Gaunt's interview with Alfric the plowman. Walter had indeed been meticulous in his notetaking, Chaucer reflected with some elation. He had even managed to record a somewhat rueful comment of Alfric's that he hoped they would find the murderer soon, as the pilgrimage hadn't even begun yet and he had already been away from his fields far too long. He had been a week on the road before he even reached the Tabard in London—because he lived on a farm near Leeds.

Leeds. In Yorkshire. Near Kirksdell Abbey.

"Thank you very much, Simon," he said softly. "Your help has been invaluable. You can go now. But as you go, please send Don John in."

Simon nodded, then hurried out the door, obviously anxious to escape the glowering stare of Sir Richard. A moment later the monk entered.

Chaucer had avoided making the acquaintance of Don John. He disliked monks, believing that they were all corrupt and hypocritical, and while he realized that was probably an unfair prejudice, he had in the course of his life met very few who didn't fit this stereotype. Don John had come on a holy pilgrimage wearing a cloak trimmed in fur pinned with a gold brooch, carrying in his pack such outrageously luxurious foods as roasted swan—hardly in keeping with the customary monastic vow of poverty. Chaucer had immediately tarred this man with the same brush with which he had painted all monks.

"Don John," Chaucer began without preamble, "by your habit, I gather that you are a Benedictine monk. Is that correct?"

"Yes," said Don John, cocking an eyebrow quizzically.

"Do you have any dealings with Kirksdell Abbey, in Yorkshire, near Leeds?" Chaucer queried.

The monk frowned. "I myself am an outrider for that monastery," he replied. "Why?"

"I understand that there is a Brother Nicholas in residence at Kirksdell. Do you know him?"

"I do. Though not well. He is overseer of the library, in charge of copying manuscripts and supervising illuminations. A very brilliant and well-read man. He is a gifted calligrapher and illuminator; Kirksdell is very proud of his books and manuscripts. Why do you ask about him?"

"Did he know about this pilgrimage?" asked Chaucer.

"Indeed he did. He had planned to come himself, and I was surprised not to find him present. I do recall that one of his copyists fell ill. Perhaps Brother Nicholas was forced to take his place until the man recovered."

"What more can you tell me about him?"

"Nothing, Master Chaucer. I told you I didn't know him well. I am an outrider, in charge of the Abbey's outlying property. Brother Nicholas spent most of his time in the library. There would be no chance for us to grow well acquainted."

"Thank you, Don John," said Chaucer abruptly. "You may go."

Don John didn't need to be told twice. He was gone before the others knew it.

"That bastard knows more than he's telling," said Chaucer grimly.

"Geoffrey, you're always ready to think the worst of monks!" said John of Gaunt. "What makes you think he knows more than he's telling?"

"I feel it!" Chaucer insisted. "Can't you tell he's holding something back? I'm beginning to think this Brother Nicholas is pivotal to what we need to know."

"How could he possibly be pivotal?" Gaunt demanded. "He's cloistered in a library up in Yorkshire! The girl was killed down here!"

"Nonetheless, so far, four people who were on this pilgrimage knew him, and one of them is dead," said Chaucer. "Don John, Alfric the plowman, Father Harold, and Sophia. Possibly there were more. What about that damned friar? My lord, I am forced to ask you one more favor!"

"I would gladly do anything, if it will clear this mess up and allow me to return to London!" said Gaunt. "What do you want me to do?"

"Take Walter with you, and go talk to Friar Hubert. Find out what he knows about Brother Nicholas. I have four gold crowns that say he knows something about him!"

"You're on!" cried Gaunt. "Come, Master Walter, let us find this Friar Hubert and take his mind apart!"

Walter nodded eagerly, and would have followed Gaunt out the door had Agatha not burst in at that very moment. All eyes were suddenly focused on her. She was beaming, attractively flushed, excited.

"Geoffrey!" she cried. "You must come at once! Peter Adams and Deputy Sheriff Canty have returned! They're riding in now, and they've found the summoner!"

Eight

Chaucer and the others followed Agatha down the stairs and out the front door. It seemed that all the pilgrims were standing in the yard, gathering around a rustic wagon drawn by a tired old horse. One of Wulfstan Canty's sergeants was driving the wagon, his own mount tied behind. Peter Adams, preening himself importantly, was leading the way. When he saw John of Gaunt, he immediately steered his horse over to meet his master.

"We found your man, my lord Duke," Adams said pompously.

"Good!" was all Gaunt could say.

Chaucer pushed his way through the crowd until he was close enough to the wagon to peer into its bed. Jack the summoner, his head lolling, lay atop a pile of empty sacks. Chaucer looked over at Peter Adams in some alarm.

"Is he dead?" he demanded.

"No, he's not dead," Adams responded. "But he's suffered a severe beating."

Chaucer caught sight of Walter standing beside him. "Walter, fetch Master Richemont!" he said.

"No need. I'm right here," said the physician, pushing his way over to stand by Chaucer. He glared at the crowd hovering around. "Go on about your business! Leave the poor man alone!"

"Yes!" said Peter Adams, taking up the cry. "Let the doctor do his work unmolested!" He brandished his sword menacingly. The pilgrims, disappointed at having to miss anything, dispersed. Walter, hoping to be of service to Chaucer, hovered in the background.

William Richemont stepped up on the wheel, then hoisted himself into the wagon. He put his hands on Jack's neck, then felt of his arms and rib cage. He frowned. "The guard was right, he has been abominably abused. This arm is broken in at least one place, and so are several of his ribs. I only hope that none of the broken ribs has pierced a lung."

"Can he be moved?" asked Chaucer.

"If it's done carefully. Walter! Fetch two blankets! Then I want four of the biggest men available to each take an end! They can carry him up to my room!"

Walter rushed into the inn, almost crashing into Jenifred Atte Wood.

"Good heavens, what's your hurry?" she asked.

Disconcerted by her presence, Walter almost forgot his mission, then he realized that she could help him. "They've found the summoner—the man who ran away last night. He's been given a hellacious thrashing. Master Chaucer needs two blankets, so that the soldiers can carry the man upstairs."

"Come with me," said Jenifred.

Walter followed her into the back of the inn, where she opened a rough pinewood chest and took out two dun-colored blankets of coarse homespun. "These should serve you well," said Jenifred, handing the blankets to the clerk.

Deliberately he took them from her in such a way that both his hands touched hers. Their eyes met and locked. Hers were a strange sea-green color, ringed by long, thick brown lashes. She smiled tentatively, never allowing her gaze to waver from his.

"This all must be very upsetting for you and your family," Walter ventured.

"On the contrary, it's the most exciting thing that's taken place here in years," said Jenifred. "Nothing ever happens in St. Mary Cray. It's so—so—*boring!*" She said the last word with such vehemence that Walter's heartbeat quickened. Did this mean she would not be averse to leaving? She then caught her breath, as though suddenly remembering the seriousness of the situation. "Of course, it's terrible about that girl who died. And it is awful that a murderer sleeps under this very roof. But until we know who it is, it's going to seem—" She floundered, as though groping for a word.

"Unreal," Walter said helpfully.

She smiled up at him again, her face beaming. "Yes! That's what I meant!"

They stared at each other for a few moments, then Walter gingerly put his hand up and touched her face. "I had better get these blankets to Master Chaucer," the clerk finally said.

Jenifred nodded. "I'll come with you," she said. "My name's Jeni," she added as an afterthought,

"Walter. I'm a student at Oxford, on pilgrimage."

Jenifred fell into step beside him as he carried the blankets outside, where Chaucer immediately directed the soldiers to ease the injured man onto them and pick up the corners and carry him back into the inn. Obligingly they did as he said, and the little procession stalked into the inn, leaving Walter and Jenifred standing alone in the inn's front yard.

When the door had closed behind Chaucer, Jenifred turned to Walter. "My mother has been pressing me to do a load of washing," she said. "The time will pass much more quickly if you would talk to me while I was doing it."

A wave of warmth passed through Walter. She liked him! Then suddenly he recalled his self-imposed duties. "Certainly. I mean, I would love to, but what if Master Chaucer needs me?"

"It's a small inn," said Jeni. "He can find you." She took his arm; together they walked back inside.

Jack groaned a few times while they were moving him, but remained unconscious. Richemont had stayed downstairs; Chaucer dismissed the men who had carried the summoner up, then knelt beside him. When Jack was laid on Master Richemont's straw mattress, his eyes popped open. Suddenly he sat up.

"Where am I?" he cried fearfully. "Where am I?" Chaucer put an arm around the man's shoulders and eased him back onto the bed. "You're back in the inn at St. Mary Cray. The Duke's men found you and brought you back. You've been badly beaten. Remember me? Geoffrey Chaucer? Master Richemont is here, he is a physician, and he is going to take good care of you. He's downstairs now, fixing an herbal cordial for you. Calm down. You're safe."

Jack sat up again, making motions as though to get out of the bed. "No, I'm not—no, I'm not. Sophia's dead. They killed her! And now they're going to kill me!"

"Sit still!" Chaucer practically had to hold the man down. "You've got a broken arm, broken ribs, and quite a crop of bruises! You're in no fit condition to go anywhere. Now who are 'they'?"

Jack sank into the straw, giving in to his weakness. He choked and coughed; Chaucer winced at the stench of his foul breath. "They who would wipe us out. They who wish to do away with the clergy. Sophia—she knew—"

"There is no one here who would dare to hurt you. Why one of the greatest men in England is with us now! The great Duke of Lancaster himself!"

"The Duke! God save us all!" A look of morbid fear came over the summoner's face.

On an impulse, Chaucer asked, "Jack, who is Brother Nicholas?"

He was unprepared for the summoner's response. "Brother Nicholas? Oh, no!" His eyes closed and he lay still, unconscious again.

At that moment Master Richemont entered, holding in his hand a mug of hot wine simmered with healing herbs.

Chaucer stood. "The man is terrified," he told the physician. "He is delirious; he rambles—talking about how 'they' will kill him. He even acted as if he were frightened of the Duke of Lancaster!"

"Many are afraid of John of Gaunt," said Richemont. "Not everyone in England can remember when he was a mere stripling, as you do, Master Chaucer, and thus it is hard for some to view him as anything but a Titan. I will rouse Jack briefly, long enough to give him this cordial, and then I will set his arm and bandage his ribs.

Then only sleep can help him. If a lung has not been punctured, he will recover. If so—well, there isn't much hope. Only time will tell."

Chaucer nodded, then left the physician to do his work. As he stepped outside the door, he found himself facing Robert and Agatha, who stared at him expectantly. He repeated what Master Richemont had told him.

"Oh, and I did learn one more interesting fact," he added.

"What was that?" asked Agatha.

"I must tell Walter to note in his book that here is one more person who knows Brother Nicholas."

"So what do you think of Sir Richard de Burgoyne?" Chaucer was asking.

The Duke of Lancaster waved a contemptuous hand. "He is stalwart enough. He is thoroughly awed by my presence here, and wasted no time in swearing lifetime devotion to me and any cause I may espouse. I'll accept his fealty, if that is what he wants, but I doubt if he's as devoted to me as he is to his own ambition. My armies are full of Sir Richards. All very handsome, all highly skilled in the art of warfare, all dedicated to the cause of chivalry—and all with an ambition that almost matches mine."

Chaucer reflected upon his initial suspicions of Sir Richard as a possible murderer of Sophia, and mentioned them to his friend. He then informed the Duke of his interview with the knight. "Sir Richard may be ambitious, my lord Duke, but he makes no bones about his love for his son," he added. "I doubt if Sir Richard was involved at all, even peripherally."

"I thought we'd have everything solved by now," said John of Gaunt, shaking his head in some concern. "But all we seem to come up with is more questions. Now who is this Brother Nicholas you seem to be so fixed on, Geoffrey?"

"I only wish I knew," said Chaucer.

John of Gaunt had ousted the Atte Wood family from their modest home behind the inn, handed the landlord a purse full of gold coins, and then demanded a dinner fit for a king. He had invited Chaucer, Sir Oliver, Walter, and the Willards to join him. Master Atte Wood, gratified, and never losing sight of what it might do for his reputation to have successfully served the great Duke of Lancaster, had promptly gone to his stores and pulled out every herb, every vegetable, every bottle of fine wine, and a side of his best beef, while his wife, aided by Jeni, had hurried to bake fresh rolls and pastries. The dinner had indeed been superb, and now the six of them were finishing off the last of the landlord's best French wine.

"What do we have here now, Walter? Tell us all," Chaucer invited.

"Sophia came from the north. So did the monk Don John, so did Father Harold the parson and Alfric the plowman. All of them seem to have made the acquaintance of this Brother Nicholas."

"Don't forget the summoner knew him as well," put in Agatha.

"Yes," Walter continued. "The physician believes that Sophia was once a nun, and Madame Eglantine insists that if she were, she would have had to have joined the Poor Clares, because no other order would take a girl with no money. This means that she might possibly have known the friar, as he, a Franciscan, belongs to an order close to the Poor Clares."

"Don't forget, the friar lusted after Sophia," put in Robert Willard.

"That damned friar! In all the bustle over the return of the summoner, we forget to ask him if he knew Brother Nicholas!" said Chaucer.

"Don't worry, I'll speak to him tonight!" said John of Gaunt.

"But why did Sophia leave the order?" asked Walter.

"I think that's obvious," said Agatha dryly. "That girl liked men far too well!"

"Jack the summoner was scared out of his wits when I mentioned Brother Nicholas," Chaucer mused. "According to Simon, Sophia spoke of him with some affection. According to the notes you have here, Walter, Alfric also seems to have at least borne Brother Nicholas no ill will. Don John even seemed cordial towards him—called him brilliant, said he was a fine librarian. So why would the summoner be so frightened of him? And who are 'they' that Jack insisted were close by and trying to kill him?"

"Probably those who would keep the secular clergy honest," said John of Gaunt sourly. "Brother Nicholas is probably one of them. Such scum as those who work as summoners would be wise to fear people such as that!"

"My lord, with all due respect, this pilgrimage lacks anyone of that caliber!" said Chaucer. "Look at who we have in this party besides ourselves! Two nuns, three priests, a monk, a friar, a pardoner, a summoner! A lawyer so full of self-importance that he's useless, even in a case like this! Several tradesmen, whose minds are mainly concerned with profit! A physician, skilled at his art but cold and unapproachable! Do you know Master Richemont told me that he once aspired to be a priest, and that he still hoped to join an order of hospitallers? How can a man with his temperament possibly be attracted to the idea of ministering—either spiritually or medically—to the poor, filthy, scabrous, and lice-infested? He has to be attracted to the power and wealth of the church! So how can any of these people be the type of person Jack would fear?"

"Perhaps it was Sophia," said Walter helpfully.

"Sophia?" Everyone in the room stopped talking and stared at the clerk.

But Walter had taken the idea with both hands and was finding that he liked it. "Yes! Sophia! Suppose she left the convent out of disillusionment rather than because she liked men. Look at the two nuns we have with us! Dame Eglantine certainly is more concerned with this world than with the next! Look at the clothes she wears—the airs she affects! That little gold medallion she wears, the one that says 'Amor vincit omnia'—hardly a badge of humility! And Sister Cecily! She's lovely, yes, but her piety is overblown and ostentatious. How sincere is she?"

"You may have a point, Walter," Chaucer mused. "Sophia had passion—and I don't think it was primarily passion for men, although it may have seemed that way. Sophia loved life—she enjoyed everything about it, whether it was riding, flirting with men, telling stories. If she had felt she had a religious calling she would have thrown herself into it with all the fervor of a saint. She would have had little patience with people like Dame Eglantine or Sister Cecily."

"But how could an insignificant gypsy girl have any influence with those who would keep the clergy honest?" asked Gaunt.

"She probably couldn't," said Chaucer. "But perhaps Brother Nicholas could." Suddenly all were silent.

"So now we return to the question of who is Brother Nicholas?" said Agatha.

John of Gaunt then spoke up. "He is probably more than he would seem," he said. "A mere librarian at a remote northern abbey probably would be more interested in his books than in the ethics of his peers. I wonder if there is among those books a copy of the Bible, translated into English?"

No one said a word. Gaunt was referring to Wyclif's Bible. John Wyclif, an Oxford cleric branded a heretic by the Church, had several years before sponsored the translation of the Bible into English so that all people, even those not schooled in Latin, would have personal access to the Holy Word. He publicly berated the Church hierarchy, lambasting the same corruption and abuse that caused Chaucer to distrust church officials. Wyclif charged that men who had supposedly dedicated their lives to service to God and their fellow beings used their influence and power to feather their own nests, and to live in luxury, decadence and debauchery equal to that for which the cruel and sinful King John had been famed.

Wyclif's charges fed the flames of the growing fires of anti-clericalism that had slowly been growing in England and France for the past hundred years. People flocked to his speeches and promptly became fervent devotees of Wyclif's doctrine, eventually being dubbed "Lollards." Encouraged by the widespread interest in his ideas, Wyclif dared to go a little farther. He advocated doing away with the church hierarchy, limiting church officials to bishops and parish priests. He made speeches recommending that peers whose grandfathers had bequeathed lands to the church should reclaim them—for an organization dedicated to good works would not require the wealth and power that came with the ownership of land.

It was at this point that John of Gaunt had become interested in Wyclif's philosophy. His father, grandfather—in fact, all of his ancestors within the past six or seven generations—had all been kings or prominent nobles, and all had at one time or another either given or bequeathed vast stretches of fertile, productive lands to the church. If the Duke could legally reclaim them, then he would be far wealthier and more powerful than any one man deserved to be. In fact, acquiring more wealth would enable him to raise enough troops to finally gain the one ambition that had always eluded him: to become a king. Through his wife, he could claim title to the crown of Castile, but a usurper now held that throne and would have to be driven out. For political more than spiritual reasons, John of Gaunt became an open advocate of Lollardy and began lavishing vast sums of money to John Wyclif and his organization.

As fond as Chaucer was of John of Gaunt, he was all too aware of his friend's ruthless, driving ambition, and secretly believed it would be better for all if the Duke of Lancaster secured no more power than he already had. Though Chaucer had sympathized with much of Wyclif's ideas—including Wyclif's anti-clericalism and the need for an English translation of the Bible—he had wisely remained neutral, saying nothing openly either favoring Wyclif or condemning the Church, continuing to attend Mass regularly, as a good Church member should.

Six years ago, the Vatican had declared John Wyclif a heretic and his views a blasphemy worthy of excommunication—or worse. His followers had been forced to go underground, but everyone knew that they were still as active as ever, still seeking the ears of interested noblemen, still securing funding from the wealthy—though John of

Gaunt had supposedly ceased his gifts to Wyclif—and still plotting to stop the abuses of the church hierarchy by doing away with it.

Everyone in that room suddenly became aware of new implications to their seemingly insignificant little murder. If this Brother Nicholas were suspected of involvement with the Lollards, and if Sophia were a friend or even a relative of Brother Nicholas, then stories of the wantonness and gluttony of Friar Hubert, the extravagance of Madame Eglantine and Don John, and the pompous self-righteousness of Father Matthew could reach his ears and thus the ears not only of the Lollards, but of influential noblemen and concerned church officials as well. The consequences of such exposure would be disastrous. All of a sudden, everyone knew now that there were a number of people on the pilgrimage who might fervently have wanted Sophia dead.

Agatha was the first to speak. "It may have even been one of the nuns who killed her!" she exclaimed. "Not only did they have reason—they were in the room where she was sleeping!"

Chaucer shuddered at the idea of either the dignified Madame Eglantine or the beautiful Sister Cecily creeping stealthily toward the sleeping Sophia, dagger in hand, raising a graceful, shapely arm...

"But what about the dagger?" said Walter.

Everyone stared at him blankly. "What dagger?" asked Robert.

"The dagger that killed Sophia. The one that was stolen from the dyer. Could Madame Eglantine be the thief? She would have had to have stolen her own stirrup!"

Chaucer sank down in his chair, red with embarrassment. They had all been so excited about Brother Nicholas that they had totally forgotten about the thief.

He sighed, reached into his pocket and pulled out the manuscript page on which they had drawn the astrological chart for the time of the finding of Sophia's body. "Robert," he said, passing the page down to his friend. "Take a look at that chart. What does it tell you about the murderer?"

The light was growing dim; Robert had to lean close to a candle to be able to see the chart at all, and his eyesight was growing weak. He studied the paper for several seconds.

"Well, I can ease your mind in one area," said Robert. "The Moon is in Leo, in the eighth house, ruling money."

"I know. Which means that the murder had something to do with money," said Chaucer.

"It means more than that," said Robert. "Leo, as you know, is a sign associated with luxury. The Moon is not only in the eighth house, she is in an excellent aspect to the Sun, which approaches the cusp of the second house—also ruling money."

"Which means?" Walter's eyes goggled.

"Which means that our killer is a wealthy person. He or she has no need of trinkets such as those that were stolen. I would say that his possession of the dagger was incidental—as was the summoner's possession of Father Matthew's cross. I doubt very seriously if our killer and the thief are the same person."

Simon the squire sat with his back to the fire, with the rest of the party of pilgrims sitting around him in a circle. Harry Bailey had insisted that the tale-telling contest continue, as it would give everyone something else to think about besides the murder. Simon had drawn one of the lots for that night, and so, in spite of his state of mourning, he had bravely girded himself and said that he would tell a tale of the Orient, that he had heard on one of his journeys with his father.

"At Tzarev, in the distant land of Tartary, there lived a great and noble king named Cambuskan," Simon began. "He made war on Russia, and thus gained many honors thereby. His subjects loved and held him in very high esteem. This noble and excellent monarch had two sons, Algarsyf and Cambalo, and a daughter, the lovely Lady Canacee." Simon's voice faltered slightly as he began to describe the virtue and beauty of Lady Canacee; tears began to glisten in his eyes.

He's thinking of Sophia, Chaucer told himself as he sat in the back of the crowd.

John of Gaunt sat at the very rear of the room, in an ornate chair specially carried in for him by the landlord. He was restless, anxious; many problems demanded his attention at Westminster, and Chaucer knew he ached to return to solving them. Geoffrey would have told his friend to go on, return to Westminster, get on with your duties, but he knew that Gaunt would never leave him if there was any chance that he would be accused and jailed—and possibly hanged—for murder. The only course of action open to Chaucer was to find the killer as soon as possible.

That card, Chaucer reflected. That damned Tarot card. What was its purpose? Why did the killer sneak into my room to steal it, then leave it near the body? Was it a deliberate attempt to implicate me?

Behind him, John of Gaunt stood, clearly less interested in the story Simon was telling than in the problem that faced him in the real world. He hied himself over to the side of the room where Friar Hubert was sitting, grabbed the man by the shoulder, then dragged an appropriately shocked Franciscan into the back room. Chaucer shook his head and suppressed a smile. I'll wager that was something Friar Hubert never dreamed would happen to him!

A hiss from the same door caught Chaucer's ear. He turned; Master Richemont was signaling to him. Sighing, Chaucer stood and walked over to the physician, who led him to a place in the hallway safely out of earshot of the pilgrims who were still enthralled by Simon's story.

"Jack the summoner is dead," Master Richemont informed him solemnly.

Chaucer reeled a moment. This was indeed a shock.

"Apparently the worst that I suspected was true—one of his broken ribs pierced a lung. When that happens, there's nothing any physician or herbalist can do except make the person comfortable and wait for the end."

"Damn! There goes a crucial witness!" said Chaucer. Immediately he felt ashamed of himself. Would no one grieve Jack's passing for the man's own sake?

"And not only that, the landlord here is concerned about the presence of dead bodies in his inn," Richemont went on. "Sophia still lies in what was once the women's common sleeping-room, and now there's the summoner's corpse in mine. It is spring, after all, and decay will set in soon. Master Atte Wood has asked when we plan to bury the dead."

"I'll get some of the Duke's guardsmen to carry the departed down to the barn for tonight, and tomorrow we can bury them," said Chaucer. "I don't think there's anything more we can learn from the bodies, and so there is no need to postpone giving them the Christian burial they deserve."

The physician visibly relaxed, breathing a sigh of relief. "Thank God you agree! I didn't know what I'd tell the landlord if you had insisted on keeping them! At least I can sleep in my own bed again! Tell me, what do you intend to tell everyone about Jack?"

"Nothing, at the moment," said Chaucer. "There is no need to interrupt the tale-telling with such dire news. Let the pilgrims forget murder and death for awhile. I'll go speak to the guardsmen about removing the bodies now. I'm sure they can do it swiftly and quietly, without attracting attention."

The physician nodded. "Thank you. I've drawn a lot to tell my story tonight as well, so I shall be occupied."

"The tales! God's teeth!" Chaucer hurried back into the main room, stepped cautiously through the tables until he reached the table where Walter sat with Robert and Agatha. With some interest Chaucer noted that Jenifred Atte Wood sat close to Walter. He was holding her hand.

"Walter! Agatha!" From his pocket he took the manuscript book in which he had been keeping his notes of the tales. He shoved it in front of Walter. "Would you take care to remember all you hear of the tales tonight? I have much to do, and will only be able to peek in from time to time! Walter, if you don't mind, you could take notes for me."

"Certainly, Master Chaucer," said Walter, dropping Jeni's hand, taking the book and opening it to a clean page.

"And I'll help him!" whispered Agatha. "You won't miss a word, I promise you!"

"Thank you!" said Chaucer, starting to head back towards the door. But a catch in Simon's voice stopped him. He was telling about how the powers of a magic ring had enabled the Princess Canacee to understand the language of a hawk and deduce that the hawk had been jilted by her mate. The mate had then taken up with a beautiful kite, condemning the female hawk to languish in sorrow, wandering aimlessly, her health declining rapidly.

"And then the Princess Canacee—the lovely, kindhearted Princess Canacee—took the heartbroken lady hawk back with her to her father's castle, and nursed her back to health—the compassionate, beautiful Lady Canacee—" His voice broke audibly; he was apparently choking back a sob. "And now—and now," he said, raising his voice slightly, "I will tell you how the magical mirror, horse and sword affected the lives of King Cambuskan and his sons!" The squire tried to blink back his welling tears and choke back his sobs, but his success was minimal.

The franklin, a wealthy landowner who had drawn the lot determining that his story would follow Simon's, then broke in. "Perhaps you had better save the rest of your tale for your next turn," he suggested gently. "I can take over here if you want. You are indeed an admirable young man, my dear Master Burgoyne. You tell a fine tale and you have the heart of a saint. I only wish my own sons were as genteel as you."

"Enough!" said Harry Bailey, realizing that the franklin's compliments were only serving to embarrass Simon that much more. "If you are going to tell your tale now, sir, get on with it!"

The franklin nodded. Gratefully, it appeared, Simon left his place by the fire and pushed his way through the tables. Chaucer noted with some satisfaction that Sir Richard, an intense look of compassion on his face, briefly clasped his son's shoulder before the youth left the room.

Out of the corner of his eye Chaucer spied John of Gaunt conferring with the physician in the hall, and hurried over to join them. As he left the room, the franklin began to tell the tale of a faithful wife, deserted by a husband traveling in foreign lands, and courted and tempted by a lovesick neighbor.

John of Gaunt looked at Chaucer impatiently. "Master Richemont here has told me of our landlord's request that we remove the bodies. I have already dispatched Oliver Radley to see that it is done. I have also spoken with our friend the friar. He claims to know nothing. He swears he never saw Sophia before he met her on this pilgrimage, and that he never heard of Brother Nicholas. I couldn't shake his convictions, no matter how I menaced or threatened. Either he's telling the truth, or he's a highly skilled liar and a very brave man. Now how are we going to learn more about this matter with the summoner dead?"

Chaucer shook his head regretfully. "We'll have to do the best we can with what we have. But don't lose heart, my lord. We also need to bear in mind that someone in this little band is a murderer. With every moment that passes, that someone grows more nervous. He does not know how complex the matter is growing, nor does he know how frustrated we feel. And there is also the thief to consider. We can only hope that eventually one—or both—of them will crack under the strain of keeping silent while everyone suspects and do something foolish."

"Yes, but how long will that take?" said Gaunt. "I don't have time to wait—"

"My lord Duke," said a voice from the top of the stairs. "What do we do with her?"

Peter Adams stood with two of the four guardsmen. The two carried a tightly wrapped form between them.

Quietly Chaucer stepped over and closed the door between the main room of the tavern and the hallway.

"Take her to the barn," John of Gaunt directed. "Then come back and get the other, and do the same with him."

Peter Adams turned and gestured to the guardsmen, then the three of them walked carefully downstairs, their bundle balanced equally between them. When they reached the bottom of the stairs Chaucer held up a hand to halt them for a moment, then he parted the blanket to stare once more at Sophia.

There was just the beginning of the stench of putrefaction about the body; her face was beginning to look like death. Her once lovely and glowing skin was now an ashen blue-gray; her eyes, closed as if in sleep the last time he had seen them, had opened slightly; her mouth had stretched into a death grimace. Chaucer's chest tightened as he unwillingly recalled how hungrily that mouth had devoured Simon's.

How quickly earthly loveliness fades, Chaucer reflected sadly. *Sic transit gloria mundi.*

He passed a gentle hand over her now-pale brow and closed her eyes once more, then covered the face again and nodded for the guardsmen to continue. Recalling Simon's agonized tears and his inability to continue with his story, Chaucer's own eyes began to fill with moisture.

"She must have been beautiful," said John of Gaunt.

"Yes, she was," said Chaucer. Unconsciously he turned away from his friend and returned to the main hall. The franklin was just finishing up his tale, to an enthusiastic round of applause. Wordlessly Chaucer took a place next to Agatha as Master Richemont stepped up to tell his story.

"My god, the man can actually smile!" Agatha hissed.

Curiously Chaucer looked up. Well, it wasn't really a smile, he reflected; it was more of a self-satisfied upturning of the corners of the mouth. At that moment Master Richemont settled himself into a comfortable position, moving his head slightly. The motion stirred Chaucer's memory slightly. Where had he seen that gesture before?

Master Richemont, finally settled, seemed pleased to be before the group, taking his turn at entertaining. He took a deep breath, then spoke.

"I will tell you a tale handed down to us by Titus Livius," the physician began. "A long time ago there lived a knight named Virginius, He had only one child, a lovely fourteen-year-old daughter. As well as beauty, she possessed all the other noble virtues: patience, humility, kindness, chastity, and temperance. As all parents should, Virginius took the time to set an example for his child, and so he—as should all parents and others who care for children—lived the most exemplary of lives.

"One day the girl and her mother went into the nearby town. On the street a corrupt judge named Appius laid eyes on the daughter, and immediately was seized with lust for her. After puzzling over how to satisfy his lust, he sent for the town's most despicable blackguard, a man called Claudius, and paid him well to assist in Appius's nefarious plan.

"Claudius then accused Virginius of having stolen a maidservant from his house many years before, and had ever since passed the girl off as his daughter. Before Virginius could protest, Appius the judge ruled that the child must be brought to him immediately as a ward of the court.

"Virginius was not fooled by the judge's scheme. He went home and sadly called his daughter into his presence. She must, he said, accept either death at his hands or shame at the hands of Appius. She said that she was his child, to do with what he would, and then cried, 'Blessed be God, that I shall die a virgin!' Then, in order to spare his daughter the ordeal of being violated, he seized his sword and cut off her head. Holding the head by the hair, he took it to the judge. Appius then ordered that Virginius be hung for murder, but the citizens immediately knew the culpability of the judge and threw him into prison. Claudius was exiled. And thus," Master Richemont concluded, "one can see that all should forsake sin, or else sin will forsake them."

The room was silent. The first sound everyone heard was Agatha, rising, barely able to control her temper. "I think I'm going to lose my dinner!" she hissed at Chaucer. With that she strode out of the room.

Harry Bailey then stood. "By God's blood and nails! This judge was about as corrupt as they come! A pox on all like him! Because of him this innocent maiden is dead!"

Chaucer roused himself from the spell woven by the tale, and looked around him at the faces of his fellow pilgrims. All had been moved by the strange story, but Alisoun of Bath, like Agatha, seemed angry.

"My beloved wife," Robert said softly, standing and briskly moving his cramped legs, "would argue that the girl is dead because of her father. Agatha despises all men who think the value of the lives of women is secondary to the value of their purity. Especially when the men are hardly pure themselves!"

Chaucer shook his head. "I tend to agree," he said, rising and leaving the room beside his friend. "I am of the minority of men, I am afraid, who value the lives of women, children, men and beasts far more than any abstract concept."

He bade Robert a sober good night. Slowly he climbed the stairs to his room, where he entered, lit a candle, and sat at his desk. Incongruously, throughout Master Richemont's story, Chaucer had imagined the chaste young martyr as possessing Sophia's face. A sob escaped his throat as he recalled the delightful young woman; alive only the night before, who had liked him so much, and whose stiffened corpse had only an hour before been unceremoniously hauled out to the barn. He leaned his head on his hands.

No! He suddenly pulled himself erect, quickly gaining control of his emotions. Sophia would not be forgotten!

He groped in his pocket, then cursed. Walter had his manuscript book—and was probably using it right now to update his notes of the tales told that night. Well, no matter! Geoffrey could always recopy them later!

In his pack were a handful of bills of lading which had been discarded at the customs office and which Chaucer had retrieved for his own use, as paper was costly. He pulled them out, turned them over so that he could use their backs, and began to write.

Elation passed through him as he realized that he felt within his heart the thrill of the audience as Sophia had told her tale, and at the same time identified with Sophia's own love for her story and the characters therein.

The candle grew smaller; the sounds of footsteps climbing the stairs intruded upon Chaucer's consciousness; his hands began to ache, but he did not stop writing. Words were flowing through him like rainwater through a rich and fertile field; images and emotions filled his mind and kept his pen moving. Page after page was completed and tossed into a pile on the floor beside him. The myth of Isis and Osiris came to life as no other story he had written ever had.

When he finally put down his quill, well after midnight, Chaucer knew that *The Gipsy's Tale* was a masterpiece.

No matter how great the other tales told here will be, he reflected, *my retelling of them will never match this one. Many generations to follow, perhaps even into the next millennium, will still be fascinated with Sophia.*

Despite the tragedies of the past two days, despite the increasing complexity of the situation surrounding him, that night Geoffrey Chaucer slept like the dead.

Nine

Wulfstan Canty fired up his forge, dreading the heavy day of toil that lay before him. He was an ironmonger by trade, and in a small village like St. Mary Cray a man of his skills was forced to serve as both blacksmith and armourer. His duties as deputy sheriff, however, always took precedence over his own work, and thus with all the excitement yesterday over the murder at the inn, the orders he had not yet filled had piled up. He had been behind to begin with, due to the illness of an apprentice, and thus he was beginning to anticipate and fear the inevitable wrath of his customers.

He found the entire matter of the murder very confusing. To him, it was obvious that the poet from London had killed the girl. He had simply dropped his card in the process and not known it. Who else would bother with such a thing?

And why was the famous Duke of Lancaster interfering with the due course of justice in the death of an unknown gypsy girl?

"Master Canty!"

Wulfstan set his bellows aside, cursing as he did so. It was the voice of one of his sergeants, riding up quickly to the door of the foundry and dismounting.

"What is it, Will?" Canty demanded.

"We've found another body—hidden under a bush, out in the woods near the road to London. It was stabbed, like they told us the gypsy girl was, and you'll never guess what we found beside the corpse!"

"What?" asked Canty impatiently.

"A card!"

"A card!" Suddenly Wulfstan was interested. "What kind?"

The man reached into his pocket and drew from it the card that had been found beside the body. Wulfstan Canty scrutinized it carefully, but the picture meant nothing to him. "Where is the body?" he asked.

"Ben and Jehan are bringing it, Master Canty."

Wulfstan Canty sighed. His orders would have to wait another day. "Ride back, meet up with them and tell them to take it not to the foundry, but to the inn. The gentlemen from London had better be told about this."

The party of pilgrims stood solemnly in the early morning fog. Over their heads the spire of the century-old Church of St. Mary reached towards the sky; below their feet stretched the graves of Sophia the gypsy and Jack the summoner. Father Harold, at Chaucer's request, had read the service.

Early that morning Peter Adams and the guardsmen had risen early, gone to the churchyard and, with the vicar's permission, dug the two graves. Osewold the reeve, also a carpenter, had hastily carved two crosses. But no one knew much about either Jack or Sophia, and so the two crosses bore only the names "Sophia" and "Jack" and the date "1382."

Simon—flanked by his father, who had gripped his son's hand in a conspicuous show of support and sympathy, and Alisoun of Bath, who welcomed any excuse to put her arm around a handsome young man—had unashamedly sobbed throughout the ceremony. Agatha had wiped tears away several times, clinging tightly to Robert. Walter stood at the back of the crowd, with a sober Jenifred Atte Wood clutching his arm. The three priests who had accompanied the nuns—all rankled over the fact that Chaucer had asked the simple country parson to preside—stood stiffly off to one side, crossing themselves dutifully.

Now they were all leaving, and Chaucer, alone, lingered behind. A tremendous weight of sorrow hung over him, and not just because of the loss of beauty and youth. All had mourned Sophia. But few—other than Father Harold—had spared any words or shed any tears for Jack.

Chaucer stood over the grave, staring at Osewold's skilled but roughly carved cross. "Jack, 1382." Scant testimony to a man's entire life! Poor repulsive, ugly, corrupt Jack! Had the man ever known any happiness? Geoffrey doubted it. He was probably born poor, with no prospects and no future, and so he took the only road he could to a life without starvation: thievery. Somehow he had managed to secure employment with the Church, in the much-feared role of summoner, and did as most summoners do: sought survival through taking bribes. Therefore, though many had feared him, and some probably hated him, few, if any, had loved him.

And Chaucer couldn't help feeling contempt for himself. Why hadn't he been able to feel compassion for Jack when the man was still alive?

Well, Jack, Chaucer thought, though you never could have done so in life, in death you will have the company of the young and the beautiful. Sophia will sleep beside you until Gabriel's trumpet awakens us all.

His reverie was rudely interrupted by the sound of approaching horses and shouts from the crowd. Quickly he turned around and began following the others back towards the inn. Walter, with Jeni at his heels, caught sight of Geoffrey and hurried to meet him.

"What is it?" Chaucer asked as Walter fell into step beside him.

"It's the local deputy—Master Canty—and his men," said Walter. "Something's happened!"

They quickened their pace and hurried to meet the horses. Peter Adams was arguing heatedly with Wulfstan Canty.

"The Duke cannot possibly be disturbed now!" said Adams arrogantly. "Surely a body found in the woods cannot possibly have any connection with the murder here! See to it yourself—I cannot possibly disturb the Duke!"

"Master Adams, what is happening?" asked Chaucer, striding up to stand by Peter Adams. Wulfstan Canty caught sight of him, and a look of relief passed over his face.

"You!" Canty called loudly to Chaucer. "Tell this half-witted arse-hole that this murder is important because a card was found by the body!"

"A card?" Chaucer was thunderstruck. "What kind?"

"Here!" Wulfstan Canty reached into his pocket and drew it out. "Take a look!" He tossed the object over to Chaucer, who caught it deftly.

He stared in sheer wonderment. It was indeed a Tarot card. It was totally unlike his—not the work of Jacquemin Gringonneur, not even a painted card, just the cheap stenciled type which were the only cards that the middle-and lower classes could afford. But he recognized it nonetheless, and was all too aware of its meaning. The Wheel of Fortune implied sudden, unexpected changes in the life of the querent—for good or evil.

He stared intently into Canty's eyes. "Where's the body?"

"My men are bringing it."

"Where was it found?"

"In the woods, between here and the road to London. Hidden under a bush."

Chaucer glowered at Peter Adams. "Go for the Duke!" he demanded. Adams, chagrined, hesitated, opened his mouth as if to protest, then changed his mind and left. A moment later he disappeared into the landlord's little house behind the inn.

The pilgrims, curious about the new development, were gathering in the front yard of the inn, keeping a discreet distance from Chaucer and the deputy's men so as to avoid being sent away. They drew back even farther when three horsemen came leading a third horse, across which a shrouded form had been tied.

Chaucer's heart sank. *We started on this pilgrimage in order to seek hope from the shrine of the saint. And all we have encountered so far is despair and death.*

The sergeants pulled their horses to a stop just as John of Gaunt sauntered through the innyard towards the horse bearing the body. Chaucer opened the blanket that covered the figure and laid his eyes on a face he had never seen before. A middle-aged man, tonsured and obviously a monk, with a thin, spare face, his hair and skin both brown and very nearly the same color.

Geoffrey directed the sergeants to remove the body from the horse and lay it on the ground, then he turned around and called for Master Richemont, though he didn't need the physician's aid to discern the cause of death. A dagger with a carved silver handle—clearly the work of a skilled craftsman—stuck out of the man's breast. The rough brown monk's robe that the corpse wore was stained with blood.

And a Tarot card had been found beside it…Chills swept through Chaucer's body. He looked up at a scowling John of Gaunt.

"The same man killed him who killed Sophia," said Chaucer. "There is no doubt."

Gaunt turned to Master Richemont. "How long has he been dead?" he demanded.

Gingerly Richemont moved the man's limbs. "Was he found face up or face down?" he asked one of the sergeants.

"Face up, Master."

"Then I would say he's been dead several days—four or five, at least. His body is totally flaccid, and decay has definitely set in; I'm sure you can smell it. The blood has settled to his back and has begun to solidify; see how the undersides of his arms are purple and black?"

Chaucer breathed a sigh of relief. "Then that clears me, at last," he said. "Four or five days ago I was busy at work in the customs office, and every one of my employees can vouch for me!"

A wave of longing for his home, and even for his job, swept over him. What on God's green earth had possessed him to come on this pilgrimage?

"I am tempted to return to London, but I still won't feel safe until we find the murderer," said John of Gaunt. "Bring the man into the barn!"

Four of the sergeants and guardsmen standing by took each a corner of the blanket and carried the body into the barn, laying it in an empty stall.

A sudden thought occurred to Chaucer. He turned around to see Walter standing behind him; Jeni had disappeared, probably recalled to work by her mother. "This man died unshriven," Chaucer said to the clerk. "Fetch Father Harold. The victim was obviously a man of God, and deserves the Last Rites, anyway."

Nodding obediently, Walter left the barn, returning a few moments later with Father Harold in tow. Father Harold removed from his pocket his prayer missal and rosary and prepared to perform his ritual. But when he saw the man's face, he gasped.

"May God save us all!" he cried. "It's Brother Nicholas!"

"Both daggers are of very high quality," said Wulfstan Canty, weighing the dagger that killed Sophia and the one found in the body of Brother Nicholas in his hands. "Yet I doubt very seriously if they were made by the same person. Other than the fact that they both have silver hilts, they are not alike at all. This one is an Italian stiletto. I don't think they are made in England, at least not in quantity. You can tell by the blade—it is long, thin, and conical in shape. This one, on the other hands, is a good old Saxon dagger, short, flat, and three-sided, with a point and edge honed to a razor-like sharpness."

Wulfstan Canty was the only one among them knowledgeable in the art of weapon making, and so he had been called upon to give his opinion of the implements of death used in the two murders.

"So does this mean that the murders were committed by two different people?" asked John of Gaunt.

"No," said Chaucer.

They were sitting in Master Atte Wood's parlor. Walter was taking scrupulous notes, while Jeni hovered in the background, pitcher of ale in hand. Wulfstan Canty, William Richemont and John of Gaunt were sitting by the fire, while Henry de Coverly, ever desiring to impress the great Duke with his own importance, stood leaning against the wall with his arms folded. Chaucer stood on the hearth, pacing back and forth, his mind buzzing like a bee.

"I doubt very seriously if there would be two murderers on the entire Continent of Europe, much less in the vicinity of St. Mary Cray, who would virtually 'sign' their work with Tarot cards," Chaucer went on.

"But one card came from your deck, which you said was quite costly," Gaunt went on relentlessly."and you said the other was from a cheap pack stenciled with black ink."

"True. But you're forgetting that one of the decks belonged to me. When the first murder was committed—that of Brother Nicholas—the killer didn't even know me, much less that I owned a deck of Tarot cards. This Wheel of Fortune card came from a deck that was probably the property of the murderer himself."

"Then what are we waiting for?" demanded Wulfstan Canty, jumping up and standing as though in readiness for battle."Let us search the belongings of every person in this inn until we find the rest of the cards!"

"Relax, Master Canty," said Chaucer."Robert Willard deduced from my astrological chart that the killer is not a man lacking money. These card packs are commonplace, at least in France, and quite inexpensive. The killer is far too clever to keep such incriminating evidence in his possession. He has undoubtedly discarded the rest of the pack by now."

"But why use two different daggers?" demanded Gaunt."Why not remove the first dagger from the body and keep it? He was forced to steal one!"

Master Richemont then spoke up."I think that I can tell you that," he said."If he had removed the first dagger from the body of the monk immediately after death, it would have released a large quantity of blood, which would have undoubtedly left a trail that might have enabled someone to find the body. He had to leave it behind."

Chaucer pressed his hand to his mouth, thinking."I believe," he said."that my dear friend Robert was mistaken when he said the thief and the murderer were probably not the same person. That information was not intrinsic in the chart; he only surmised it because he discerned that the murderer was a man of some means. I think that the thefts of the stud, the stirrup, and the haberdasher's brooch—and even my silver candleholder—were blinds to cover the theft of the dagger. That is why nothing but trifles were taken. The man was not looking to sell the items for money—he only wanted us to think that was his intention."

"You're probably right," said Henry de Coverly. "So where does that take us?"

"Well," said Chaucer, "we have deduced that the death of Sophia—and probably that of Brother Nicholas—was connected in some way with those who would seek to purify the clergy, possibly the Lollards or those within the true Church who would monitor the behavior of its officials so as to disprove the claims of the Lollards that the Church is corrupt and decadent. Master Richemont has surmised that Sophia was a defrocked nun. We have the statement of Simon that she knew Brother Nicholas. So did several of the other members of this little band of pilgrims—Father Harold, his brother Alfric, Don John the monk, and Jack the summoner. Others among the party may have known him as well, though they're not admitting it.

"It is all quite possible that someone on this journey—possibly one of the church officials—did not want Sophia reporting to Brother Nicholas that certain members of the clergy, probably one of the people present here and now, were living and behaving in a rather un-churchmanlike manner. Brother Nicholas may or may not have been a Lollard sympathizer, but according to Don John he was highly respected at Kirksdell and his work was known all over England, or at least in the north. It doesn't take much imagination to discern that he probably had the ear of a number of bishops, perhaps even archbishops."

"But doesn't the discovery of Brother Nicholas's body give the lie to your theory?" asked De Coverly. "If the murderer had already killed Brother Nicholas—thus ending whatever chance he might have had to report what Sophia had seen to the church hierarchy—then there was no need to kill Sophia."

Chaucer's face fell, as though he had been bereft of a cherished possession. Slowly he collapsed onto a small stool on the hearth. "You're right," he finally admitted.

Walter then spoke up. "But there may have been more to it than simply a churchman—or church woman—concerned about his or her reputation with the ecclesiastical hierarchy, or any sort of penance that might have been assigned. This is murder, not bribery or graft. If the killer is connected with the church, I would think that it would take more than fear of discipline or humiliation to warrant risking eternal punishment for murder in the fires of hell. Sophia was a gypsy, after all. Defrocked nun or not, a few gold coins might have easily purchased her silence. She had to make her way in the world now, after all. And Brother Nicholas—who knows—his presence in this area may be no more than coincidence. He has traveled a long way, after all, leaving his monastery, which was his home, his spiritual sustenance, and his livelihood. Would he do this simply to check on the behavior of such reprobates as Don John and Friar Hubert? Hardly, I think. Master Chaucer, your theory may be inaccurate in some ways, but I think that basically you are correct. We just need to delve more into the motivation for these crimes."

Chaucer's face was relaxed once more. He lifted himself off the stool, walked over and clapped the clerk on the shoulder. "Bright boy, Walter! Bright boy! I am proud of you! Clearly there is more to this than we even suspected." He turned to the other men in the room. "Money," he said tersely. "The astrological chart was very clear on that point. The murder was motivated by money. But what money, what purpose, and from what source, and how was it connected with Sophia?"

John of Gaunt suddenly sat straight up in his chair and cast an appreciative eye on Jeni. "Fill my tankard and that of Master Chaucer, dear girl, then get on with your other duties," he said. Imperiously

Gaunt stood and glared at those surrounding him. "Leave us! Every one of you! I want everyone in this room except Master Chaucer out of here in two minutes!"

Disgruntled and insulted, De Coverly and Master Richemont strode proudly over to the door, the bubble of their self-importance plainly burst. Wulfstan Canty hesitated a moment, then shrugged and followed the other two. Walter, crushed, stood slowly, manuscript book in hand, and glanced questioningly from Chaucer to Gaunt, then back to Chaucer. It was obvious that Gaunt had included him in his dismissal. Chaucer nodded encouragement.

"Take a break, Walter," said Geoffrey reassuringly. "You have worked hard and done well. Take the book into the tavern and write down all you've told us. I'll speak to you in a few moments."

Jeni finished refilling the tankards of ale, then took Walter's arm. "I'll go with you," she said. "I'm sure there's something for me to do in the tavern. There always is."

With one last backward glance at Chaucer, Walter allowed Jeni to lead him from the room. Gaunt seemed totally remorseless with regard to Walter's injured feelings. He merely stared into the fire.

After a few tense moments, he finally spoke up. "I'm afraid I have not been totally honest with you, Geoffrey."

Chaucer merely looked at him. *Since when have you ever been totally honest with anyone, old friend?* he thought. To Gaunt he only said, "Yes?"

"I truly did come here out of nothing more than concern for your welfare, my friend. But my remaining here was also motivated by something else."

Like Walter, Chaucer suddenly felt stricken. It did not surprise him that Gaunt had been motivated by other concerns than their friendship. Yet Chaucer was still human, and it hurt that the Duke had continued to give the impression that his remaining in St. Mary Cray had been for the sole purpose of exonerating Geoffrey—while all the time he had other problems.

"And what was that?" Chaucer queried, trying hard to keep his voice steady.

Gaunt stood, walked over to the fire, and leaned his head on the hearth, not daring to look at Chaucer's face. "I knew about Brother Nicholas," he finally said. "You are right in suspecting that Brother Nicholas had Lollard sympathies. He was a simple man, motivated by desire to serve his fellow man in the best way he could. As Don John has told you, Brother Nicholas's primary talent lay in the creation of beautiful books and manuscripts. He wondered why only the clergy, who had little need of it, were allowed access to Holy Writ, while the fearful and unawakened common people were denied it. When Master Wyclif appeared on the scene, Brother Nicholas was quite taken with his philosophy, and secretly attended a number of his lectures.

"Brother Nicholas did not like the idea of totally breaking with the church. But he believed wholeheartedly in purging the Church of corrupt clergymen, and in making the word of God available to all. When Master Wyclif published his Bible, there were vast numbers of copyists devoted to his cause who were all too willing to work day and night to put out inexpensive editions for everyone—like your stenciled Tarot cards. But Brother Nicholas and a few of his monks who were more devoted to him than to the church hierarchy worked diligently in secret for several months, putting out several copies of a beautifully inscribed and illuminated edition of Wyclif's Bible for anyone wealthy enough to buy one. I myself have one in my library—though I have to keep it a secret from my pious Spanish wife! The money raised from the purchase of these illuminated Bibles went to finance Wyclif's cause."

"How do you know all this?" asked Chaucer, frowning.

John of Gaunt sighed. "Well, here is where the story grows rather sordid by your standards. You always were too much of an idealist, Geoffrey—expecting too much of the sinful folk living in this difficult world. In the beginning, Brother Nicholas was involved only in his production of the magnificent Bibles. However, through contacts which he made while selling them, he became involved with Wyclif's cause in a more mundane way. When Master Wyclif and all his followers were declared heretics, Brother Nicholas's sympathies were still unknown and unsuspected by all outside the Lollard circle, and by many within it. Therefore he became—much against his will, I might add—a sort of go-between delivering messages from one Lollard nobleman to another who didn't dare contact each other openly. They were developing plans for a *coup d'état* that would advance the cause of Lollardy far more than anything else possibly could."

"And what was that?"

"My elevation to the throne of Castile."

Chaucer sighed; involuntarily he rolled his eyes. How like John of Gaunt to use the spiritual hunger of others to fire his own ambitions!

His expression did not go unobserved. "You disapprove, Geoffrey, and I am more aware of your reasons than you believe. But consider! Other than Italy itself, of course, can you think of any nation on Earth more deeply mired in the prejudices and self-righteous dogmatism of the Roman Church than Castile? For centuries Christian Spanish kingdoms have had to hold fast their faith against the onslaughts of Moslem infidels and prolific Jewish scholars. As a result, they have been forced to justify their faith to others and to themselves. They have done that not by seeking spiritual strength from God and Christ, but by becoming enslaved to the rituals and the rigid, unyielding dogma of Rome! Some have even taken up such insane and barbarous practices as severe asceticism, and actively seeking martyrdom!"

He paused for a moment, then continued. "Religion is supposed to bring hope, succor and joy, but do you know anyone more unhappy than my wife Costanza? Do you know of anyone more consumed by her religion? Of course you don't! She fasts all the time, eating only enough to keep her alive. She has abandoned all concern for the body, even for keeping it clean, which doesn't make it easy for me or anyone else to live with her! She attends Mass seven times a day, constantly prays and says her rosary, and is highly condemning of anyone who doesn't. Yet she is miserable, Geoffrey. And I refuse to believe that God sent us all here to Earth to be miserable!"

Chaucer could not argue that point. It was one of his most fervent arguments with the more fanatical members of the Church.

"In Castile, Geoffrey, Costanza is not unusual. At least half the Spanish population—probably more—live their lives exactly as she does. Master Wyclif once pondered if that was perhaps the reason why, in the early years of the last century, so many Spanish flocked to the Cathars! I would stop that, Geoffrey. By making the words of Master Wyclif available to Spanish Christians, I would give them the means to allow their Christ to bring joy into their lives. And so the Lollards are working hard, night and day, to raise enough funds to finance my campaign, and bring the words of Master Wyclif to southern Europe!"

Chaucer was totally flabbergasted, though a part of his mind realized that he shouldn't be. How so like John of Gaunt to rationalize fulfillment of his own desire as representing a holy spiritual crusade, solely for the benefit of the religiously oppressed people of Castile!

Holy Crusade, Holy Crusade…Why did that phrase ring a bell in Chaucer's mind? Suddenly he remembered. "My lord Duke—John—hasn't the Pope in Rome also declared your cause a holy crusade?"

Gaunt smiled wickedly. "Yes! Isn't it insidiously wonderful?"

Chaucer chuckled, shaking his head in disbelief. "You certainly take the prize for sheer gall, old friend." His mirth was abruptly replaced by confusion. "But what does all this have to do with the murders of Brother Nicholas and Sophia?"

"Brother Nicholas had obtained leave from the Abbot of Kirksdell to go on pilgrimage to Canterbury. He was, in fact, probably planning to accompany this bunch. But it was no more than a pretext. Brother Nicholas was carrying a message to one of my Lollard contributors in Kent. I am not sure what information the message actually contained, but it was vital to my campaign. The originator of the message had arranged to secure funding from my contributor and travel to the Continent to arrange for the hiring of a large number of Swiss mercenaries."

He sighed. "There are those who would stop me, Geoffrey. The Bishop of Norwich, for one. God only knows what possessed him to take holy orders, for he is a warrior at heart. He has his own quarrels with France and thus has taken it upon himself to retrieve more of our French lands that were lost during the reign of King John. And that damned pope in Rome has declared his cause a holy crusade as well, because he despises the French king's championing of the false pope in Avignon! And devotees of the Roman Church are contributing to Norwich's coffers like mad. The Bishop would do anything to stop me, Geoffrey, because not only have I been known to sympathize with the Lollards, I am collecting financial and other contributions which he fancies would otherwise have gone to him. He is a dangerous man—the enemy of anyone and everyone who would stop him."

Suddenly the implications of Gaunt's message hit Chaucer like a kick in the solar plexus. "My god, John, do you know what this means?"

"Of course I do. Brother Nicholas never delivered the message. And someone connected with the Roman church is aware of everything that has been going on both with me and with some on this very pilgrimage."

Ten

Geoffrey Chaucer closed his eyes and breathed deeply before saying anything more. Finally he spoke. "John, do you realize that this puts all of us here in danger? That includes you!"

"No one would dare treat me as they did Brother Nicholas and the gypsy girl!"

"Her name was Sophia." Chaucer was finding it difficult to hide his exasperation with his friend.

"Yes—yes, of course. I meant no disrespect," said Gaunt impatiently. "I am here for one reason and one reason only. To find a murderer. And to nip any conspiracy against my campaigns in Castile in the bud before word reaches the pope that high-ranking Lollards are financing them! If the pope finds that out and publicly denounces me, it would kill every chance I have of being crowned King of Castile!"

"My lord, I am certain that the pope would just as soon see you dead in Castile as murdered in an obscure English inn," said Chaucer bluntly. He realized wryly that he was perhaps being foolish. John of Gaunt was his old and dear friend, yes, but he was also the most powerful man in the kingdom—and he was well known for his hot temper. He switched to a more diplomatic tone. "We don't know for certain that whoever killed Brother Nicholas knows what was in the message he carried. I doubt if a man of Brother Nicholas's reputed intelligence would carry a written letter. He must have memorized the message. If anyone asked, he would have claimed to be no more than a humble Benedictine monk going on pilgrimage to Canterbury. The killer's mission may have been no more than to stop the messenger."

"It's possible. But not all that certain," said Gaunt. "We can take no chances, Geoffrey. We must find this murderer immediately!"

"But undue haste will not help us," Chaucer cautioned. "It would do us no good to arrest the wrong man. Not only would a murderer escape, but your ambitions would be placed in jeopardy. And we must realize: no one—with the exception of you and myself, and certainly Robert and Agatha—that is now present in this inn is above suspicion."

Walter was standing outside the back door of the tavern, drawing a bucket of water for Jeni, uneasily watching the door of the Atte Wood house and wondering what Chaucer and the Duke of Lancaster were discussing inside. He lifted the bucket, now oppressively heavy with the weight of the water he carried, hauled it into the tavern kitchen and hefted it onto the kitchen table, where Jenifred was preparing a huge pot of soup for the pilgrims' supper.

"My father is exceedingly happy," said Jeni as she helped Walter empty the water into the iron soup kettle that hung from the spit over the fireplace.

"Why?" asked Walter. The bucket was now empty. With some relief he placed it on the floor.

"He has made more money since your party of pilgrims has been here than he expected to make in the entire year," Jeni replied as she bent to light the fire. They watched for a moment in silence as the sparks from Jeni's tinder box set the kindling alight and the flames began to stretch up toward the kettle.

Jeni waited until she was sure the fire had caught, then walked over to the pantry and opened its doors. Her voice rang from its interior as she walked inside. "The Duke of Lancaster's payments alone amount to more than we made all of last year—not to mention what the pilgrims are paying us." She emerged from the pantry carrying a large earthenware pot. "The wealthy among them expect to be pampered and are willing to pay for it. Until the murderer is found, this newfound prosperity is bound to continue—at least for another day or so. So my father is making great plans for what he wants to do with the money."

"And what are his plans?" Walter watched in fascination as Jeni dumped the contents of the pot, which appeared to be lentils, into the soup kettle.

"He wants to expand the inn, first of all," Jeni replied, taking a bone with fragments of meat sticking to it and dropping it into the soup kettle. "Secondly, he wants to buy some gifts for my mother—she works so hard, for so little reward. And he also wants to establish a dowry for me."

"A dowry!" Walter's spirits plummeted. "Are you betrothed?"

"No, of course not." She returned to the table, picked up a knife, and began chopping onions. Their fumes wafted over to Walter and caused his eyes to sting. "But I will be some day," Jeni continued. "And my father wants me to have a better life than he or my mother have ever had. Up until now it has appeared that I would never be able to do better than any of my cousins did—that I would probably marry a local farmer's son, live a poor and meaningless life, and be dead of hard work or in childbed before I reached thirty-five, without ever having set foot outside of St. Mary Cray."

A wave of fear passed over Walter as he imagined such a dreadful fate for his lovely new friend. Then inspiration struck him. "Jeni, why not come with us to Canterbury? If your father wants you to have better prospects, then surely he cannot object to your traveling with a band of respectable pilgrims? Making a pilgrimage would add to your experience, and thus make you more appealing to the worldly and successful! There are a number of respectable women here who would be glad to chaperon you—Dame Eglantine, Sister Cecily, Mistress Willard." Wisely he avoided mentioning Alisoun of Bath. "And there are plenty of men here who would go down fighting before they would allow harm to come to you. Sir Richard de Burgoyne, Simon, their yeoman, Alfric the plowman, any of the tradesmen, Master

Chaucer." Not to mention myself, he avoided adding."You would be quite safe. And it would all be very proper."

Jeni stopped chopping onions for a moment and stared at the wall ahead of her, a faraway look in her eyes."To travel to Canterbury, to see the cathedral, and to set foot on the same stones as the holy martyr—oh, Walter, that would be wonderful. But in spite of all you say, my father would never consent. There is too much work to be done here. Father expects our inn to continue to prosper, even after the pilgrims leave. It has not taken long for word to spread about what's been happening here. My brother went into the village yesterday. A minstrel was there, playing a harp for coins in the street. He did well, for he was singing a ballad about the tragedy of the lovely murdered Sophia, and of how the Duke of Lancaster himself came to avenge her death.

"And then he moved on—he was on his way to the fair at Bromley, he said. A fair at Bromley! Do you know how many people go to such a fair? If he plays that song there, other travelers to Canterbury or Dover could well make a point of passing through St. Mary Cray just to see the place where Sophia died! There are even those who whisper that her ghost haunts this inn; my brother said that some who have never visited this tavern nonetheless swear to have seen Sophia's ghost appear in one of its windows! People will come, Walter. And my father will need my help."

Walter was immediately filled with anger over the idea of Jeni being forced to remain here as unpaid labor when she could be traveling with him. But he forced himself to control it."I'll have Master Chaucer speak to him," he finally said."He can be very persuasive. Don't lose heart, my dear Jeni. You may reach Canterbury yet!"

She smiled at him—a bewitchingly beautiful smile. Walter smiled back, somewhat uncertainly, and thought he saw a blush stain her fresh young cheeks. Turning resolutely away, Jeni added the chopped onions to the soup, took a long-handled wooden spoon and stirred it slightly, then began shelling fresh peas. The delicious aroma of bubbling soup began to fill the kitchen. Walter couldn't help fantasizing that this was *their* kitchen, *their* home. For a brief moment he was blissfully, ridiculously happy.

"Jeni!" came an angry voice from the door. "What are you doing?"

Jeni and Walter both looked up with a start—and then felt overwhelmingly guilty. It was Mistress Atte Wood. "What is that young man doing in here?"

"Mum, he was only helping me draw some water!"

"You know very well that guests are not allowed in the kitchen!"

"I'm sorry, Mistress Atte Wood," said Walter. "I was only trying to take some of the heavier work off Jeni's hands—"

"Jeni's hands will be far stronger if they are left to do the work God gave to her! Now get on out of here, young man, and find somewhere else to waste your time!"

Walter spun around and stalked out of the kitchen door, humiliated. And he had dared to entertain the thought that he could entice Jeni away from a woman like that! If Mistress Atte Wood had her way, she'd keep Jeni there working for the rest of her life! His previous happiness gave way to despair, and he leaned against the water pump, closing his eyes.

"You're falling in love with her, aren't you?"

Startled, Walter looked up to see where the voice was coming from. Simon de Burgoyne stood before him, dressed in a rich blue tunic trimmed with gold braid, his waist encircled by a finely tooled leather belt.

"Don't fall in love, my bookish friend. It only brings you pain."

"Why do you say that?" said Walter indignantly. Then he remembered. "Oh—I forgot. I'm sorry. I'm so, so sorry."

"Ah! What is there for you to be sorry about? You didn't kill Sophia. You didn't even know her."

"But I did know her—though not well. I know enough about her to be sorry that she is dead. And, though I hope you will take no offense at this, because one man's love is murdered doesn't mean that all romance is destined to end in pain and suffering."

"You're right," said Simon. "In fact, it is very ironic, isn't it? If my love had not been murdered, we would not be stuck at this godforsaken inn and you would never have had a chance to make the acquaintance of the lovely daughter of our landlord."

Walter's face stung at this rebuke. "Perhaps not, perhaps so. If two people are meant to be together, God will bring them together no matter what the circumstances—so perhaps even if Sophia still lived I would have managed to meet Jeni some way."

"Ah, what an innocent you are!" said Simon with a superior air. He suddenly realized how ridiculous those words must seem, as he and Walter were just about the same age. He hastened to explain himself further. "I mean, you have spent most of your life sequestered in the safe haven of books. I have been out fighting wars with my father, traveling in foreign lands. I have seen much of the world—perhaps too much. Very little of real life is conducive to the affirmation of faith in God." He said the last line bitterly. Walter suddenly felt very sorry for him.

"I know nothing can bring Sophia back to you," said Walter gently. "It is hard to have faith in God when one's dearest love is snatched away by death—and such a brutal death, at that. But justice will be done, I assure you. Master Chaucer is the smartest of men—and the Duke of Lancaster the most powerful. They will find Sophia's killer, I promise you!"

"Master Chaucer! All he has done so far is talk!" said Simon harshly. He stared Walter straight in the eye. "I'm planning to do more than talk," he said more quietly.

Walter eyed him suspiciously. "What's that?"

"I'm going to go out to the place where they found Brother Nicholas's body," said Simon. "Would you like to go with me?"

Wild fantasies suddenly galloped through Walter's mind. He, Walter Locksley, would find the one puzzle piece that brought it all together. Master Chaucer would be so grateful, he would offer him a post at the customs office. Walter would then be able to provide the prosperous life for Jeni which Master Atte Wood wanted for his daughter...He returned to earth with a crash, facing Simon's somewhat mocking gaze.

"How do you know where the place is?" Walter queried.

Simon rattled the moneybag hanging from his belt. "A few silver pennies bought the knowledge from one of that idiot deputy sheriff's half-witted sergeants," he replied. "Now do you want to come with me or not?"

"Yes!" said Walter excitedly.

"Then get your horse and let's go!" Simon cried, showing more zest for life than he had on the entire pilgrimage.

He dashed off towards the stable. Walter, exhilarated, hesitated only a moment before running after him.

"So it seems that we are all caught up in something which started long before this pilgrimage," Chaucer was saying.

He was leaning against the window, a small diamond-paned glass model which must have cost Master Atte Wood a month's profit. The sun had just passed over the meridian, and was now slanting its powerful rays through the glass. John of Gaunt had retreated from the ensuing heat into the shadow on the opposite side of the room, and was sitting in the most comfortable chair available.

"Who of all the pilgrims are the most likely to be involved with such an affair?" Chaucer continued. "Of course we're going to think first of the churchmen here. I don't think the nuns would be involved."

"But Master Richemont pointed out that Sophia must have been a nun once," the Duke of Lancaster pointed out.

"True, true," Chaucer acknowledged. "Still, I'm more inclined to believe that the men are more likely to be involved in a political conspiracy than the women. Don John, the monk, is also based at Kirksdell, where Brother Nicholas lived and worked. What is your impression of him?"

"He's an arrogant, self-righteous, pompous ass," said John of Gaunt promptly. "He likes good food, fine clothes, and the best of wines. He may have taken a vow of poverty, but he certainly has access to money somewhere—as do all corrupt churchmen. Yes, I can see him seeing Master Wyclif and all Lollards as a threat to the life he loves so well. But he also seems like a scared rabbit—too timid to participate in murder."

"An accurate appraisal," said Chaucer. "He impressed me the same way. Don John also probably knows more than he's telling. He never seems to be able to look me straight in the eye. Now, what about the three priests?"

"Father Matthew is dogmatic, inflexible, and rigid," Gaunt replied. "He likes his luxuries as well, but somehow he doesn't seem as attached to them as Don John. He probably thinks of Wyclif and his followers as heretics and blasphemers, but I believe he would be motivated more by his own judgmental and self-aggrandizing brand of piety than by politics. If he killed Sophia, it was not because of any connections she had, with Brother Nicholas or anybody. It was because she was a gypsy, and he saw her as demonic and evil."

"So it is unlikely that it was he," said Chaucer. "because it appears, at least, that the same person killed Brother Nicholas that killed Sophia. What about the other two priests?"

"They are ineffectual," said Gaunt. "Both very young—probably not very long since they were consecrated. Still very idealistic—still full of faith and totally innocent in the ways of the world. I am far more inclined to suspect Friar Hubert."

"Ah!" cried Chaucer. "On that we are fully agreed! I am so glad you said that, as I have disliked the man intensely since we started on this pilgrimage, and I couldn't help suspecting that my reasons lay in my own instinctual dislike of all friars. The friar is every bit as corrupt as Don John, he is not easily frightened, he lusted after Sophia, and possibly he knew her before we all met at the Tabard. If anyone on this pilgrimage fits the profile of a murderer, it is Brother Hubert!"

"Still, we must not be hasty," warned Gaunt. "According to the notes kept by that paragon of a clerk, Friar Hubert was in the men's common sleeping-room throughout all the time in which Sophia could have been murdered. No one saw him leave. As you yourself pointed out, it would do us no good to arrest the wrong man."

"Or woman," added Chaucer. "But we are focusing so strongly on the churchmen we are forgetting the others. All those that weren't in the common sleeping-room. What about Master Richemont, or Henry de Coverly?"

"Master Richemont seems interested only in the functioning of bodies," said Gaunt. "De Coverly, however, is another matter entirely. He is a sharp lawyer, and all lawyers are politicians. I imagine that he would follow political trends and battles very closely, and declare his loyalty to whatever side seemed most likely to win. Since John Wyclif and his followers were declared heretics, I can't help believing that Master de Coverly, even if he had sympathized with the Lollards in the beginning, probably has now totally thrown his allegiance in with the Church. He doesn't strike me as being fanatical enough to commit murder. Still, we cannot in all good conscience eliminate him."

"And Sir Richard de Burgoyne?"

"Of course he is not the murderer! He would never declare war on women under any circumstances, and by offering me his fealty he has already subtly, if not openly, thrown his lot in with the Lollards. No, if Sir Richard is the killer, then our reasoning is totally wrong. If he killed Sophia, it was an act of passion, not politics, and the Tarot cards at both murders are no more than a bizarre coincidence."

And that, Chaucer told himself, is highly doubtful.

They had much more to discuss. There still remained the two nuns, and Alisoun of Bath, and every other pilgrim on the journey. He sighed. It was going to be a long afternoon.

Walter and Simon had dismounted, tied their horses to a tree and carefully tiptoed over to the area where Wulfstan Canty's sergeant had said Brother Nicholas was killed. A wide spot opended right after a slight bend in the road, where bushes were more plentiful than trees, and where an old tree with a monstrous trunk and gnarled roots grew back about ten feet from the path.

"This has to be the place," said Simon almost reverently.

Walter nodded his agreement. The bush where they were standing had many small broken branches underneath, as if something unusual had lain in that spot. A few spots, dried liquid of some kind now dark reddish-brown in color, dotted a tiny area near the broken branches.

"Blood," Simon speculated.

Carefully Walter bent low, lifted the branches and stared at the place where Brother Nicholas's body must have lain.

"Nothing," he declared, dropping the branches and standing up. Then a thought struck him. "Where's his pack?" he asked.

Simon stared blankly at his companion. "What pack?"

Now it was time for Walter to flaunt superior knowledge. "Even monks who travel on foot carry some kind of pack," he said wisely. "They have to have some place to store their food, and any money they may need while on the road. Usually it's a small leather bag attached to their belt. But I saw Brother Nicholas's body. There was no pack on him."

"Perhaps the murderer took it," suggested Simon.

Walter shook his head. "It's possible, but doubtful. To carry away the pack of a murder victim? He might take the money inside, he might even take the food, but the pack? To my mind that would be too dangerous. No, it has to be somewhere around here. Let's find it!"

Scrupulously the two youths searched all around the bush, backs bent, their eyes glued to the ground. They searched the area twice, all to no avail.

Walter, however, not one to accept easily the defeat of a brilliant theory, crossed over the path, strode by the gnarled old oak and found a small clearing, dotted with stones and small wildflowers. A few minutes later his diligence was rewarded.

"Simon!" he cried. "I've found it!" A moment later he was waving a worn old leather wallet, with a hole poked through the top of it for a belt to be threaded through. As Simon rushed to meet him, his face fell. "There's nothing in it, though," said Walter, who had secretly hoped to find some clue inside the bag.

"Well, so what?" demanded Simon. "You yourself said the murderer probably would have taken any money or food there was inside. He killed Brother Nicholas, stole whatever he had, then tossed the pack over here."

"No," said Walter, his quick eyes surveying the land around him. "Brother Nicholas was killed here."

"Why do you say that?" asked Simon.

"Look!" said Walter, pointing. "See where those stones have been upturned? They lie on grass—grass which has been growing for a long time. But next to each stone there is a bare spot of earth. It looks as if Brother Nicholas did not go easily—he put up a fight. And in the course of that fight he—or the murderer—kicked over those stones." He pointed to an area beyond the stones, between them and the path. "Look! See the trail of flattened grass! The killer dragged his body from here to the bush!" Eagerly Walter followed the trail, with Simon close at his heels.

"But what does all this matter?" demanded Simon. "What do you expect to find?"

"This!" Walter cried triumphantly. "Look!" He held up a small piece of rough black homespun cloth which had been caught on a hollow log near the flattened grass.

"But that's just a piece of Brother Nicholas's habit," argued Simon. "As the killer dragged him back towards the road, the dead monk's clothes got caught on the twig and a little piece was torn off."

"No," said Walter, looking closer. "The killer stopped to tear it off the twig himself. He probably was unable to pull the body any further as long as it stayed caught—this is tough cloth. And in the process of freeing the body he left a memento of his own." Walter bent and carefully removed something he had almost missed from the earth near the log. If it had not caught the few remaining rays of the sun, he would have missed it. It was very tiny—a link of a finely crafted silver chain, broken at the seam, but nonetheless costly when it was new.

"That could have been here for ages," objected Simon.

"No," Walter insisted. "It's clean and bright still—not encrusted with dirt at all. It was on the surface of the grass—it had not yet even sunk between the blades. And it was near the fragment of Brother Nicholas's habit. It can't have been the monk's—it is far too valuable for a humble Benedictine. No, it must have belonged to the killer."

"So what do we do with it?" Simon demanded.

Grimly Walter placed both objects into the pack, then tied the wallet to his belt. "We take everything to Master Chaucer."

Meekly Simon followed him as they returned to the road and untied their horses.

As their horses stepped out of the wood, towards the road that led to the inn, the sun, now barely above the horizon, shone full into their eyes, blinding them. At that moment they heard a chorus of angry shouts.

"There they are! They who have brought the devil to our village!"

"The one wearing the sword—he's the one who lay with the pagan gypsy witch!

"If it weren't for those so-called pilgrims St. Mary Cray would still be a peaceful village."

Vaguely Simon recognized the voice of the man who had given him the directions to the murder site. He exchanged a glance of alarm with Walter.

"Get them!" cried a rough voice.

Almost in one motion Simon and Walter kicked up their horses and rode at a full gallop past the band of angry villagers who had waited in ambush for them. Simon's swift warhorse sped on ahead; Walter's old palfrey was much slower, and so he began swatting him mercilessly with his riding crop. The hoof beats of the men following them sounded fearfully close. The clerk whipped his horse that much harder.

It seemed an eternity before the roof of the inn appeared in sight.

Eleven

"To arms! To arms!" Simon cried as he and Walter galloped at full force into the inn courtyard. "Outlaws! Outlaws!"

From the stable emerged Sir Richard, alert to the sound of his son's voice. Peter Adams and another of the Duke's royal guardsmen followed him. A number of the pilgrims came running out of the inn itself, including Robyn the miller, the four guildsmen, Osewold the reeve and Alfric the plowman. They all dropped their jaws in shock as they caught sight of the furious mob chasing the two young men.

"There's at least fifty of them!" cried one of the guildsmen.

Walter, quickly dismounting, realized that the guildsman was right. No more than a dozen had confronted him and Simon outside the wood; other angry farmers and villagers must have joined them on the chase back to the inn.

Sir Richard, Peter Adams and the guardsman drew their swords; the others, unarmed, looked around for whatever they could use for weapons. Robyn the miller let out a loud guffaw of satisfaction as he located a shovel off to one side of the inn. He picked it up, swung it at the first angry enemy that came close, and knocked the man off his horse to lie insensible on the ground.

Simon dismounted, smacked his horse on the hip and set it running for the stables. He drew his sword and began swinging it as the outlaws began attacking him.

"Incubus!" cried one. "He sleeps with demons! The gypsy whore's ghost haunts the inn because of him—"

He said no more. Simon's angry sword thrust right through to the man's heart and left him lying in his own blood.

The dead man's companions cried out in fury and ganged up on Simon, four of them confronting him. Sir Richard jumped in and swung his sword mightily in defense of his son. Between the two of them they managed to disarm one man, kill still another and chase the others off.

"A fine show of courage, son!" cried Sir Richard. "I'm proud of you!" Without wasting any further time the knight went to rescue the besieged Walter, who was bravely trying to fight off three men with the lid of a barrel.

"Good show, friend clerk! Good show!" cried Sir Richard, as he beheaded one of the attackers and sent the others running away in terror. "I've never seen a king with more courage!" He turned toward the youth and winked, then ran to aid Simon once more.

Walter nodded his thanks to Sir Richard, then hurried back to the Atte Wood house and pounded on the door, frantically looking behind him as though fearing he'd been followed.

Geoffrey Chaucer opened the door slightly, smiled at the sight of Walter, then gasped as he spotted the mêlée going on in front of the inn. "Good God, Walter, what is happening?" he cried.

"Simon and I rode out to examine the spot where Brother Nicholas was murdered," Walter related. "On our way back we were chased by a band of angry villagers. They don't like murder, I suppose—unless they themselves commit it! Now everyone out there is fighting them!"

Behind Chaucer appeared John of Gaunt, his face dark with rage. "Where's that damned deputy sheriff?" he bellowed.

"I don't know, Your Grace," said Walter miserably. "But there's a few dozen men out there, all of whom have decided that we pilgrims are bringing the devil down upon their village."

"Well, I'll show them who can bring the devil down on them!" cried Gaunt. His sword and scabbard hung from a peg near the door; he took them down and strapped them around his waist. With Chaucer and Walter at his heels, he half strode, half ran into the courtyard. "I am John of Gaunt, Duke of Lancaster!" he bellowed. "Stop this immediately!"

But the only people who paid any attention to him were the pilgrims. The outlaws went right on fighting, unimpressed by his name or rank.

A short, dark, ugly peasant suddenly confronted Chaucer, waving a club. Deftly Geoffrey dodged to one side, then skillfully kicked out at the backs of the man's knees, in a maneuver he had learned as a soldier. The man crumpled to the ground, loosening his grip on his club, which Chaucer seized, then threw to Walter. "Tie him up!" Chaucer barked. "Or beat him senseless, I don't care!" The poet then turned to fight off another attacking villager in the same way.

John of Gaunt had drawn his sword and was fighting next to Sir Richard, laughing all the way. Chaucer was impressed by Sir Richard's bravery and skill; the knight could well hold his own with a dozen Saracens, Geoffrey reflected. These ignorant peasants were nothing to him. Nor were they any match for John of Gaunt.

Walter had dragged his prisoner into the barn and bound him to one of the horse's stalls wherein was tied a very skittish horse. He returned to Chaucer's side, still holding the man's club. "They just keep coming!" Walter gasped. "There weren't this many before at all!"

"Superstitious louts!" hissed Chaucer, shaking his head. He watched as Harry Bailey disarmed a wizened little man who had attacked him with a dagger. "Good show, Harry!" Chaucer shouted, then grabbed the club from Walter and ran to join his friend.

Walter hurried inside the tavern's kitchen door, oblivious of Mistress Atte Wood's previous banning of guests in the kitchen. He found Jeni standing by the fireplace next to Agatha Willard. A huge pot of water was boiling; Jeni and Agatha were filling iron kettles. Alisoun of Bath stepped out of the shadows, took one of the kettles, then ran out of the kitchen.

Without disturbing the women or asking what they were doing, Walter's eyes darted around the kitchen, looking for a suitable weapon.

His eyes fell on a poker that stood by the fireplace. He seized it, catching Jeni's questioning eye, nodded wordlessly to her and ran back out to the courtyard.

The clerk managed to intercept two hideous peasants who had set their sights on the kitchen. Gritting his teeth, he knocked both of them unconscious with his poker, then ran out towards the front, where the Duke of Lancaster, Sir Richard de Burgoyne, Simon, and all the guardsmen seemed to be bringing a large number of the renegades under control. The ground was littered with bodies. Some were dead, but more were alive and bleeding, groaning with pain.

Directly in front of the door to the tavern Harry Bailey, Robyn the Miller and Henry de Coverly were battling off angry farmers. A brief movement at one of the windows on the second floor caught Walter's attention. He looked up; a plump figure leaned out: Alisoun of Bath.

"I am the ghost of the gypsy witch!" she cried eerily. "I will show you what I do to those who would thwart me!" She leaned as far forward as she dared, held the iron kettle out in front of her and poured its contents out on the heads of those attacking the defenders. They screamed in pain and collapsed onto the ground, their heads and faces horribly scalded.

"Anybody want any more?" Alisoun called invitingly, threatening to tip the kettle once more.

"And I've got some too!" cried Agatha, appearing at a second window. Everyone—Harry Bailey and the other two pilgrims as well—hastily moved away from the tavern walls.

At that moment Wulfstan Canty, accompanied by a number of his sergeants, came riding into the courtyard. "Stop!" he shouted.

Hearing the voice of one of their own, the remaining outlaws stopped fighting.

"What is going on here?" Canty thundered.

The angry peasants clumped together, then shoved the tallest of their number forward, apparently choosing him as their spokesman.

"We wanted to get rid of these people, Master Canty," the tall man said. "They have brought murder into St. Mary Cray. The ghost of the heathen gypsy witch now haunts this inn, and thus defiles our village. They have brought great evil, all in the guise of a holy pilgrimage. We wanted to chase them and their evil away from St. Mary Cray forever!"

John of Gaunt then pushed his way forward. "You idiots!" he shouted. "It is not the band of pilgrims that has brought the evil! It is one person, one man, who has committed murder and thus put you in fear of your lives! You have acted unwisely—as people of your sort always do!"

Chaucer realized that his friend was recalling the Peasants' Revolt of the year before. Fourteen-year-old King Richard II had, through sheer charisma and bravery, forestalled a bloody civil war—thus making John of Gaunt and the other regents, who would have mowed all the rebels down like stalks of wheat, look like fools. Gaunt had yet to forgive King Richard—or the peasants—for his humiliation.

"Well," said Gaunt, with some satisfaction, "you have brought more evil and death upon yourselves. Some of your companions lie dead or dying at your feet. And you will soon follow them into eternity. I hereby charge you all with treason, as you have attacked a royal regent! You will be escorted to London in chains, by my men, where you will be duly tried and hanged!" A wail rose from the crowd of assembled peasants.

Chaucer then stepped forward and drew his friend aside. "My lord Duke, do you want to bankrupt the village of St. Mary Cray by executing all her men, all her farmers? Do you want to create widows and orphans of all the citizens of this little village? Some of the peasants here have already paid with their lives; others have been grievously wounded. All have lost brothers, sons, companions. To hang them all because of a desire for vengeance would do little for your own soul and nothing for theirs. Surely a little forgiveness is called for here."

"Never!" shouted Gaunt. "I won't rest until I see every one of these arse-holes dangling by the neck—"

"Do you want word to spread throughout Europe of the cruel tyranny of he who would be King of Castile? Or do you want to be known for your mercy?"

Realizing the wisdom of Chaucer's words, John of Gaunt stamped his feet in frustration. "One of these days you're going to be right once too often, Geoffrey, and I'm going to lose my temper and break your jaw! Very well!" He turned to the assembled throng in front of him. "I have reconsidered. Justice here would be served better by forgiveness than vengeance. I realize you were only acting out of fear. Return to your homes. Take the bodies of your dead and wounded with you. I give you my word: He who committed the murders and brought such evil into your village will be found, and will pay with his life! Now go!"

Relief replaced the despair on the faces of the renegades, then suddenly unease took over again as they all realized that the good Duke was perfectly capable of changing his mind; they had better go before he did so again. Quickly they all dispersed, some taking time to carry the bodies of their dead and wounded companions to their horses, others mounting up and escaping without another word or gesture.

"Master Chaucer?"

Geoffrey, who had been rapt in watching the departure of the outlaws, started. He turned to find Simon de Burgoyne standing beside him, looking worried.

"What is it, young man?"

"It's Walter, Master Chaucer. He's in the Atte Wood house. I carried him there. He's taken a bad gash on the left arm. Master Richemont is with him, but—

Chaucer didn't hear another word. Immediately he pushed past Simon and ran to the back of the tavern toward the Atte Wood home, the squire at his heels.

Walter sat in the front room, near a window so as to enable Master Richemont, who was stitching up his wound, to see clearly. Jeni Atte Wood was holding Walter's other hand; Agatha stood close by, handing the physician tools and herbs as he needed them. Sir Richard de Burgoyne stood by the door, as though keeping watch. The clerk gave a cry of pain as Chaucer entered; Master Richemont had just taken another stitch. When Walter opened his eyes, he found Chaucer smiling at him.

"Well, my esteemed assistant," said Chaucer, patting the youth on the shoulder. "it is well that it is your left arm that is hurt. I shall continue to need your right hand to help me to find a murderer. How did this happen?"

Walter grimaced. "I hit one of the peasants with the poker, and thought that I had knocked him senseless. However, I hadn't; he took his dagger and sliced me open like a pheasant. If Simon hadn't found me when he did, I would probably have bled to death. But I am glad you're here! Simon and I have much to tell you. Ugh!" Master Richemont had taken another stitch.

"Well, perhaps you had better remain still and let Simon tell it," said Chaucer. He looked expectantly at the squire. "What is Walter talking about?"

Briefly Simon told him the story of their trip to the site of Brother Nicholas's murder, elaborating greatly upon how Walter's quick eyes had found the true site of the murder and the two clues. Chaucer's ears pricked up. "Where are these two artifacts?" he demanded.

Walter nodded to Simon. "Outside, in the stable. I hung the pack on my saddle when we arrived here." Simon immediately ducked out of the door and ran to the stables.

"Ouch!" cried Walter. Master Richemont had taken still another stitch. "When are you going to finish that?" he demanded.

"I already have," said Master Richemont. "That's all you're going to need. I need only dress and bandage it now. Mistress Willard, would you please hand me some chamomile so that I can dress Master Locksley's wound?"

Agatha did so, but frowned. "Chamomile? Isn't that rather ineffectual for what Master Locksley suffers? Wouldn't echinacea or comfrey be better?"

"Possibly, yes, but I have none with me, and chamomile is an herb that can be used for nearly every ailment." He pressed the leaves against Walter's arm, then tied a bandage around it. "You're going to have a scar there, my boy. But at least you'll live to tell your grandchildren how you got it!"

Simon then returned. Without a word he handed the dead monk's leather wallet over to Chaucer. Geoffrey opened the pouch, reached inside and took out the two tiny objects. "A fragment of cloth from Brother Nicholas's habit, and a tiny link from a silver chain," he mused. "What could they possibly mean?"

"I can tell you some!" said Walter excitedly. His brow was becoming sweaty and his voice weak. Chaucer could tell he was exhausted from the experience and still suffering pain.

The latter was not lost on Master Richemont. "Mistress Willard, would you brew a cordial for Master Locksley? Willow bark and valerian in wine, to ease his pain and make him sleep. Sleep is what he needs now." Agatha nodded and left the house for the main kitchen at the tavern.

"But I must tell Master Chaucer!" Walter protested. "He needs to know now! That little link—it caused me to remember! Master Wyclif—he lives in Oxford, you know, and so do I! Many of us at the University know of his activities, and follow them closely even if we are not totally accepting of them. But there are those who are hostile. There is one group in particular; I learned of it quite by accident, when one of my lecturers got drunk and loose-lipped one night. Members of this group call themselves the Brothers of the Sacred Silver. It is a secret society, said to be limited in its membership to proven descendants of those who destroyed the Knights Templar and the Cathars. Their mission is to preserve the Church of Rome and to protect it against assault by heretics at all costs. They appropriate all treasure from any heretical group—particularly silver! Some they give back to Rome, but more they keep for themselves. The Brothers have tried to kill Master Wyclif many times, but all attempts have been unsuccessful. All the

Brothers wear silver chains, which are no more than trophies made from silver treasure stolen from groups or individuals that they consider heretical and dangerous to the Church. The chains identify them to the rest of their membership. One of their numbers is here, Master Chaucer, and he killed Brother Nicholas and Sophia!"

Chaucer's brow knitted. He had not been aware of such a society, and he prided himself on keeping up with such matters. But if the society were secret, and knowledge of it limited to those at University—well, it was a long time since he had visited Oxford.

"This could indeed be valuable knowledge," said Chaucer. "You say they take silver from those whom they consider heretical? Do you mean that the thefts of silver suffered by this group could fall into such a category? But Dame Eglantine, a devout Dominican nun, was robbed, as were Mistress Willard and our friend the haberdasher, neither of whom has any interest at all in religious matters beyond Sunday Mass. Myself—well, there are those who brand me as a blasphemer because I use classical themes in my poetry, and because I am friends with John of Gaunt. Nevertheless, I am not an active participant in any religious group."

"Ah, but the members of this society are lunatics," said Walter. "Like those who destroyed the Templars, they see heresy where none exists. Who knows how their minds work? I think we should consider this information before we investigate any further."

Agatha then returned, cordial in hand. She gave the mug to Walter. "You'll be doing no investigating for the rest of today, Master Locksley," she said, taking a motherly tone. "Master Richemont says you need sleep, and sleep is what you're going to do!" She turned to Jeni. "Where can we put him?"

"In my room," said Jeni promptly. "It is in the very back of the house, away from the tavern, and well protected from any noise. He can rest quietly there."

Sir Richard de Burgoyne then stepped forward. "But wouldn't His Grace the Duke object?"

Jeni cast the knight a withering look. "The Duke will have to accept that Walter needs quiet, and we have no more rooms available at the inn. And I am certainly not going to banish this poor young man to the stables, as the innkeeper in the Bible did to the family of Our Lord! The good Duke sleeps in my parents' room, after all. This is my room!"

Sir Richard retreated, wisely avoiding saying anything more.

Chaucer held Walter up on one side, Master Richemont on the other, as they helped him walk into Jeni's bedroom. With Jeni's help they tucked him into bed.

The girl then took up a mass of needlework on the bedside table, sat down in a nearby chair and began to work. "I shall sit with him in case he needs anything," she said.

No one dared to argue with her. All left the room. Chaucer went to inform John of Gaunt that Walter was sleeping in his commandeered quarters, as everyone else was afraid to do so.

John of Gaunt, as usual, stayed way in the back of the room when it came time for that night's tale telling. The pardoner, a thoroughly insidious character, was due to tell his. He had promised to tell a moral tale, and so he had embarked upon a confession that he was a hypocrite and a con artist, that he liked money, rich food and good living, but even if he was not of a moral nature, his tale would be.

"In Flanders, in the days of the Black Plague," the pardoner began, "three young men, rioters all, sat in a tavern drinking, gambling and swearing. As the night prepared to pass into day, they heard the sound of a bell, which told them that a coffin was being carried past the inn. The three rascals asked the servant to go find out who it was that had died.

"The servant replied there was no need to ask, for he knew who the dead man was. He had been stabbed in the back only the night before by some sneaky thief called Death. This was the same thief that had caused the plague to take so many lives in the next village.

"The three rioters realized that Death might still be lurking in the neighboring village, and so they decided to seek him out and slay him. On their way, they met a very old man dressed in rags. The three young men commented on his advanced age, and he told them that he must wander the Earth until he can find someone willing to exchange youth for age. Until then, not even Death would take his life."

While Chaucer found the Pardoner an especially disgusting sort, he was nonetheless fascinated by the man's skill at tale-telling and role playing—for he assumed different voices and inflections for each and every one of the characters, and was especially dramatic in his portrayals of the three greedy students. The voice he assumed for the old man was as cracked and weak as that of any octogenarian of Chaucer's acquaintance.

"The three students asked the old man where they might find Death. The aged one replied that he had last seen Death under a tree at the end of the lane.

"Our friends then rushed to that tree, but instead of Death, they found eight bushels of gold coins. Immediately they forgot their mission and decided to keep the gold for themselves. Still, they were afraid to remove the gold in the daytime, and decided to wait for night. To pass the time, they decided that one of them should go back into the town for food and wine to entertain them until nighttime.

"They drew lots, and the youngest of them drew the short straw, and thus he was elected to return to the village. However, on the way, he began to think that he would be a fool to share all that gold with his friends when he could have it all for himself. So he went to a chemist and purchased the strongest poison the man had, and put the poison in two of the wine bottles.

"Meanwhile, back at the tree, his two companions had decided to kill the youngest and divide the gold two ways instead of three. So when they saw him coming, they hid behind the tree, then jumped out and stabbed him in the back. Then they decided to celebrate and drank all three bottles of the poisoned wine. Their bodies tumbled lifeless to the earth.

"So you see, then, the old man had been right. Our three rapscallions did indeed find Death under the tree at the end of the lane."

A hush descended upon the company.

How intelligent the man is, how well read, how talented, Chaucer exclaimed inwardly, marveling. How ugly, how effeminate, how crooked! Ah, what a wonderful Creation is man!

"And now!" the pardoner was crying, "And now! All of you who want to avoid ending up as the three rioters did! I have pardons to sell! Just a small amount of money, my friends—and not only are your sins forgiven, you become the owner of the relic of a holy saint!"

A cry of outrage came from the pilgrims, with Sir Richard vainly trying to restore order. Few of those present believed in the power of a pardoner, Chaucer realized with some satisfaction—although Sister Cecily did seem inordinately interested in what the skinny little man had to sell. Chaucer began taking notes furiously. He sadly missed Walter.

The shipman then stood up; it was his turn. Before he could start, however, Agatha sidled into the room through the kitchen and sat quietly down by Chaucer. "Walter's wound has turned septic," she reported.

Chaucer's eyes opened wide with concern. "Master Richemont is not here. He was weary, and went early to his bed."

"Praise be to God! Leave him be before he does any more damage! I have already dressed the poor boy's wound. I cleansed it with wine and threw away that useless chamomile, then dressed it with comfrey as it should have been in the first place. Physician my arse! Men! How dare they even presume to call themselves healers!"

"But Master Richemont said he had no comfrey with him—"

"Bah! Comfrey grows wild nearly everywhere! All I had to do was walk out to the tavern gardens and there was a healthy patch of it! Anyway, Sister Cecily had been sitting with Walter so that Jeni could have some supper, then Jeni returned to the poor boy's side and relieved

Sister Cecily in time for her to return to hear the pardoner's tale. Jeni likes Walter—a little too much, if you ask me, and so she was more inclined than Sister Cecily to notice that he was moaning in pain and tossing restlessly. The girl is very bright, Geoffrey. She sent for me instead of that self-important tomfool who calls himself a physician!"

"How is Walter doing then?" Chaucer asked.

"He is as well as we could expect. If you keep that Master Richemont away from him, he should recover fully. Now I had better be getting back to him. Jeni has to get herself a good night's rest, poor lamb. Mistress Atte Wood has made it all too clear that she has no intention of allowing the girl to shirk her duties and watch by the bed of the boy she loves!"

Chaucer couldn't help smiling as Agatha rose and tiptoed out of the room. The shipman was lost in the intricacies of his story, a grossly immoral tale of a thieving monk. This was the kind of story Chaucer loved, but he had to go see Walter for himself. Sighing, he handed his notebook and pen to Robert Willard without a word. Equally silently Robert accepted it and nodded his assent. He would take notes tonight instead of Walter—in spite of the rheumatism that plagued his aching hands.

Feeling a rush of affection for his old friend, Chaucer grinned his thanks, rose, and left the room.

Twelve

Chaucer found Walter looking far paler even than he had that afternoon. The bloody, pus-soaked bandages had been tossed into a corner; Mistress Atte Wood, looking none too happy, was gathering them gingerly into an old sack. She cast Chaucer a withering look as he entered the room, as though to say it was all his fault, then carried the unsavory bundle out to the rubbish heap.

The youth's eyes were swollen and red, as though he had been fighting to suppress tears of pain. Jeni was holding his right hand, stroking it gently. Geoffrey's gaze fell on her. "How is he?" Chaucer asked.

"He is quiet now," said Jeni. "Mistress Willard is making him another cordial. He will sleep soon."

Chaucer sat on a stool by Walter's bedside. "Young man, you have to stop doing damage to your arms," he said heartily, yet gently. "Like I said, I'm going to need them. Tell me, Walter, when do you graduate from Oxford?"

"In September," said Walter weakly.

"September! Perfect! That is the time of year when merchants start importing delicacies for the Christmas holidays—close enough to the festivities, but at a time of year when the weather is still fairly warm. The customs office will be very busy then. I could use a bright young clerk like you. Would you consider moving to London and taking a position there?"

All the color rushed back to Walter's face. "I would, if 'twere with only a moment's notice! Oh, Master Chaucer, I would be ever so grateful!"

"Nonsense, my friend. It is I who should be grateful. You would be shocked at the idiots I am forced to employ because there is a dearth of bright, educated men. When you recover, I shall give you a letter attesting to the fact that when you graduate, you will be gainfully employed by the Office of the King's Petty Custom. And if you let her know in advance, I am sure you would be welcome to lodge in Mistress Willard's inn."

"You will indeed!" Agatha entered with the cordial. "But for now, Master Locksley, you are going to do what I say and drink this down!" She put a motherly arm around the youth and propped him up so that he could drink.

Tactfully Chaucer withdrew. Jeni followed him into the hall. "Master Chaucer, that was very kind of you. Your offer did more for him than any cordial or herb ever could."

"Well, I doubt that," said Chaucer, "but I know he needed something. And it's all true—I do sometimes want to toss my clerks into the Thames. Walter is more intelligent than all of them put together."

"But what will you do with your clerks? You surely won't discharge them?"

"Not at all. I'll pick the best of the lot, then promote him to inspector. It takes more brains to be a clerk than to be an inspector!"

Jeni giggled, then her expression sobered. It was hard for Geoffrey to read the look on her face, but it appeared to be a combination of gratitude to him and concern for Walter. She gripped his arm briefly, then returned to Walter's bedside. Chaucer stepped out into the cool, clear, brisk night, and paused a moment to look at the vast panorama of stars. The moon was nearly full, and now it was high in the sky. No wonder the villagers had gone berserk! And unless he was mistaken, that doleful yellow-brown star just over the horizon was Saturn, and the red one beside it, Mars. No wonder Walter had grown feverish. A chill passed down Chaucer's spine. If these planetary aspects were any measure, their hardships were not over yet.

But there! Soon the Moon would conjoin Spica, the star of good luck—perhaps then there would be a break in the mystery!

Harry Bailey emerged from the tavern, half drunk. "Geoffrey, m'boy! It's time for you to tell your tale!"

With a sinking heart Geoffrey remembered that he had drawn one of the lots to tell his tale that night. And he simply was not in the mood. "Harry, I don't think I should. I am no closer to finding the murderer—

"Sooth! The murderer isn't going anywhere—that would be the easiest way to tell us who he is! Now you agreed like everyone else to tell a tale, and tell a tale you shall! Come on, Geoffrey—no excuses! Come on in and tell us a story! You're one of the most famous poets in the world, after all!"

"Not in the world," Chaucer objected as Harry grabbed his arm and dragged him into the tavern.

Geoffrey wanted to sink into the earth when he walked in and everyone applauded. God's bones! He didn't want to be here—he wanted to be up in his room, pondering Walter's notes, studying the astrological chart for the finding of Sophia's body, trying to puzzle out anything—anything that would shed some light on the identity of the murderer before he—or she—could strike again.

"Who might this fellow be?" demanded Harry Bailey. "Why, he is the best tale-spinner in the kingdom! Let us hear what he has to say!"

Well, I won't say much, Chaucer told himself grimly. I'll tell them a story so bad they'll beg me to leave off!

He began:

"Listeth, lordes, in good entent,
And I wol telle verrayment
Of myrthe and of solas:
Al of a knyght was fair and gent
In bataille and in tourneyment,
His name was Sire Thopas.

> "Yborn he was in fer contree,
> In Flaundres, al biyonde the see,
> At Poperyng, in the place.
> His fader was a man ful free,
> And lord he was of that contree,
> As it was Goddes grace…"

Chaucer was improvising, and trying deliberately to do so poorly. His story was a parody of the popular tales of chivalry such as that told by Sir Richard. It included every cliché known to romance writers, including Elf Queens, three-headed giants, and impossible challenges. Intentionally he used the most affected language he could think of. As Chaucer had foreseen, long before the tale would have been finished Harry Bailey broke in. "Good God, Geoffrey, surely you can do better than this! I am exhausted by such moronic rhymes!"

Chaucer gazed at him reproachfully. "But Harry, these are the best verses I've ever written!"

Someone in the audience choked back a laugh; Chaucer knew it was Agatha.

"Well, now is not the time for them! Tell us something in prose!"

"Very well," said Chaucer. He sighed; he was not to get off so easily.

Suddenly he began reciting a translation of a very boring French story he had heard only recently. It was a moral tale, laced throughout with proverbs and aphorisms. It concerned Sir Melibeus, his wife Dame Prudence, and their daughter—who, ironically, was named Sophia. The story concerned a moral dilemma: Is it in keeping with the laws of God and man to avenge a violent injury by more violence?

During the absence of Sir Melibeus and Dame Prudence, three burglars broke into their home and seriously injured their daughter Sophia. Now: should they take revenge upon the burglars?

While he was expounding upon this theme at great length, citing law, philosophy, and other high-flown schools of thought, Chaucer sensed a hush on his audience. The subject of the tale of Melibeus was a bit too close to their current situation for comfort, and so, in spite of Chaucer's attempts to make it as boring as possible, they hung on every word.

"Consider the words of the Apostle Paul," Chaucer droned on. "He says: Do not yield harm for harm, nor wicked speech for wicked speech, but do well to him that doth thee harm, and bless him that sayeth to thee harm…Solomon said, 'He that fears and thus hardens his heart shall thus attract all evil,'"…and Ovid said, 'The little weasel shall slay the great bull and the wild hart,' and the good book said, 'A little thorn shall prick a king full sore, and a hound shall hold off the wild boar.'…And yet Cicero said, 'If you begin an action, consider it carefully first, as its consequences will haunt you forever.' Thus one should expect to reap the harvest of what he has sown. And yet Cicero also said, 'If you take vengeance for any action, be assured that still another vengeance will be taken upon you.

Chaucer paused a moment to scan the faces of everyone in the room. All were waiting to hear what he would say next.

"Finally," he went on, "the three burglars were captured and brought before Dame Prudence, who shocked and yet delighted the three evildoers. She suggested that no vengeance upon them should be taken; a peaceful resolution would be found. Sir Melibeus proposed that the burglars be let off with a fine, but Dame Prudence rejected that idea. Therefore, Melibeus forgave the burglars, chided them harshly, then praised himself for his own virtue. And that is the end of my story."

No one said a word. Chaucer merely rose and walked out into the courtyard, amazed at himself for what he had just said. Yes, a person who does evil should expect the just consequences of his actions. And yet: What happens to the person who exacts such vengeance? Does he become as evil as the one he punishes? Does he who forgives place himself in danger of becoming as self-righteously sanctimonious as Melibeus?

A large shadow appeared in front of him, looming between Chaucer and the Full Moon. Geoffrey turned; John of Gaunt stood behind him.

"What did you mean by that sermon in there?" Gaunt hissed. "Are you trying to tell us that we shouldn't try to find the murderer?"

"No, of course not, my lord Duke," said Chaucer. "No one who kills as wantonly as Sophia's murderer should be allowed to run free. Yet the question of vengeance is a moral dilemma we all need to ponder. Do two wrongs make a right? Does a second act of violence cancel out the first, or does it simply compound the evil? Forgive me, my dear Duke John. It is only the philosopher in me rearing his head."

"Well, let's hope that whoever the killer is thinks you're serious and relaxes a little!" Gaunt put both hands on his hips and glared at his friend. "And let's also hope your philosophy doesn't get in the way of finding the murderer!"

Chaucer walked toward the barn, watching the moon curiously. It had almost reached the exact conjunction with Spica. What would it bring? "No, John," he finally said. "The murderer must pay for his deeds. He wantonly destroyed the lives of two people—two exceptional people. Sophia, with her whole life ahead of her, beautiful, bright, by all accounts a talented dancer, and by my own observation a skilled storyteller. Brother Nicholas, known far and wide as one of the finest calligraphers and illuminators in the kingdom, capable of producing Bibles worthy of the saints themselves. This killer deprived the world of two fine talents, which could well have enriched the world had they lived. And Jack, the summoner, and all those peasants killed this afternoon died indirectly as a result of the murderer's deeds. No, Dante's final circle of Hell, the three mouths of Satan, is far too good for this monster. I will do all I can to discover him, my lord Duke, I assure you. But I don't have to like it!" With that he deliberately turned his back on the duke and stormed back into the inn.

The tale-telling contest was breaking up; no one wanted to follow Chaucer's thinly disguised moral metaphor of their own condition. Geoffrey bade good night to all he met, then entered his room and closed the door. By the light of the full moon he lit his candle, then took out the astrological chart for the moment of the discovery of Sophia's body. It told him nothing more than he and Robert had already discerned.

Frustrated, Chaucer cast the chart aside. Then, in a fit of inspiration, he searched through his pack until he found the chart he had drawn up for the start of the journey.

Little had changed in the two days from the beginning of the journey to Sophia's murder. The Sun, Mercury, and Jupiter were still in Aries; Venus was still in Pisces; Saturn and Mars were still in Cancer. But the Moon—the Moon at the beginning of the journey had been posited at the 29th degree of Gemini. The 29th degree was an unhappy degree in any sign.

Chaucer frowned. At the start of the journey, he realized, he had not remotely conceived that the nefarious events along the way would include murder. But now, looking at this chart, he saw it easily. Venus was posited in the twelfth house, the twelfth house of the secret enemy, while the malefic planets Saturn and Mars were conjunct in the fourth house of the grave, signifying the end of a life.

And the Moon…the Moon in Gemini, sign of the twins…and Venus, the esoteric dispositor of the Moon, located in the ominous twelfth house, in Pisces, sign of the two fishes…Pisces and Gemini are both double signs…

The thought hit Chaucer like a bucket of cold water. He stared ahead at a knothole in the wall. Could there be two killers?

No, his logical mind insisted. It's impossible. The murders were too much alike: the daggers, the Tarot cards…

But in his heart he knew that it *was* possible. In fact, if his interpretation of the first chart was correct, it was probably true.

An uncomfortable doubt then spread through his mind. If there were indeed two separate murders, then could the murder of Brother Nicholas be coincidence—nothing to do with anyone on this pilgrimage?

That was hardly likely. Too many people on this pilgrimage knew Brother Nicholas—and one of them had been Sophia. There had to be a connection somewhere.

And then of course there was the irritating coincidence of the Tarot cards. What was the point of leaving them behind?

The first murderer's motive in dropping the card near the corpse of Brother Nicholas was unfathomable. But the second killer could well have been imitating the first—perhaps even hoping to cast suspicion upon him.

Which meant that the second killer knew about the murder of Brother Nicholas before he stabbed Sophia. Which meant he knew about the first killer.

Which brought the motivation back to John of Gaunt and his ambitions for the throne of Castile.

And how did the thefts fit into all this? Were they, as Walter had suggested, connected with the Brotherhood of the Sacred Silver?

Chaucer rubbed his forehead; his head ached, partly from studying the astrological charts in dim light, and partly from the strain of all the events of the day—not to mention the uncomfortable idea of two murderers. What would Gaunt say to that?

Geoffrey tiptoed down the hall, to the room Agatha shared with Robert. The light was on; he could hear their voices, discussing Walter's condition. Good!

He knocked on the door. Surely Agatha had some herbs stashed away that could ease his headache…and allow him to sleep in spite of an overactive mind.

The thief was frightened—on the verge of cracking, of running to Geoffrey Chaucer and confessing all. There were times when the culprit had caught the poet's gaze, fastened tightly to the thief's own.

He knew, the pilferer fretted. How could a man of Chaucer's intelligence not be able to spot the anxiety of one so obviously guilty?

Oh, if I had only remained at home—if I had only never become involved in all this intrigue! I would be happy, among my own friends, in my own house, never to have to bother with dishonest doings, or with terrible men like John of Gaunt!

Oh, God, help me! Should I go to Master Chaucer and confess all? I would go to prison, be disgraced, never see those I love again. But at least all this miserable fear would be past.

And yet, if I did that, I would betray all I stand for, risk losing every advantage I have gained for our side, play false all those who have depended upon me.

No. I cannot do it. I must be brave and steadfast, continue to behave as though I were innocent, and pretend to be calm and happy. Blessed Mother, please help me!

The thief sighed. *One such as I is not worthy of the aid of the Blessed Mother. I am involved in stealing, in murder, in the sin of Judas.*

But there is something I can do—something that might protect me from discovery. I can get rid of the items I stole.

Suddenly exhilarated, the frightened felon ran for the cache of stolen trinkets. By St. George, they would be hidden—hidden in so unlikely a place that even a man with Chaucer's mind would never find them!

A few moments later a dark, hunched form slinked from the back door of the inn.

Agatha Willard frowned as she stepped silently out the kitchen door and headed for the Atte Wood house. She had promised to relieve Jeni at Walter's bedside after the tale-telling was over, but first she had had to deal with Geoffrey's headache and overactive mind, The poor man—he had come here to escape the hard days at the customs office, and had ended by working harder than ever! While stirring some soothing herbs in wine for Geoffrey, she had decided to make a second cordial for Walter as well in case he needed it, and thus she would be later than she had promised. Agatha hoped that this would not cause Jeni any trouble with her mother. Well, if it did, Agatha vowed, I'll have a word with Mistress Atte Wood myself!

A brisk wind had picked up; Agatha pulled her cloak closer around her. Her quick eyes caught sight of a shadow moving over by the stables. Instinct caused her to retreat behind the outer wall of the inn; curiosity impelled her to peer around and see whose shadow that was.

The shadow crept over to the well, peered down inside, then carefully lowered a bundle—what could it possibly be?—into the well, using something so thin that it was only by the figure's motions that Agatha could even deduce that it existed. Then the creature, relieved of its burden, began to walk quickly away from the well, its back to Agatha.

In spite of the full moon, Agatha could see nothing but a murky shape slithering from the barn to the inn's front door.

Blast being fifty-two! My night vision is growing worse every day!

There was something familiar about the body, but Agatha was unable to discern its identity. *Of course it's familiar,* she told herself. *It has to be one of the pilgrims. But which one? And what is he—or she—doing sneaking around out here at nearly midnight?*

The person—whoever it was—disappeared into the inn. Agatha felt no desire at all to follow—it could, after all, be the murderer—but she could possibly, just possibly, sneak over to the stables and look into the well.

I must tell Geoffrey. But not now—the poor boy needs his sleep. And Jeni is still waiting, poor child.

Whatever it is that has been hidden in that well, it'll still be there tomorrow. I'll wake Geoffrey at dawn and take him out there. For now I must see to Walter.

With determination Agatha strode towards the front entrance of the Atte Wood house. It bothered her not at all that by entering that way she might disturb the great John of Gaunt.

Walter lay asleep, the light of the full moon shining through the window and illuminating his face. Jeni gazed down upon him, a warm feeling spreading through her body. What a beautiful young man he really was, she thought. He was too thin, true, but good food would fix that. His hair desperately needed a trim by a skilled barber, and his clothes left much to be desired—but all of those faults could be easily remedied.

He was certainly the only young man who had ever caused her to thrill to the sight of him, whom she had actually wanted to touch her, who had ever really shown her any true caring or compassion. All the farm boys in or near St. Mary Cray were stupid, insensitive louts who saw her as little more than a lump of meat to be used and discarded.

His eyelids fluttered and opened; a look of sheer adoration passed over his face as he saw Jeni looking down at him. "Are you still here?" he said weakly.

"Yes. But I must go soon, or Mum will be angry. Mistress Willard is coming soon, to sit with you for the rest of the night."

"I feel guilty, taking her away from her husband," said Walter.

"When our comrades are ill, sacrifices must be made," said Jeni. "And most good people are happy to make them."

She suddenly felt uncomfortable; Walter was unashamedly staring at her. Her skin began to prickle; she felt an overwhelming desire to bend down and take him in her arms. But such behavior would not be seemly, and *Mum and Dad would hate me for it.*

"You are so beautiful, here in the moonlight," Walter finally said.

Embarrassed, Jeni lowered her eyes.

"Jeni, I love you," he finally said. "Will you marry me?"

Jeni gasped and clutched at her apron. "Oh, Walter, it is too early—"

"But I have to speak now! Don't you see? Master Chaucer will find the murderer soon, and then we will be on our way to Canterbury, and if I say nothing I will probably never see you again! Oh, I know it's only been a few days that we've known each other, but I have never felt about any girl the way I feel about you! In fact, I've never noticed girls before—which makes you that much more special! And in those few days we've spent many hours together. Why, we probably know each other better than some married couples! I can't simply ride away and never see you again!"

Jeni couldn't stand the raw desperation in Walter's face. She turned away from him, facing the opposite wall. She stood for a few moments, breathing heavily, trying to absorb all that he was saying. Finally she spoke. "Mum and Dad would never approve."

"Why? What's wrong with me? You said your father wanted a better life for you. I will be working for the king himself—under the supervision of Master Chaucer! I will be able to give you a house in London! I am an educated man, and I will go far in the civil service! You could even be presented at court! Are you telling me your mother and father would prefer to see you with coarse ruffians such as those who attacked us today?"

"Such men would not take me away from them!" Jeni cried.

An ominous silence filled the room. "But what do you want, Jeni?" Walter said quietly. "I do not want to marry your parents. I want you. I want Father Harold to perform the ceremony—tomorrow, if possible. I want you to ride away from here with me, to Canterbury. Mistress Willard will be glad to look after you. I want you to return with me to Oxford; you can live at my mother's house, outside the city limits, and I can visit you on Sundays. Then in September, I want you to move with me to London, where we can be near Master Chaucer, and Master and Mistress Willard, and make new friends as well. What do you want?"

Jeni practically had to choke the words out. "I—I want to go with you. I don't want you to leave me. I have very strong feelings for you, and I don't believe I will ever feel this way about anyone again—especially anyone from St. Mary Cray! Oh, Walter, my parents will never let me go—but I want to! I want to, so bad!"

Walter struggled to sit up, his face now a testament to total happiness. "Then that's all that matters! Somehow I'll convince them to let you come with me! I love you, Jeni, and we're going to have a good life together!"

She spun around to face him again, her face beaming. "Walter, can we really make it happen?"

"I will, I promise!" He was now sitting stock straight up. "Kiss me, Jeni, my darling! Hold me—quick! Mistress Willard will be here any minute—we can't let her find us like this!" Jeni hesitated only a moment, then she bent down, threw her arms around Walter and kissed him—clumsily at first; she had never before kissed anyone other than relatives. Nor, for that matter, had he. But then their lips grew accustomed to each other, and they managed to use their instincts to kiss the way men and women in love had done for generations before them.

Their love hung heavily in the air around them, like a warm comforting fog. Walter's good arm reached up to encircle Jeni as she nestled close to him.

Finally Jeni pushed away. "I must go," she whispered. "Mistress Willard will be here directly, and my mother will be furious with me for being so late!"

Reluctantly Walter let go of her hand. "Will you be here in the morning?"

"Yes," said Jeni. "I promise."

"Well, now that that's settled, can a man sleep in this house?" came a rough voice behind Jeni. She gasped, quickly spinning to face John of Gaunt. Her face turned white. Walter collapsed onto the bed again, pulling the covers up to his chin.

"I'm sorry, my lord Duke," Jeni muttered. "I'm so sorry!" With that she ran from the room and then from the house, passing Agatha Willard on the way.

Agatha gazed at the Duke reproachfully, heedless of the fact that he wore only a thin towel around his waist.

"Cheap—very cheap!" she snapped. "You spoiled what should have been a wonderful moment for them. You had no right to do that, Duke or no!" Airily she brushed past him and went to check Walter's arm.

Chuckling softly to himself, John of Gaunt retreated to his own room.

She's right, he reflected. *It was very low of me to intrude on their time together. I really should make it up to them in some way.*

I'll speak to the girl's father, that's what I'll do. I'll convince him of the boy's brilliant prospects.

What more could I do?

Thirteen

"You want to marry Jeni?"

Chaucer was staring down at a radiant though somewhat defensive Walter. He had been dismayed, though not really surprised by Walter's statement.

Agatha had awakened him before dawn, just as tiny fingers of sunlight were beginning to permeate the black of night. She had told him that she had something vital to show him, but Chaucer had insisted on checking on Walter first. Now, in spite of his embarrassment in front of John of Gaunt the night before, Walter seemed as if he would burst with happiness.

The clerk wasn't pleased at Chaucer's reaction to his announcement. "Why do you react that way?" Walter cried. "It's not like Simon and Sophia. I am poor—I have no lands or title to leave to anyone, so a pure bloodline is no consideration. And Jeni is my social equal. We are both of the merchant class. My father was a skilled bookbinder, and her father is a hardworking, prosperous innkeeper. Furthermore, she is a lovely girl, and though I am now poor I am an educated man, with good prospects. You yourself have offered me solid employment with chances for advancement. So why does everyone seem to have reservations about our loving each other and wanting to be married?"

Chaucer took a deep breath. "Everything you say is true, Walter," said Chaucer. "If I seem shocked, it is only because the two of you have known each other for a mere three days."

"How well did you know Mistress Chaucer before you married her?" Walter challenged. "And how happy are you with her?"

Chaucer cast an accusing glance at Agatha. Dear Mistress Willard! so eager to advance the cause of young love! Surely, unless Agatha had talked, Walter could not have known that Geoffrey and Philippa had hardly known each other at all when they were married—the marriage had been arranged by the late King Edward's queen. And yet Chaucer loved Philippa with all his heart, and could not imagine life without her.

"Undoubtedly you know that already," Chaucer finally said. "Oh, I have no problems with your marrying Jeni, Walter. Except possibly for one."

Walter frowned. "What's that?"

"Your tale," said Chaucer. "We have been so concerned with this murder that I have not kept my promise to you—that I would tell you what I thought of your tales, to see if you have any gift for poetry or not. I'll keep that promise now. Your tale told of a man who caused his wife a great deal of pain for no other purpose other than to test her loyalty and devotion to him. Why, you even gave your hero your own name! Your heroine, Griselda, bore every bit of tortuous pain your fictitious Walter dealt out to her with a patience that few can expect of any human being—least of all a wife. He humiliated her publicly, demanded total obedience, even took away her children and deprived her of watching them grow, then denounced her before her people and repudiated his marriage to her. And yet she still meekly accepted his harsh treatment without complaint and rejoiced and ran eagerly back to his arms when he revealed he had only been testing her loyalty. I'm sure Agatha would say Griselda would have been justified in breaking his head open! I trust you wouldn't expect behavior resembling that of the mythical Griselda from your flesh-and-blood Jeni."

Walter was indignant. "Never!" he cried. "You're forgetting, Master Chaucer, that I said at the end of the story that women should not try to be like Griselda, nor should men expect their wives to be like her. That was a story, Master Chaucer—the only story I could think of besides children's fables of talking rabbits and winged fairies. I read it in the works of Petrarch—and remembered it precisely because the hero had my name. You're not being fair, Master Chaucer! Of course I wouldn't expect Jeni to be like Griselda! I wouldn't love her so much if she were!"

"Well said, my friend," said Chaucer. "Any man with brains expects a woman with backbone. And I believe your Jeni has that. I only asked because it is my experience that people often choose to tell tales that reflect them in some way. I am glad for you, Walter. Quite glad."

Agatha was glancing nervously out the window; dawn was now breaking. "Geoffrey, I do think we'd better go out to the well now, before it gets any brighter," she said. "We need to see this before it's fully light."

Chaucer nodded his good-bye, then followed Agatha outside. There was an ominous chill in the air, as if Chaucer were about to be confronted with a reality he wasn't yet ready to face. The ground seemed uneven, dotted with lumps of rock and little rises that threatened to trip any living being that tried to walk over them. Geoffrey shivered and huddled into his cloak as he tried to keep up with Agatha. Robert was waiting for them at the well.

"As far as I know, no one is up yet," the mathematician reported. "I have stood guard here since shortly after Agatha went to fetch you. No one has come out, or even appeared at a window."

"Good," said Agatha. She stepped over to the edge of the well and felt around with her hand until she found a thin leather thong hanging down into the depths of the water. Whatever was on its other end was lost in the murky blackness. "Last night, Geoffrey, when I went out to relieve Jeni and take Walter his cordial, I saw someone drop something into this well. Don't ask me who it was—it was too dark for me even to see if it was a man or a woman. But it was definitely someone with something to hide." She pulled up the leather thong. "And I am sure that something is on the other end of this line."

"Pull it up," Chaucer directed.

Agatha tried, but with difficulty; Robert then reached over and gave her a hand. A moment later the two of them hauled up a waterlogged potato sack.

Chaucer jumped forward and put both hands on the sack; it was heavy, and the leather thong had been stretched to the point of breaking. He hauled it out onto the ground, opened it without ceremony, and dumped its contents on the grass. The three of them gasped.

The pale light of dawn draped itself over the objects and caused them to shine—faintly, to be sure, but enough to reveal exactly what they were. A small silver bridle stud. A brooch. A detached stirrup. And a silver candleholder. In addition, the bag had contained a number of other silver objects that none of them recognized.

"Jesus, Mary and Joseph," Chaucer swore. "Put these back in the bag—right now!"

Robert and Agatha hastened to do as Chaucer directed. Geoffrey, meanwhile, walked back over to the well. The sun was now completely above the horizon, and the light was gradually spreading over everything in the yard. Chaucer bent low over the ground immediately surrounding the well; to his consternation he saw that the dew the night before had been quite heavy, and that any footmarks the thief might have left had been obliterated by the weight of the moisture. There would be no clue, then, to the thief's sex, weight, or occupation such as a footprint might have left.

"Well, whoever it was must have been badly frightened," Chaucer finally said. "He or she wanted to get rid of the loot—but was still clever enough to make it possible to retrieve it at a later time."

Robert was shoving the last of the cache into the sack, when Chaucer's eyes fastened upon something that still lay on the ground. Eagerly he seized upon it. It was a small silver cross that apparently had at one time been fastened to a chain, as one broken link still remained in the ring at the top.

"This looks like a type of cross that Don John wears," said Chaucer. "Don John's is gold, but it's still the same type of cross. It is meant to be fastened to a belt. I have often seen Benedictine monks wearing them. I wonder if by chance this belonged to Brother Nicholas."

He turned his face toward the barn, then hurried towards the door, with Agatha and Robert, who still carried the bag, following in his wake. Agatha realized with trepidation that Chaucer wanted to examine the body of Brother Nicholas.

He did. Taking care to leave the dead monk's face decently covered, Chaucer unwrapped the blanket around him just enough to allow him a solid look at the man's belt.

It was made of the same rough cloth as the rest of the habit—except for the broken silver chain at the left side. Agatha, wrinkling her nose at the stench of death, realized that they had just learned something important.

"This cross," Chaucer breathed, "belonged to Brother Nicholas. Then we were wrong, dear Robert. The murderer and the thief are indeed one and the same person."

Robert raised his arms in a gesture of surrender. "I never claimed to be infallible," he stated.

Chaucer then frowned, staring straight ahead of himself. What was wrong with the body of Brother Nicholas? Something was not right—something about the monk's habit...Suddenly his eyes narrowed and he turned his full attention to the hem of the dead monk's robe. He looked at it closely, examining it inch by inch, then studied with equal thoroughness the rest of the garment.

"Good God, I would never have guessed!" he exclaimed. "Robert—Agatha—I think I know who the murderer is!" Throwing the blanket over Brother Nicholas again, Chaucer jumped to his feet and ran out of the barn. After exchanging a glance of sheer bewilderment, Robert and Agatha followed.

Sir Richard de Burgoyne was at the pump, washing his face and dampening his hair. He looked up in surprise when he saw Geoffrey running from the barn.

"Sir Richard," Chaucer panted, "would you be so kind as to awaken Sir Oliver Radley and inform him that we need the assistance of Peter Adams and the guardsmen, and the good Duke himself if possible. I know who the murderer is and I do not want to confront him without witnesses."

Sir Richard hesitated only a moment before nodding and hurrying back to the Atte Wood house.

"Now hold on here, young man!" said Agatha. "How do you know who the murderer is? Who is it? You said 'he'—does that mean that Alisoun of Bath and the nuns are cleared?"

"It does indeed," said Chaucer. "And it is all thanks to your brilliant work—and to Walter and Simon, those brave boys! Once this is all over, we must inform Walter that his being wounded was not in vain! If he and Simon hadn't gone out to the murder site—if you hadn't had the presence of mind to watch when that person came out to the well last night—"

"Geoffrey, calm down!" Agatha cried, her frustration mounting. "You're talking in circles! Who killed Sophia?"

"Agatha, don't be so impatient!" admonished Robert. "Obviously Geoffrey doesn't want to say anything until everyone is present!"

Chaucer shot Robert a grateful glance. "Yes, that is it!" he said. "You shall know, my dear Agatha, but all in good time. Even walls have ears, as you know. How do we know the killer is not awake and listening somewhere? If we say his name then we could give him a chance to escape!"

Disgruntled, Agatha closed her mouth. It seemed as though an eternity would pass before she would know the solution to the mystery.

But within a few more moments Sir Richard, accompanied by Peter Adams, the three guardsmen and John of Gaunt, emerged from the door of the Atte Wood house. The soldiers joined Geoffrey and the others; Gaunt gazed quizzically at Chaucer. "Where do we find our murderer?" the Duke asked, almost disbelievingly.

"In the men's common sleeping-room," Chaucer replied. "Let's go!

The members of the household not already awake were roused by the noise of the band of heavy-booted men storming up the stairs. Jeni, who had been helping her mother in the kitchen, ran out to see what was going on. Agatha hesitated, looked longingly at the band of soldiers following Geoffrey, then cast a reassuring glance at the girl. "This will all be over very shortly, Jeni, my love," she said. "You'll know all in a few minutes!" Agatha then hurried to catch up with the soldiers.

The men asleep on the straw pallets of the men's sleeping-room were shocked awake, their eyes bleary with sleep, their brains fogged from the kind of sleep that follows heavy drinking. As Chaucer, followed by the knights, stormed through their ranks, stepping over their prostrate forms, they shrank back under the covers, fear written over all their faces. All breathed a sigh of relief when Chaucer stopped in front of one particular bedroll.

"Don John," he said loudly. "I hereby accuse you of the thefts of a number of silver objects, and of the murders of Brother Nicholas and Sophia!"

The monk looked small and helpless. Two of the Duke's guardsmen had dragged him out of the men's common sleeping-room, and, at Chaucer's direction, had hauled him downstairs to the main tavern, where he now huddled on a bench, his face resembling the scared rabbit to which John of Gaunt had compared him. He had said nothing, neither affirming nor denying Chaucer's accusation of him.

"How did you learn," Gaunt was saying, "that it was Don John?"

"Well," Chaucer began. "last night my dear friend Mistress Willard witnessed someone stowing a heavy bundle in the Atte Woods' well. When we retrieved it this morning, we found a bag full of silver objects, including everything stolen from the pilgrims and a number of other items. Among those items was a silver cross, a type which I had seen worn by a number of Benedictine monks, hanging from their belts."

All eyes went accusingly to Don John's belt. Instinctively he clapped his hand over the gold cross that hung there.

"I wondered if it might have been taken from Brother Nicholas," Chaucer went on. "So Robert, Agatha and I went to the barn and learned that, if he had had such a cross, it had since disappeared. But there was still a fragment of a broken silver chain hanging from his belt. I then remembered the fine link that Walter and Simon had found at the murder site—and indeed, the remaining links seemed to be fashioned in the same way as that one link.

"Then I remembered that Walter and Simon had also discovered a fragment of cloth which appeared to be torn from a Benedictine habit. Instinctively, my eyes glanced at Brother Nicholas's robe. But it appeared to be fully intact. Just to be certain, I examined it closely. And it was intact. Not a scrap, not a thread was missing. It was not torn in the least." He paused.

"And then I wondered," he went on. "Could the scrap of cloth have been torn, not from the robe of the victim, but from that of the murderer? You, Don John!" He raised his voice dramatically, turning and pointing directly at the cringing monk. "Is your habit as unmarked as that of Brother Nicholas?"

Agatha, followed by Peter Adams, immediately rushed forward and lifted the hem of the monk's robe. Everyone caught their breath.

As she turned the fabric through her fingers, Agatha suddenly stopped and silently held it up for everyone to see. Toward the back of the robe, a sizable amount of fabric had been torn away, leaving a gaping hole.

John of Gaunt was the first to speak. "So we finally know," he said. "Now we can all go home! Oliver! Send one of the guardsmen out for Wulfstan Canty! Let us turn this hypocritical blackguard over to the authorities!"

"No!" Don John suddenly cried. "Wulfstan Canty has no authority over me! I demand to be turned over to the nearest bishop!"

"Bishop!" John of Gaunt thundered. "This isn't heresy—this isn't embezzling church funds! This is murder! Two murders, no less!"

"No!" cried Don John again. "All right? I admit I stole the silver objects! I am a Brother of the Sacred Silver! I am dedicated to the preservation of the True Church, and have no intention of allowing heretics like Brother Nicholas and other Lollards—"here he glanced pointedly at the Duke of Lancaster—"undermine the sacred duty of the

Church to spread the Word of God!" Here he lowered his voice. "And I did kill Brother Nicholas. He and I traveled here to set off on this pilgrimage. I knew what his purpose was in joining this band. I had been instructed by an agent of my Master, the Bishop of Norwich, to make certain that Brother Nicholas never delivered his message to them who awaited it! I never intended to kill him. I only wanted to stop him. I confronted him, and warned him that he should do no more than to travel to the shrine of St. Thomas like any other pilgrim. But he had his beliefs, and his duty—the same as I. We struggled, then he managed to elude me, and started back towards the road. So I leapt forward and stabbed him in the back. Then I took his cross, and left the Tarot card. But I didn't kill Sophia! I hardly knew the girl. Why would I want to kill her?"

"Why did you leave the Tarot card?" asked Chaucer curiously. "How do you explain the fact that another Tarot card was found near Sophia's body? If not for the timely intervention of the Duke of Lancaster, that could have gotten me hanged!"

"I confiscated the pack of Tarot cards from a parishioner because I thought they were evil," said Don John. "I shoved them into the pocket of my cloak and forgot about them. Then, after Brother Nicholas died, I remembered that the Master—the Bishop of Norwich—had instructed that Brothers of the Sacred Silver, when forced to eliminate heretics, should leave some kind of message as to what happens to them. So I fished around in my pocket till I found the cards, and used one of them that seemed appropriate for that sort of message."

"The Wheel of Fortune," Chaucer mused. "Ay, Don John, you could hardly have picked a better one. But how do you explain why one of my cards was stolen and left by Sophia's body?"

"I can't!" Don John blubbered. "I don't know why! Can't you believe me?"

"Who, here on this pilgrimage, knew about your mission?" Chaucer demanded. "Whom did you tell about leaving the Tarot card near the body of Brother Nicholas?"

The monk's face turned to stone. "No one," he said woodenly.

"You're lying!" John of Gaunt thundered.

"No!" cried Don John. "No, my lord, I am not lying! I told no one! Master Chaucer merely dropped his card! Perhaps Sophia herself took it! I don't know!"

Chaucer decided to drop the subject. "Very well, Brother John. But how do you explain the use of Master Dyer's stolen dagger to kill Sophia? You have already admitted to stealing it!"

"I can't! Any more than I can explain the card!" The monk was crying by now, though bravely trying hard to stifle his sobs. He took a few deep breaths and pulled himself together. "The dagger I used to kill Brother Nicholas was mine. I am an outrider for Kirksdell Abbey, in the depths of the Yorkshire forests, and my duties often take me through places where outlaws are known to lurk. I bought that dagger from a merchant who had recently returned from Italy. But when I stabbed Brother Nicholas, I didn't dare pull it out. So after I took Master Dyer's dagger, I kept it close by me, in the pocket of my habit. But the morning after Sophia's death it was gone. Someone had stolen it from me."

"A likely story!" shouted Gaunt. "Adams! Take him to the wine cellar, then go for Wulfstan Canty! Bishop indeed!"

Peter Adams and two of the guardsmen leapt to obey the Duke's orders, grabbing the monk by his arms and demanding that Aleyn Atte Wood direct them to the cellar where they could confine him.

Fairly glowing with relief, John of Gaunt sauntered over to Chaucer, who had collapsed onto a bench, suddenly seeming lost in despair.

"So now we have our murderer!" Gaunt said enthusiastically. "Finally, I can go home, and you can continue with your pilgrimage!" Suddenly he noticed Geoffrey's glum expression. "What's wrong? You should be proud! It was your keen insights that solved this case!

Chaucer took a deep breath. "No, my lord, it's my stupidity that nearly got an innocent man—at least in one sense innocent—accused of a crime he didn't commit. Oh, Don John is a thief and a murderer, all right. He did confess to killing Brother Nicholas. But I'm afraid that, as far as Sophia goes, he is telling the truth. He didn't kill her."

An angry cloud descended over Gaunt's face. "What do you mean? Of course he killed her!"

"My lord," said Chaucer patiently, "why would he deny killing Sophia and admit killing Brother Nicholas if he had committed both murders? Even if the secular authorities do retain custody of him—which I doubt they will—a man can only hang once!" He sighed. "My friend Robert, I have done you a great wrong. You said that the thief and the murderer of Sophia were not one and the same. You were right. This morning, I was so pleased with myself over discovering Don John's guilt, I completely forgot that last night I studied once more the astrological chart that we erected for the discovery of Sophia's body. I also studied the chart which I calculated for the start of the pilgrimage. Jeni!" he shouted.

Jenifred's winsome little face appeared in the door between the tavern and the kitchen. "Yes?"

"Be a dear, my love, and run up to my room. On the table are two pieces of paper, with strange drawings on them. Could you bring them to me?"

Jeni nodded and ran up the stairs. Chaucer then turned his attention once more to Robert. "From the chart I deduced that there were, not one, but two murderers. When Jeni returns with the chart, look at it yourself and tell me what you think."

"See here!" said John of Gaunt. "How dare you judge the outcome of this investigation on some hocus-pocus that you see in the stars? That makes no sense at all! Brother John has confessed to one murder, and is probably guilty of the second as well, no matter what he says!"

"It isn't only the chart, my lord," Geoffrey replied. "You yourself questioned those who slept in the men's common sleeping-room the night Sophia was killed. And you have read Walter's notes of that evening, several times, I believe. Do you not recall that everyone in that room—including Father Harold and Alfric, whose integrity I at least would never question—stated positively that during the time in question, no one—and they mean no one, including Don John—left that room?"

Stunned by the truth of Geoffrey's statement, John of Gaunt collapsed onto a heavy chair in front of the fireplace. At that point Jeni returned with the charts. She held them out to Chaucer, who directed her to give them to Robert.

Robert's brow puckered as he studied the earlier chart carefully. Finally he spoke. "I would have to concur with you," he stated. "The Moon in Gemini, and Venus in Pisces in the twelfth—it seems clear that there must be two murderers. Our job is not yet done, then, it seems."

"So I'm not free," said Gaunt, a black look on his face. "I still have to stay until we find still another murderer!" He stood up and stomped over toward the window. "God knows I may stoop to committing murder myself if I have to remain one more day in this Godforsaken place!"

No one else said a word. It was all too clear that the Duke indeed was right.

At midmorning Peter Adams and the guardsmen removed the body of Brother Nicholas from the barn and carried it to the churchyard, where the local gravedigger had dug a hasty grave next to that of Jack the summoner. Father Matthew read the service this time, while all the pilgrims but Don John—who was still safely locked in the winecellar—devoutly stood by listening. Even Walter had felt well enough to leave his bed, leaning on Jeni's arm.

After the service, Master Richemont walked over to Walter and asked about his arm. "It seems as if while I slept my patient was appropriated by Mistress Willard," he said.

"Mistress Willard is quite skilled with herbs, and didn't want to disturb you," said Walter diplomatically. "But my arm is better, thank you, and I should be able to be up and about soon."

"Not too soon!" protested Jeni. In fact, Walter's face was a little pale, and he appeared to be somewhat dizzy.

"Come, young man!" said Master Richemont. "It was good of you to attend the funeral, but now you must rest some more! I'll take you back to your bed."

Walter suddenly felt faint. He was quite glad to let go of Jeni and lean on the physician's arm. The three of them left the churchyard, heading for the Atte Wood home.

Agatha, dropping a clod of dirt on Brother Nicholas's body, scowled at the sight of their three retreating backs. "The boy would likely be dead if he were still in his care;" she muttered. "But far be it from me to interfere with the business of a physician!" she hissed sarcastically.

Robert patted her arm, then gazed around them. The funeral was clearly over; the party of pilgrims was starting to scatter. Agatha took one look back at Chaucer, but Robert hastily led her away before she could interrupt their friend's thoughts. Chaucer's face wore that look which Robert had long since learned meant he needed his solitude.

Oblivious to the desertion of his friends and of everyone else in the party, Chaucer lowered himself onto one knee and gazed at the stark bare earth which covered Brother Nicholas—a man whose work could have beautified the Christian world for another twenty years at least.

One murder had been solved. But another still remained wide open. How many more answers would have to be found before they could all get on with their lives?

Fourteen

"What do you mean, I can't arrest him? He's a murderer, ain't he?"

Wulfstan Canty, hastily summoned by Aleyn Atte Wood, stood before Chaucer in the main room of the tavern. Next to the poet stood Father Matthew. Looming in the back of the room were Sir Richard de Burgoyne and John of Gaunt.

"I am the ranking churchman here," declared the priest. "The secular authorities have no authority over those consecrated to the Church. Brother John is in my custody and under my protection. I have sent a message to the nearest bishop. As soon as I have his permission, I will escort Don John to the church authorities and he will be duly tried there."

"We'll see about that!" said John of Gaunt, stepping forward. "I suppose you pilgrims to the shrine of St. Thomas have forgotten that the question of church versus secular authority was what gained him his martyrdom!"

"Is that a threat, my lord Duke?" demanded Father Matthew. "Perhaps His Holiness the Pope would like to know more about the religious practices of those whose ambitions he declares to be holy Crusades!"

Gaunt's face turned purple; unconsciously his hand went to his sword.

"Stop this at once!" shouted Chaucer. "Threats and innuendoes will get us nowhere. I suggest that we all stop treating Don John like the child in the story of King Solomon and the two mothers, and concentrate on finding Sophia's murderer! I suggest the monk be taken nowhere until that killer is found, for the monk could well possess some information that could be invaluable to us. Master Canty, if you would be so kind as to remain with us for a few hours, we might yet have a killer for you to lock away in your gaol!"

Sir Richard then stood beside Chaucer, his eyes sweeping the room. "Master Chaucer is quite right, you know," he said respectfully. "The question of whether the church or the crown takes custody of Don John should wait until Sophia's murderer is unmasked. Then perhaps we shall all see things more clearly."

Gaunt sank onto a bench before the fireplace, his color returning to its normal ruddiness. "Just once—just once," he muttered, "I would like to resolve a dispute by removing my opponent's head instead of being forced to resort to the wisdom of Solomon!"

"So what do we do then?" demanded Wulfstan Canty.

"I must think," said Chaucer. "Give me some time." Leaving everyone else in the room staring at him in bewilderment, he crossed to the stairway and wearily trudged upwards.

The door to his room was wide open; Jeni had finished cleaning it. A fresh candle had been placed in the retrieved silver candleholder, which was now back in its place on the table. Gratefully resolving to thank the girl at the first opportunity, Chaucer took a taper from a torch in the hallway and lit the candle, then collapsed into the chair.

The astrological charts lay on the table before him, but Geoffrey's eyes couldn't quite focus on them; besides, he and Robert had milked them for every piece of information they could possibly offer. Angrily Chaucer swept them off the table and leaned on it. What else could he do? Besides astrology, what other tools did he have that could possibly shed light on the vast quantities of pieces of information that now swum around mockingly within his befuddled mind?

Then he remembered.

The Tarot cards.

Was it true what Jacquemin Gringonneur had told him—that in Italy, diviners used the cards as keys to the unknown? Could they possibly tell him anything new about this murder?

Feeling strangely disembodied, Geoffrey went to his pack and removed the wooden box which contained his treasure. Almost reverently, he returned to the table, took the cards from the box, and shuffled them carefully. Searching his mind for whatever tiny recollections he still possessed of his conversation with Gringonneur, Geoffrey laid the cards out on the table, in three rows of five: Five cards which explained the past; five outlining the present; and five predicting the future.

The first row was uncannily accurate. The first one was the Death card, followed by the Ten of Swords, which Chaucer deduced meant a great sorrow of some kind. Oddly enough, those two were flanked by the Popess and the Devil, which Gringonneur had said meant not only evil, but also lies and deception. The serene painted face of the crowned nun mocked Chaucer; could the pairing of these two cards hint at deception on the part of one of the nuns? The card that followed those was the Six of Swords, which Geoffrey recalled implied the overcoming of difficulties. Well, that was a good omen, anyway!

The next row—the row of the present—was intriguing. Its first card was The Lovers, followed by the Page of Coins and the Maiden of Cups, then by the Ten of Cups, which Gringonneur had explained meant marriage and great happiness. Was that Walter and Jeni? But the last card in that row was the House of God—an ominous card meaning the revelation of secrets, the overturning of opinions, and a world turned upside down. Did that mean that the secret of Sophia's murder would soon come to light?

The last row—predicting the future—began with The Fool. *Well, that's me, I'll warrant,* Chaucer told himself ruefully.

Or perhaps what is to be revealed will make me feel like a fool.

After The Fool came the King of Swords. John of Gaunt? No. The Emperor would most likely represent him. But then who was it?

Whoever it was, the person was headed for a fall. The following card was the Eight of Swords, which meant crisis and imprisonment. The Six of Staves, connoting a victory or triumph of some kind followed that card. The last card in the row was Justice.

Well, that's good to know, Chaucer told himself. Justice will triumph in the end, then. But who is the King of Swords?

What had Gringonneur explained? A man with brownish hair, hard-visaged and grim by nature—an enemy to be reckoned with. Perhaps he was skilled with the swords, or with blades of some kind. God's bones, that description could fit half the men on the pilgrimage!

Chaucer studied the cards intently, one by one by one, then by gazing at the entire layout, memorizing the place of each one.

The cards were telling him something, he knew—but what it was eluded him. Yet future events, future knowledge gleaned, could well shed light on the message of the cards—and all could come together at once.

When Geoffrey felt that he had memorized each and every position, he picked the cards up and replaced them in their box.

He had already seen enough to convince him that Gringonneur's assertion that the cards could be used for divination was true.

A soft knock sounded on his door. Geoffrey started, then bellowed, "Enter!" His eyes grew wide with concern when he saw Walter enter.

"Walter!" he cried. "Shouldn't you still be in bed? I can tell you're still weak!"

Walter stumbled over to Geoffrey's bed and sat heavily upon it. "That's not my arm, that's Master Atte Wood," he said bitterly.

"You spoke to him about Jeni—"

"Yes. And he told me that nothing—not a message from God himself—would induce him to allow his daughter to marry a penniless clerk whom she'd only known for three days."

"Did you tell him that you had a post waiting for you as soon as you graduate?"

"Yes. But that meant nothing to him. He mentioned all these local farm lads who were younger than I and yet already had their own farms. Never mind that they are boring, mindless louts whom Jeni detests!"

"He's her father, Walter," said Chaucer, remembering his own daughter Katherine. "She's his only girl. You must expect that he would be reluctant to let her leave with a virtual stranger—particularly when that stranger was taking her as far away as Oxford. He'll come around, my friend. He only needs to know you a little better."

Walter tried to get up and pace, then grew dizzy, collapsed back onto the bed, and then pounded on the coverlet in frustration. "Perhaps, but when could that happen? You will find the murderer soon—I know it. And then we will all continue on our way to Canterbury, and I will never get the chance either to become friends with Master Atte Wood or to court Jeni properly. And I, like Simon, will be as bereft of my love as if she were dead, like Sophia!"

"I may not find the murderer as soon as you think," said Chaucer grimly. "I must admit I am totally in the dark." Suddenly he remembered the cards, and said no more. The House of God had appeared on the row representing the present.

But so had The Lovers, and the Page of Coins and Maiden of Cups, and the Ten of Cups. Geoffrey smiled. "Don't despair, my dear Walter. I firmly believe you will win the hand of your Jeni, and soon. But I need you to regain your strength—you will have to help me with the records if I really am to find this murderer so that we can all get on with our pilgrimage—nay, with our very lives. So I am going to take your arm and help you back to your room. Master Richemont and Agatha may not agree on much, but I am sure they are in accord on one idea: you must rest."

Walter didn't argue. He stood, leaned on Geoffrey's shoulder and walked meekly down the stairs with him.

They found the main room of the tavern in total uproar. Robyn the Miller, accompanied by two of Wulfstan Canty's sergeants, was advancing threateningly on Father Matthew and Brother Hubert.

"What do you mean, Don John won't hang?" Robyn was snarling, his country accent that much more pronounced by his anger. "He killed Sophia, didn't he? Don't men who murder deserve to hang?"

Father Matthew, trembling with fear but trying hard to be brave, summoned what authority he could muster and responded clearly: "Don John will be fully disciplined by the elders of the Church. He has committed a grave sin. But the Holy Father would look with dire displeasure upon the execution of one of his flock by the secular authorities. Do you want England to be placed once more under an interdict?"

All had heard terrible stories of the days under King John, when the Pope had placed England under an interdict. He had, in effect, excommunicated everyone in the kingdom for the sins of its king. The dead had remained unburied, confession went unheard, marriages went unsolemnized, children died unbaptized. For a brief moment Robyn and the others balked at this possibility. But it only lasted a moment. Robyn bared his teeth once more and the three of them again moved closer to the churchmen, their thick, muscular arms raised menacingly.

"Master Richemont!" Chaucer called. The physician, who had been standing at the back of the room watching, started, then went over and took Walter's other arm. "Take Master Locksley back to his room!" Chaucer directed.

Nodding, Master Richemont obeyed; he and Walter disappeared into the kitchen. Chaucer then turned to Robyn and the two sergeants, stepping in front of the two churchmen. "Stop this nonsense immediately!" he bellowed. "Unless perhaps you want to join Don John in the cellar!"

Robyn stopped, somewhat bewildered by this turn of events. "That monk killed Sophia, and now this sniveling little worm of a priest says he's going to escape punishment!"

Chaucer sighed. "First of all, Master Miller, Don John did not kill Sophia. He murdered Brother Nicholas. You yourself were among those who swore that no one left the men's common sleeping-room during the time period in which Sophia must have been killed. Sophia's killer has not yet been found—and you certainly are not helping matters! Because Don John murdered another churchman, the Church is especially interested in his fate. This is not to say that the secular authorities will not have some say in it—it only means that the Church is determined to see that justice is served. They certainly do not want the message conveyed that men of God are free to do away with each other and still escape punishment!" He sighed. "Do not forget that our company now includes the great Duke of Lancaster. Do you think for a moment that John of Gaunt would let a murderer escape justice?"

Silence was the miller's only response.

"I understand that you're bored, and restless, and angry," Geoffrey continued. "I understand that you left home looking forward to a pilgrimage and are now delayed by a murder investigation. But squabbling among ourselves only hinders matters. Now unless any of you has some new information that you think might help us unmask Sophia's killer I ask that you find something to occupy yourselves. We are all working as hard as we can."

Robyn, somewhat shamefaced, hung his head and turned away. The two sergeants followed him. Father Matthew and Brother Hubert fled through the kitchen. Gradually everyone else left the gloomy tavern and went to find comfort in the April sunshine. Sir Richard de Burgoyne was the only one left in the room.

"You handled that very well, Master Chaucer," said the knight. "I would have intervened with my sword had you not come in. But I feel that violence should be avoided unless there is no other way."

"And I agree with you," said Chaucer. Images of the Tarot cards danced in his head. "Tell me, Sir Richard, do you know what has become of the nuns? I have not seen them for quite awhile."

"They have sequestered themselves in the women's common sleeping-room and not come out," replied Sir Richard. "That poor girl, Jenifred I think her name is, has been compelled to carry trays of food up to them whenever it suits their fancy to eat. I don't know what they do up there; I for one would die of boredom staying in one room all the time. I presume they spend most of their time praying and doing needlework and other such nun-like activities."

"And Brother Hubert!"

"Bah!" Sir Richard spat into the fireplace, his contempt for the friar showing plainly. "Haven't you noticed? He is at least twice as fat as he was when we arrived here! He has spent most of his time eating—and Master Atte Wood, who is making the most of his trapped customers, is all too eager to supply his finest victuals for a price. I am surprised our friend the friar had the guts to take Father Matthew's part against the miller in the quarrel you ended just now."

"He is probably a toady, like all friars, wanting to enjoy the good life yet stay on the good side of his superiors," said Chaucer. He and the knight exchanged a significant look, as if wordlessly admitting a mutual contempt for churchmen—and women.

Loud shouts and scuffling noises interrupted their conversation. Sir Richard hurried over to the window; Chaucer followed at a slower pace. "What are they doing?" Chaucer asked.

"Someone has blown up a leather ball, and they are now playing futball in the field across the road," Sir Richard responded. He smiled proudly. "Simon is playing with them. He will show them all what futball really is!"

"I am sure he will," said Chaucer, recalling with a rush of nostalgia how much he had enjoyed playing futball with his son Thomas, now away studying at Oxford. "Well, I'm glad they have found a way to amuse themselves for awhile. And perhaps futball will tire them out so much they will have no energy for quarreling."

Sir Richard continued to stare out of the window. Chaucer peered over his shoulder. Simon was running gleefully toward the goal line, ball in hand, vainly pursued by his fat, middle-aged fellow players. Geoffrey suppressed a smile as Henry de Coverly, the man of law, trying to stop Simon, tripped on something unseen and fell flat on the ground with a loud thump. Simon crossed the goal line easily.

Chaucer's eyes returned to Sir Richard's face. The King of Swords…There was no doubt that Sir Richard was a master of swordsmanship. Could he have been the man implied by the cards? An image of Sir Richard berating his son for his love of Sophia, on the first day of the pilgrimage, came to Geoffrey's mind unbidden.

Sir Richard had declared he would have fought to the death to protect the gypsy's life…but then Chaucer remembered the appearance of the Devil in the card layout. Lies, deception—and then there was the Popess…

At that moment Agatha burst into the tavern. "Arrogant, self-important son of a whore!" she cried angrily, shocking Sir Richard somewhat. "Who does he think he is? 'You have to leave now, Mistress Willard,'" she said in a mocking high-pitched squeal. "'I have to help Walter undress. He should stay clean in spite of his wound!' Who the hell does he think I am? Madame Eglantine? I've had four brothers, five husbands, three sons and a host of injured men who have come to me for help! Does Master High-and-Mighty Richemont actually think I don't know what men look like without their clothes on—"

"Agatha, calm down! Master Richemont is everything you say—arrogant, insensitive, and not much of a physician! But does it really matter who helps Walter bathe? Besides, we have to find our murderer before everyone here grows so bored they kill each other, and you have been far more of a help to me along that line than Master Richemont! I need you far more than I need him, so let him help Walter. Sit down with me and tell me what you think of this entire affair! You have been more than circumspect, but now it is time to speak your mind!"

Immediately mollified, Agatha sat down at one of the tables. Chaucer and Sir Richard joined her.

"Well, if you ask me," said Agatha. "whoever killed Sophia knew Don John, was involved with him in that evil Brotherhood, and knew that he had killed Brother Nicholas and left a Tarot card as his signature—whether he learned about it from Don John himself or not! He also knew that you possessed a deck of Tarot cards. Who in this company knew all that?"

Chaucer's brow puckered as he paused to think. "Father Matthew knew I had the Tarot cards," he finally said. "I showed them to him the very night Sophia was killed. He reacted to them the same way Don John said he did—he thought they were evil. He also is a stern advocate of the supremacy of the so-called True Church."

"And whether or not Sophia knew Brother Nicholas, undoubtedly Father Matthew thought of her as a pagan witch, even though she was taking part in a Christian pilgrimage!" said Agatha triumphantly. "And he was terrified when Sister Cecily went to fetch him to shrive her! If I were you, Geoffrey, I'd question Father Matthew!"

"You're forgetting one fact," said Sir Richard. Chaucer and Agatha both turned to look at him, as though surprised to see that he was still there.

"What's that?" Chaucer queried.

"Father Matthew was accommodated in the men's common sleeping-room," the knight replied.

Chaucer pounded the table in frustration. "Damn!" he swore. "How many obvious suspects we would have if it were not a known fact that no one left the men's common sleeping-room!" Shame kept Chaucer from admitting that, whether or not they had had anything to do with Sophia's death, he would gladly have seen both Father Matthew and Brother Hubert locked up in the cellar with Don John—and shut away in whatever punitive cloister the church had in mind until Gabriel's trumpet blew. Somehow he must overcome this prejudice against churchmen!

"Are we sure that no one could have left the men's common sleeping-room?" Agatha was asking.

Chaucer was suddenly alert. "What do you mean?"

"So much is made of the fact that everyone, including Walter, whom we have all elected to deem a total innocent, swears that no one could have left the men's common sleeping-room without being seen, and that no one left. But is that totally true? Perhaps there's another way to leave the room besides the main door."

The three of them looked at each other, then in one united motion rose from the table and dashed up the stairs.

Chaucer went first, peering inside the room to make certain no one was in there, then waved the others to follow him.

Each person staying here had marked off his own particular territory. Walter's, as would have been predicted, was neat and well kept, though somewhat dusty, as he had not slept there the night before. The sleeping areas of the churchmen were similar. The bedrolls of Robyn the Miller, the four guildsmen, Roger the Cook and Osewold the Reeve, however, were in comfortable disarray, with blankets entangled with cloaks, spare shirts and other items of clothing. Jack the summoner's bedroll had not been removed after his death, and appeared rather pathetic.

Geoffrey did not want to dwell on the sad fate of Jack. He turned his head quickly away and set about the business at hand. "According to Walter," he said. "the majority of those present were sitting right about here, in a sort of circle, between everyone else and the door," he said, pointing to a spot where the bedrolls were especially untidy. "Walter was there, tired but unable to sleep because of the noise. Jack the summoner was there, fast asleep. The three priests were in the back of the room—there." He pointed.

Suddenly something caught his eye. He frowned, then in three long steps was back by the priests' bedrolls.

In the darkest of the four corners of the room—which must have been even darker at night—there was a small opening which, judging from the clothes-pegs on the wall, had at one time served as a garderobe. At first glance it seemed normal, yet a small vertical sliver of light appeared at the back wall.

Carefully Chaucer crept into the garderobe and ran his hand over the wall where the light was. The board nearest to the light was slightly askew and somewhat loose. Geoffrey pushed on it gently, and it fell away. Chaucer put his head through the opening left by its fall and found himself staring into what had been the women's common sleeping-room.

The room in which Sophia had died.

He whistled. "Agatha," he said. "I knew you'd be of more use to me here than you would have been bathing Walter!"

Agatha and Sir Richard were both standing curiously behind him, peering into the garderobe. Chaucer stepped out and gestured for them to see for themselves.

"As you had guessed, my dear Mistress Willard," he went on, "there is indeed a second way out of the men's common sleeping-room."

Fifteen

"I think we had better keep this new discovery to ourselves—at least for as long as we can," said Chaucer.

He was sitting in the main taproom, at a table with Agatha and Sir Richard. None of them had said much about their find; it had been rather overwhelming to realize that one of their most firmly-believed truths associated with the investigation—that no one could have left the men's common sleeping-room without being seen—had never been true at all.

"Robert," said Agatha. "We can't keep it from Robert."

"No, we can't," Chaucer acknowledged. "Robert has been too invaluable to the investigation. But no one else should know—not young Simon, not Walter, not even the Duke. If the murderer was indeed one of those in that particular chamber, then as long as he thinks we don't know how he left the room, he will feel secure in his safety—at least for awhile."

Sir Richard was deep in thought. Finally he spoke. "From what I recall of the events of that night, Friar Hubert was deeply involved with the conversation at the front of the room. He could not have left under any circumstances—not through the main door, nor through the garderobe—without someone noticing. But Father Matthew was in the back of the room with the other priests, who could have been asleep, or they could be keeping silent to protect Father Matthew. He could easily have slipped through the loose board."

"I can't believe it!" exclaimed Agatha. "A man of God?"

"Don John too is a man of God," said Chaucer grimly. "And yet he confesses to killing another."

But the King of Swords, Geoffrey's inner voice nagged. *Not the Pope—the King of Swords. A man of the world, not of God.*

Chaucer brushed the nagging voice out of his consciousness. After all, Jacquemin Gringonneur could be totally wrong; the Tarot cards were probably useless in divining the future.

At that moment Walter burst in, carrying a bundle under his arm. He still looked weak; he also seemed in the depths of despair, as if he had lost his last friend. He collapsed into a chair between Chaucer and Agatha.

"I've been ousted," he said dolefully. "Mistress Atte Wood says I'm recovered enough to leave Jeni's room. She wants the investigation finished, and the pilgrims on their way, and is going to speak to the Duke of Lancaster. She just wants me out of the way so she can bully Jeni into marrying one of those loutish farm boys."

"Well, we'll see about that!" said Agatha, rising. "I'll go find Mistress Atte Wood and give her a piece of my mind!"

"Sit down, Agatha," said Chaucer, waving his hand. Reluctantly, Agatha obeyed.

"Mistress Willard has a point," said Sir Richard. "We have been paying Master Atte Wood quite well; I know that what the Duke alone has given him has made him a rich man. I believe our companions deserve far better treatment than she has given Walter!"

"I know, Sir Richard," said Chaucer. "But I actually would rather have Walter closer to me than he is out in the Atte Wood house. He will be safer here, with us. Still, we can't allow him to return to the men's common sleeping-room. Walter, would you have any reservations about staying in the room where Sophia died?"

"Not as long as I can lock the door," said Walter. "I don't believe in ghosts!"

"Then you need to rest," said Chaucer. "No matter what Mistress Atte Wood says, your strength is still depleted from your wound, and the infection. Agatha, would you take Walter upstairs? Don't let anyone in to see him except myself, Sir Richard, Robert, or Master Richemont."

"Or Jeni," added Walter.

"Or Jeni," Chaucer agreed.

"Master Richemont indeed!" Agatha muttered as she escorted Walter to the stairs."'Twould be far better to exclude him as well!"

"What about that loose board?" Sir Richard asked when they had gone.

"You and I will go upstairs and fix it as soon as Walter is asleep," Chaucer answered."We won't be able to secure it properly, of course, with hammer and nails, but we can barricade it with something. That should cause anyone with designs on Walter's life to think twice, anyway."

"Why would anyone want to kill Walter?" asked Sir Richard.

"Because he knows so much about that strange brotherhood," Chaucer replied."Who knows but that when his mind is not so much on Jeni, he may be able to tell us more? All facts point to the murderer's being connected to the Sacred Silver in some way. If I were the killer, I'd want Walter out of the way as soon as possible."

To their delight, Chaucer and Sir Richard discovered that there was a door to the old garderobe. It had been propped open for so long the hinges creaked ominously when they tried to close it, but they managed to do so without attracting any attention. In that door was a key; Chaucer turned it in the lock and pocketed it. At least no one would be able to use that route to Walter's new bedchamber.

When they arrived once more in the main taproom, the futball players had finished their game, and were demanding food and ale to quench the ravenous hunger and thirst that had resulted from their exertions. Sir Richard spotted an exhilarated Simon joking with the four guildsmen, and went to join him. Chaucer thought there were tears in the knight's eyes; it was the first time anyone had seen Simon smiling since Sophia's death.

Wulfstan Canty and his sergeants were exchanging serious words with Sir Oliver Radley and Peter Adams; John of Gaunt was nowhere in sight. Uneasily Chaucer realized that the sun was sinking low in the sky, and that a fourth day of investigation had now come to an end. Brother

John was locked up in the cellar, awaiting the church authorities, but they were still no closer to discovering the identity of Sophia's killer.

And today's discovery had not narrowed, but widened their range of suspects.

Chaucer ordered a tankard of ale for himself and went to sit on a bench in front of the fireplace, the better to observe the people around him. Nearly everyone on the pilgrimage was in the room—except the nuns, who still kept themselves isolated from the contaminating influence of their fellow pilgrims, and Robert, Agatha and Walter, whom Geoffrey knew to be innocent. One of them was a murderer. But which one? Chaucer's eyes jumped from face to face to face, trying to discern the thoughts and feelings lying beneath each mask. For some—such as Master Richemont—he had no luck at all, while others, like the guildsmen, the miller, the reeve, and others who were growing more intoxicated by the minute—were more obvious.

About an hour later a drunken Harry Bailey insisted that the tale-telling contest continue, and in a loud voice declared that Don John had not yet told his tale, and, prisoner or not, it was his duty to keep his word and entertain the company. After much persuasion (and a few threats) from the increasingly drunken pilgrims, Peter Adams and the guardsmen went down to the cellar with Master Atte Wood, reappearing a few minutes later with Don John, who, though his hands were still tied, seemed pathetically grateful not to have been forgotten, and relieved to be out of the cellar, even if it were only for a short while. Obligingly the monk began telling a number of stories, about heroes with great strength, such as Samson and Hercules. When he finished, he was unceremoniously returned to the cellar. Father Matthew was then called upon to tell his story.

This is very interesting, said Chaucer to himself. *We could be hearing performances by two murderers.*

One of the younger priests had gone up to the women's common sleeping-room to summon the nuns so that they might hear Father

Matthew's offering. Master Richemont, whose interest in the tale-telling contest was minimal, went upstairs to check on Walter, passing the nuns on the staircase and tipping his hat to them politely.

Once Father Matthew's tale—a comical fable about a cock and hen who outsmarted a fox—was done, Harry Bailey pointed out that Sister Cecily had not yet told a story. Obligingly the young nun began the story of the life of her saintly namesake, St. Cecilia, and her spiritual triumph over death and the persecution of Christians by Rome.

By this time Chaucer was growing restless. Sister Cecily was indeed a beautiful girl, but her storytelling style resembled that of a street preacher rather than a minstrel. Confident that Robert or Agatha would fill him in on the story, he decided to go outside for a breath of fresh air.

The night was dark, gloomy; somewhere up in the sky Geoffrey knew there was a full moon, but a thick cloud cover effectively obscured it. A brisk cold blast of wind struck his face as soon as it opened the door. Chaucer had always felt the cold and hated wind, but when he considered that his only other choice was listening to Sister Cecily drone on, he resolutely closed the door behind him.

As he stepped out the front door, his eyes fell on the stable. Guiltily he remembered that he hadn't visited or exercised Remile during the entire time they had been here in St. Mary Cray. The poor horse had spent every day confined to his stall.

His heart suddenly throbbing with pity and loneliness for his equine friend, Geoffrey headed off to the stables. Carefully in order not to startle the horses, he eased the door open. The cheery warmth projected by a small brazier combined with that of large bodies enveloped him; the comforting smells of hay, oats, and horseflesh gave him a sense of security. Someone had left a faint lantern shining; by its light Geoffrey could see the dark forms of all the pilgrims' horses. A loud yowling protest escaped a small body that had been standing or sleeping near the door; Chaucer looked down and spotted a big white cat staring up at him indignantly with luminescent copper eyes.

Chaucer adored cats—perhaps even more than the dogs and horses who served him so well. This one suddenly reminded Geoffrey of Troilus, the loyal pet who kept his flat over the Aldgate impeccably free of vermin. He bent down and scratched the animal's ears. Sensing the presence of a kindred spirit, the cat began to purr.

"Sorry I disturbed your rest, old fellow," Chaucer murmured as the cat rubbed affectionately against his legs.

The horses also sensed the presence of an intruder. Some were looking curiously in Chaucer's direction; others were nervously shifting from one leg to the other in a suspicious manner. One neighed and snorted loudly; in response the cat jumped away from Chaucer and dashed up the ladder to the loft. In spite of himself, Chaucer chuckled.

His eyes were gradually growing used to the darkness; he began to make his way down the row of stalls, searching for Remile.

Somewhere in this herd of mounts was Nicholas, the dead monk's namesake, who had carried Sophia here and would never carry her again. What would be his fate?

Would he remain here, for Master Atte Wood's use? Or would he perhaps carry Jeni away to her wedding with Walter?

He shook his head in disbelief. Clearly Jeni's parents had no intention of allowing her to go away with Walter. *I am expecting too much of the Tarot cards,* Geoffrey admonished himself.

A welcoming nicker sounded in Chaucer's left ear; he had found Remile, then. With some amusement he noticed that the white cat had followed him along the edge of the loft, going where Chaucer went, but cleverly remaining safely out of reach of the horses' hooves.

Stepping cautiously in order to avoid tripping or startling Remile, Chaucer entered the stall and found his horse's head. He petted the faithful animal's nose, crooning sweet words to him, receiving loving nuzzles in reply. With a sinking heart Geoffrey realized he should have found an apple for him.

The next moment something crashed upon his head, causing him to fall to the ground.

Remile, well trained and intelligent, quickly stepped to the opposite side in order to avoid stepping on his master. But the horse couldn't help jumping around nervously; though he loved his master and couldn't bear to hurt him, someone else was in the stall with them. Someone evil, who would willingly kill both man and beast. Remile could smell it.

Geoffrey, his head throbbing with pain and his thoughts muddled by the blow, had the presence of mind to try to roll away from Remile's hooves, but found himself hitting the barrier between the stalls. At the same time someone grabbed his collar, someone strong but wiry, someone determined to bring him out of the stall. *Someone who wanted to kill him. The man who killed Sophia now had his hands on Geoffrey.*

In spite of both Chaucer's and Remile's caution, one of the horse's nervously moving feet struck Geoffrey in the side of the head and on the chest. The murderer dragged the dazed poet out of the stall, tossing him in the middle of the stable, in the aisle between the stalls. As Chaucer lay helplessly before him, the man picked up a heavy stool that lay nearby and raised it high, as though to crash it down on his victim's head once more.

And then a loud hissing sound filled the air. Weakly Geoffrey turned in its direction.

The cat.

The cat was crouched on the edge of the loft, ears plastered back against his head, his angry glowing eyes calling to mind the Devil himself. The murderer raised the stool as though to strike the cat instead of Geoffrey, but the animal was too quick for him. It leaped off the loft's edge and onto the man's head, hissing, yowling, cruelly clawing and scratching.

The stool fell from the killer's hands and landed heavily on Chaucer's solar plexus. *But at least I know I have a champion,* Chaucer told himself.

While his opponent was trying to tear the cat from his face, Chaucer crawled into one of the neighboring stalls.

He knew he was taking a big chance; the horse inside was a stranger, and might panic and kick him to death—and in his weakened state, Geoffrey wasn't certain he could defend himself. Still, he preferred to take his chances with the unknown horse instead of the man. Luckily the occupant of the stall seemed to be sleeping heavily. Geoffrey lay quietly by the barrier, hoping that the shadows would keep him hidden.

The noise stopped; a loud thump hit the floor, as though the murderer had dislodged his vitriolic attacker from his head. *I hope the poor old fellow's all right,* Chaucer told himself fervently, thinking how tragic it would be if the cat had died protecting him. The killer, however, seemed to be admitting defeat; his footsteps seemed to be heading rapidly away from Chaucer, toward the door to the stables. A moment later the door slammed, and all was silent.

It could be a trick, Chaucer realized. *He could have simply opened and shut the door, hoping I'd come out.*

He waited a few moments, then, satisfied, carefully got to his feet.

A wave of dizziness then struck him; he grabbed the side of the stall in order to keep from collapsing. Suddenly every part of his body hurt—his head most of all. Involuntarily his eyes went to the loft, where with some relief he saw the white cat, apparently unharmed, bending over a dark shadow in a thick pile of hay. A moment later the shadow broke out in a series of hungry, high-pitched mews.

In spite of his pain Chaucer smiled. *So you're not an "old fellow" after all. How arrogant of me to think you'd risk your life just to protect a useless human like me.*

Shakily Chaucer made his way to the door, cautiously opening it and peering outside. But no one was anywhere near.

The tale-telling was apparently still going on. The lights still shone in the tavern; the loud shouts and laughter still rang from within those walls. Geoffrey thought of Robert, of Agatha, of Walter and Sir Richard, and all the others whom he had learned to call friend. Suddenly he longed for their presence, and with some determination pushed away from the security of the stable's walls and into the vast open space between the stables and the tavern. Bravely he tried to walk the distance.

He only made it as far as the rubbish heap, where he collapsed, finally unconscious. As he passed out, his hand closed over something soft and comforting.

His dreams were haunted by the images on the Tarot cards.

Sixteen

"Geoffrey? Geoffrey, wake up! It's Agatha!"

Gradually the words filtered through to Chaucer's consciousness. His head still throbbed; he tried opening his eyes, only to find they were stuck together with hardened tears. A warm, wet cloth brushed across his face; a moment later his eyelids were clear and he could open them. A sea of faces swam unfocused before him, then gradually sharpened. Agatha was the first one he saw, bending closely over him, cloth in hand. Beside her stood Robert. Dear Agatha, dear Robert! They had proven themselves true friends again and again.

Others behind them came into focus—John of Gaunt, Sir Oliver Radley, Sir Richard de Burgoyne. All wore masks of concern on their faces.

"What happened?" Geoffrey finally croaked.

"Mistress Atte Wood found you this morning, collapsed by the rubbish heap, a huge knot on your head and bruises all over your face," Agatha explained. "She immediately called for Sir Richard, and the guardsmen carried you in to your own room. Then they woke me. But why are we telling you what happened? We deserve to know, Geoffrey Chaucer, why you were out lying in the cold with your face down in a rubbish heap instead of in your own warm bed where you should have been!"

Chaucer tried to explain, but both his memory and his voice failed him. The events of the night before were cloaked in shadow; his throat was too raspy to produce coherent sounds. Finally he gave up. "Give me something for this headache, and I'll tell you everything," he croaked. "Until it goes away I can't think about anything but my aching head!"

"I've already mixed it," said Agatha dryly. "Tis the same cordial I gave young Walter—willow bark and valerian in wine. Drink it, and you'll soon be feeling your old self!"

She put a strong but gentle arm under Geoffrey's head and propped him up while he sipped, then quaffed the warm, fruity, soothing mixture. Agatha had been right, he thought with relief. Even as he lay back down on the pillow the pain in his head was already subsiding.

When it had lessened to a faint, dull throb he suddenly remembered the events of the night before. "I met the murderer," he confessed.

Five mouths gaped. "Who was it?" Robert finally asked.

"I don't know," said Chaucer. Five faces fell. "It was too dark to see. The only thing I know for certain is that it was a man." He told them the entire story of the night before. Then he sat straight up and began frantically throwing the covers off. "The horses—the cat and her kittens—I have to see them, to make sure they're all right—he could have gone back and hurt them, I have to go—"

"Geoffrey, get back in that bed!" ordered Agatha. "You're still too weak—"

But Chaucer was oblivious to her words. His shoes had been neatly placed by the side of his bed; he stepped into them, stood up and grabbed his cloak, then ran down the stairs. Robert threw his hands up in a gesture of futility, then followed Chaucer. Everyone else trailed along in his wake.

Chaucer dashed through the tavern and out the front door, then headed for the stable. The door looked so innocent, and yet so threatening as it loomed closer and closer. He threw it open and stepped inside.

Immediately thirty pairs of equine eyes turned to stare at him, including Remile's. The horses were fine, then! But the cat—that brave, heroic mother, willing to take on a murderer to protect her babies—

"Meow!"

Geoffrey sagged visibly as he collapsed against a stable pillar in sheer relief. The white cat was still in the loft, sitting peaceful and calm, which she undoubtedly would not have been had someone threatened her kittens. A few plaintive mews from another part of the loft further eased Chaucer's mind.

John of Gaunt was the first of the others to reach the stable and come to stand by Geoffrey's side. "Would you please tell me what this is all about?" he demanded.

Geoffrey pointed to the cat. "There," he said. "She saved my life last night. I just wanted to make certain—to make certain—that she was still in possession of hers."

"How can you tell if it's a he or a she?" asked Gaunt as the others opened the door and entered the stable.

"My dear Lord Duke, males don't have kittens!"

"Kittens—Geoffrey, what in the name of God and the Blessed Mother are you talking about? I'm talking about whoever's asleep in that hay up there!"

"What?" Now it was Chaucer's turn to be thunderstruck. "Someone's up there?"

"Yes, damn it!" said Gaunt. He raised his voice in a commanding manner. "Whoever you are, come out and show yourself!"

From behind a pile of hay rose the guilty face of Walter, followed by a tousled Jeni.

"We're handfasted!" Walter cried triumphantly. "Furthermore, we have lain together! Now they have to let us marry!"

The six watchers stared first at Walter, then at each other. Bewilderment was plastered over all their faces; their mouths opened and closed like fishes.

"What the hell is going on here?" John of Gaunt demanded. "Are we looking for a murderer or some starry-eyed young lovers?"

Chaucer turned his head, trying desperately hard to stifle rapidly rising laughter. "Sir Oliver," he finally said, "perhaps it would be a good idea for someone to fetch Master and Mistress Atte Wood."

Aleyn Atte Wood was clearly furious. "Did he force you, Jeni? Because if he did, I'll—"

Jeni stood as straight and tall as her diminutive height would allow. "No, Da, he did not force me. I wanted him as much as he wanted me—probably more, for he was still weak and injured. And we didn't sin—we are handfasted. We swore before God to be man and wife until death part us."

"A clerk!" cried Aleyn Atte Wood, angrily pacing back and forth in front of the tavern fireplace. "A starving, penniless clerk! Jeni, there are any number of young men here in the village you could marry—men with land, with prospects! Why a poverty-stricken student whom you've only known a few days?"

"I don't love any of those young men," said Jeni calmly, holding tight to Walter's hand. "I love Walter."

Walter then stood and faced his new father-in-law. "Master Atte Wood, I am very, very sorry that we had to force your hand this way, but you were determined not even to give me a chance. I couldn't just leave Jeni behind—I love her! And since you were determined not to allow it, we had to take matters into our own hands!" He took a deep breath. "I'm poor now, yes. But I won't always be. As I told you, Master Chaucer has a post waiting for me in the customs office in London as soon as I graduate. I'm a hard worker and I'll do right by the king and Master Chaucer. You'll see!"

Atte Wood's eyes immediately went to Chaucer, who nodded his agreement. "I shall count myself lucky to have Walter on my staff," he said. "He is bright, conscientious and well-educated, and I pay my employees well. I have to—I only want the best. I am certain that Walter will be able to provide for Jeni far better than any of the local young farmers."

"Master Atte Wood," said Walter, his courage buoyed by Chaucer's championing of him. "I shall love and cherish your daughter as any knight from Camelot would his lady. She shall never lack for anything, not while I'm alive, and if Master Chaucer instructs me as well in the ways of the world as I am sure he can, she will lack for nothing after I am gone! Your daughter will be safe, happy and prosperous with me!"

"But she'll be *gone!*" wailed Mistress Atte Wood.

Everyone in the room was quiet. Jeni let go of Walter's hand and went and put her arms around her mother. "Mother," she said gently, "you have spent all your life in St. Mary Cray, and so to you London is as far away as Jerusalem. But it is really not all that far. The pilgrims came here in two days, and that was with riding slow and stopping often. Why, my lord the Duke of Lancaster reached here in all of a few hours! I can come visit you often, or you can come see me and even see the palace at Westminster! You would like that, wouldn't you?" Mistress Atte Wood didn't answer. She was crying into her daughter's shoulder.

John of Gaunt then stepped forward and confronted Aleyn Atte Wood. "Master Innkeeper," he said, "would it help if I took personal responsibility for the well-being of your daughter, and of her young husband here, and promised to send word to you immediately if all was not well with them? And if I granted them an allowance starting now, of, say, ten pounds a year, which would be over and above what Walter would earn in the customs office? That way they would have an income now, while Walter is still at University, and would assure them of a greater standard of living once he comes to work in London. Think of it as—er—a thank-you for being such a fine landlord to us while we were all stuck here."

Agatha, flashing a knowing smile at Gaunt, then stepped forward. "I am an innkeeper, like yourself," she said. "I run a first-class tavern near the Aldgate, where Master Chaucer lives. I promise you, when Walter and Jeni come to London, they can lodge in my finest rooms until they find a house of their own. They will never be far from those who care for them."

Aleyn Atte Wood collapsed onto the bench by the fireplace, then raised his arms in a gesture of surrender. "What can I say? Obviously all of you think very highly of this young man—and of my daughter. If he is worth that much to all of you, then who am I to argue? Why keep them apart? You just make certain," he said, suddenly casting a dark look at Walter, "that she visits us at least three times a year!"

Walter's face was a testament to joy. "Yes, Master Atte Wood! Yes, I will! I promise!"

Father Harold, who had been hovering in the back of the room, then came into the light. "Shall I perform the ceremony?" he asked.

Jeni summoned all her dignity. "Yes. Tomorrow morning."

"No!" cried Walter. "Tonight! I don't want to wait another day!"

As if he'd been kept dangling for ten years, Chaucer told himself, suppressing a smile.

"But you're still weak!" protested Jeni.

"I don't care if Master Chaucer and Simon have to hold me up! I want to have the ceremony tonight!"

Aleyn Atte Wood sighed. "Very well," he said. "Tonight it is. Father Harold, is there anything special we need to do before then?"

Leaving the young lovers to plan their wedding, Chaucer, Gaunt, Agatha and Robert then walked out into the sunshine. "Well, now that is settled, tell us more about what happened with the murderer," said Gaunt.

Sighing, Geoffrey sat down on a tree stump near the walkway leading to the front door. He had been so excited during the scene with Walter and Jeni that he had forgotten his ordeal of the night before. Suddenly his head was throbbing again, and his solar plexus hurt from the stool's landing on it. He told the story of the struggle in the stables, and of the cat's fortuitous defense of her kittens.

"I must do something for that white cat," Geoffrey mused. "If it had not been for her, he would have killed me, I am certain. But while she was attacking him, I managed to roll into one of the stalls and remain still. He was too badly hurt from the scratches to spend much time searching for me."

"Then what you're saying is that whoever the killer is has a face covered with cat scratches," said Gaunt.

His face a mask of shock, wondering why this little bit of logic had escaped him, Chaucer stood up. "You're right," he said. "Why don't we go wish everyone on the pilgrimage a good morning—inform them that there is going to be a wedding tonight instead of a funeral. A face full of cat scratches will not be easy to hide without hiding oneself!"

"So anyone who doesn't come out in the open is suspect," said Robert.

"Suspect, bah! We'll drag him out in the open!" said Gaunt. "Let's go!"

They were a little late if they wanted to take the news to everyone on the pilgrimage of Walter and Jeni's upcoming nuptials. Word had spread rapidly; everyone was in the tavern drinking the health of the young bride and groom. Friendly and cordial, but vigilant, Chaucer, Gaunt, Robert and Agatha moved among the company, talking to everyone, while at the same time getting a good close look at their faces. Chaucer himself made a point of getting as close to Father Matthew as he dared, but was disappointed to see that the man's face and tonsured head were smooth and unscratched. Friar Hubert proved to be equally unmarked.

Jeni, carrying a tray laden with tankards of ale, emerged from the kitchen; Chaucer walked over to her and took it from her. "Why is a radiant bride working on the day before her wedding?" he asked.

"I may be married tonight, and I may be leaving with you as soon as the murder is solved," said Jeni, "but my father has said that as long as I am here I am still his daughter, and I still have to carry my weight. I don't mind. He's letting me marry Walter. Helping until I am rightfully wed is a small price to pay."

"You're a good girl, Jeni," said Chaucer. "Walter is a lucky man. By the way, where is the bridegroom?"

"Master Richemont took him upstairs to his room," Jeni reported. "After the confrontation with my father—plus the fact that we were awake most of the night—" here she blushed—" he was weaker than ever. And so Master Richemont decided he should go back to bed until the ceremony. They're upstairs now."

"I'll go see Walter," said Chaucer, handing her back the tray. She bustled away into the crowd.

Chaucer climbed the stairs, knocked on the door of Walter's room, and heard a muffled, "Come in."

Master Richemont was replacing the bandage on Walter's arm. He smiled thinly as Chaucer entered the room; his face, Geoffrey noted, was clear and unmarked. "Our young bridegroom here needs to conserve his strength," he said. "I have asked that Mistress Atte Wood send him up some nourishing soup. She promised she'd make her best. I presume she will, since he is soon to be her son."

"By law, I already am," said Walter sleepily. "Jeni and I are handfasted." With that he closed his weary gray eyes and nodded off.

"We should let him sleep," said Master Richemont softly. "I shall check on him again later."

Together they walked down the stairs, then Master Richemont took a tankard of ale from Jeni and congratulated her on her forthcoming wedding. Chaucer went into the kitchen, where Mistress Atte Wood was chopping onions. She glared at him; Chaucer realized she blamed him for her daughter's forthcoming departure.

She is like her cat, Chaucer realized: *passionately protective of her young!*

"Guests aren't allowed in the kitchen," she said shortly.

"Certainly, Mistress Atte Wood, and I shall leave as soon as you answer one question."

She narrowed her eyes suspiciously. "What's that?"

"Do you have a piece of fish? Clean, uncooked, with no bones in it—"

Silently Mistress Atte Wood walked outside, with Chaucer following. Slowly she pulled a chunk of filleted fish wrapped in a cloth from the depths of the well.

"The fishmonger brought it this morning," she said, gingerly unwrapping the package. "It should be fresh enough. Do you like raw fish?"

"Not particularly," said Chaucer, taking a small piece. "But I'm sure your cat does!"

"The cat?"

Leaving the woman staring strangely at him, Chaucer took the fish into the stable.

The cat, sensing the presence of her friend and smelling the fish, immediately leaped down from the loft, hurried over to Chaucer and rubbed up against his leg, purring loudly.

"Did you think I'd forgotten you, pretty one?" said Chaucer softly. "I never forget anyone who saves my life. Here—I brought you a treat."

He held the morsel of fish down to her; without hesitation she snatched it from him and bounded back up the loft. *Her kittens must be eating solid food now,* Chaucer realized. *Well, let them all enjoy it in peace.*

He left the stable and made his way back to the tavern, passing the rubbish heap on the way. *Did I really spend the night here?* he asked himself with disbelief. Vague memories of the night before danced in his head. He remembered the scuffle with the murderer, but he didn't remember collapsing by the rubbish heap.

Or did he?

A strange recollection, which he associated in some way with the cat, was hovering around the edges of his memory, as though just out of reach. Chaucer's eyes searched the pile of debris, hoping for something that would enable him to remember. Something was important—something that still eluded him. But what was it?

Suddenly, beneath a pile of castoffs that had clearly been thrown there only this morning, Chaucer saw something that seemed familiar.

A lock of black hair.

Then he remembered his hand closing on the soft black hair—soft, like the cat's fur. Distastefully, yet carefully, Geoffrey brushed aside the trash covering the hair, picked it up and held it up to the sun.

The hair was coarse, yet still soft to the touch; it was shiny and curling, and must have once been beautiful.

His eyes riveted on the lock in front of him; his jaw dropped. This hair was new; it had not been lying here long. But no member of the Atte Wood household, no member of the pilgrimage had hair that dark.

There had only been one. And that was Sophia.

Sophia's hair.

And then suddenly he realized the significance of the Tarot cards— The Devil turning up next to The Popess; The House of God and the revelations it promised.

Other bits of information suddenly fell into place. A gesture recognized, but not known from where. His own words: "It is my experience that people often tell tales that reflect who they are." Someone connected with the Church, who clearly had a stake in the fate of the Lollards. Someone who could have known he had the Tarot cards.

His mind flew back to the night Sophia died, before everyone went to bed, while Sophia was still telling her tale. And suddenly he knew who the King of Swords was.

And now that I know it, yes, it does make me feel like The Fool.

Then another revelation struck him. There had not been two murders; there had been three.

And soon there might be four.

Stuffing the hair in his pocket, he jumped up and ran into the tavern, running as though for his life.

But it was not for his life. It was for Walter's.

Seventeen

He burst into the front room of the tavern with a loud bang of the door. All eyes turned; he was so red-faced with exertion and excitement that they knew that something had happened.

Chaucer's eyes scanned the crowd until he saw the faces he wanted. "Sir Richard! Simon! Master Canty! Arrest Master Richemont at once for the murders of Sophia the gypsy and Jack the summoner, and the attempted murders of Geoffrey Chaucer and Walter Locksley!"

Bewildered, but wasting no time, Sir Richard and Wulfstan Canty advanced on Master Richemont and grabbed him, one by each arm. Simon followed, ready to act if necessary. Master Richemont sighed, as though relieved it was all over.

Chaucer pushing his way through the sea of staring faces. His searching eyes fell on Sir Oliver Radley. "Sir Oliver! Inform His Grace the Duke that the murderer is apprehended! Agatha! Robert! Come with me at once! And God grant that we are not too late!"

"What's the matter?" demanded Agatha.

"I think Master Richemont has been trying to kill Walter!" Grabbing a bottle of wine and tankard from the bar, Chaucer dashed up the stairs, followed by a breathless Agatha and a concerned Robert. Together they hurried down the hallway until they reached Walter's chamber. Geoffrey pushed on the door; when it would not open he kicked it in.

The three of them entered; their eyes immediately went to the sole occupied pallet. Walter lay sleeping, too still for normality, too pale for recovery. Agatha hurried to his side and knelt down, placed her ear to his chest and felt the vein on his neck.

"He lives," she finally said, "but something is wrong. Robert! Go down to Mistress Atte Wood and tell her to send up some burdock, comfrey and wild pepper." She began unwrapping the bandage on Walter's arm.

Robert dashed out of the room. Chaucer knelt beside Agatha. "What do you think is wrong?" he asked.

"I think that our esteemed physician gave him hemlock," said Agatha, pulling away the odious bandages.

"Hemlock!" Visions of Socrates danced through Chaucer's mind.

"Yes, hemlock. I saw a wild patch of it growing outside; some of it had been picked only recently. If Master Richemont had been accused of its use after Walter died, he would have sworn it was parsley, which is used to ease the swelling around wounds. This often happens accidentally, for the leaves of both plants do resemble each other, and I am sure it could be done and often has been done deliberately. Look here! This time Master Richemont was making sure that Walter died. He has done it again—dressed his arm with useless chamomile. See—the wound is already showing signs of growing septic once more."

"But hemlock! Doesn't that kill instantly?"

"No, it does not. Only very large doses kill for certain; smaller doses sometimes only make one sick. I doubt if Master Richemont gave Walter too large a dose—there is a distinctive odor that can arise in such cases, and the risk of detection would be too strong. I believe I smell a touch of it on his breath now. But the poor boy is weakened anyway—what with his wound, and with all the pain over Jeni, in addition to the fact that he is undernourished and not too strong anyway. I knew we should have kept that monster away from him!"

Robert then arrived with the herbs.

"Give me the wild pepper!" Agatha barked. "Geoffrey, pour a cup of that wine! There is no time to lose!"

Chaucer obeyed, pouring the wine into the tankard and handing it to Agatha. She seized the dried wild pepper from Robert, propped

Walter's head up on her lap and began to pour the mixture down the youth's throat.

Walter's eyes opened in alarm, then his expression eased somewhat when he saw it was Agatha holding him.

"Drink, lad! Drink! I know it tastes awful, but you must do it! Drink!"

Walter sputtered, then obediently swallowed gulp after gulp until the tankard was empty. He sat heaving for a few moments, then suddenly turned away from Agatha and began retching violently, spilling the contents of his stomach all over the rushes on the floor.

When there was nothing more in Walter's stomach for him to throw up, Agatha bent as close as she dared, sniffed the mess, then nodded in satisfaction. "Enough of the hemlock has been purged from his body so that I believe him now to be out of danger," she finally said. "But we must make certain. Robert, stir some of the burdock into a second glass of wine. When Walter feels ready, he must drink that. The burdock will cleanse what is left of the poison from his system."

Walter was gasping. "What is happening?" he finally asked weakly.

"Your so-called physician tried to kill you, Walter," said Agatha angrily. "If it had not been for Master Chaucer's quick thinking, you'd have probably been dead by nightfall, never to marry your Jeni. The man deserves to be hanged, drawn and quartered. Using knowledge of herbs and healing to commit murder! Why, the Devil awaits him eagerly, I'll wager!"

Chaucer finally spoke. "Agatha, please tell me: How could simply using chamomile instead of comfrey cause Walter's wound to turn septic so fast? Wouldn't it usually take longer?"

"Yes—unless the wound were contaminated with some kind of infectious substance. Such humours can be easily transferred from one person to another. I know for a fact that Master Richemont has been treating that running sore on Roger the cook's leg. It would be all too easy for a physician to save some of the pus and rub it into Walter's wound on the pretext of using a salve of some kind."

Chaucer suddenly felt as if he were going to retch. Agatha poured wine over Walter's wound, causing him to wince with pain, then she packed it with comfrey and bound it with fresh bandages. "Now rest, my lad, and allow the burdock to do its work," she said. "If you feel like vomiting again, don't worry about the mess. If Mistress Atte Wood complains about having to clean it up, she'll answer to me!"

"I'll drop a handful of silver pennies in her pocket," said Chaucer. "That should keep her quiet."

"The wedding," gasped Walter. "The wedding has to go on! I don't care—"

"We'll hold you up," Chaucer reassured him. "We'll carry you to the altar if we must. But tonight you shall marry your Jeni, I promise!"

At that moment John of Gaunt burst in, followed by Sir Oliver Radley. "Geoffrey, what is this? Oliver says that the physician is the murderer!" The Duke's face was flushed with excitement and anticipation, but it was also guarded—as though he were afraid that Master Richemont's arrest would prove to be a false alarm like that of Don John.

"Yes, he is," said Chaucer. "Not only did he kill Sophia, he also murdered Jack the summoner to keep him quiet. You can go back to Westminster now, my lord Duke."

"Oh, no!" said Gaunt. "I'm not moving a pace until you tell me everything. How, after all these days of being totally befuddled, did you finally get the blast of inspiration that told you that the physician, of all people, had killed the girl? I want to hear it all!"

"And so you shall," said Chaucer. He turned to Agatha and Robert. "Are you coming?"

"Yes," said Agatha. "I wouldn't miss this for anything. But someone should sit with Walter. Robert! Call Jeni! No!" She suddenly drew herself up short. "I don't want Jeni to see him until he is looking better. Get Sister Cecily! It is high time she came out of that room and behaved like a human being! It won't hurt her lily-white hands to clean up a little vomit in the cause of helping her fellow man!"

Robert hurried to obey. No one argued with Agatha when she was in this mood. Sir Oliver Radley stopped him. "I'll go," he said. "Perhaps Sister Cecily would be more apt to respond if he who summoned her worked for the Duke."

Robert nodded his agreement, then followed as Chaucer led the way down the stairs to the main tavern room. Gaunt, Agatha and Robert followed.

Everyone in the tavern was staring quizzically up at Chaucer as he descended the staircase. Without a word he walked over to Master Richemont, who was still being held firmly by Sir Richard and Wulfstan Canty. Someone—probably Canty—had found a pair of manacles and locked them onto Richemont's hands.

"Last night," Chaucer announced from the staircase, speaking as loudly as a priest from his lectern. "an attempt was made on my life in the stables, while I was visiting my horse. But luckily, I was rescued—by Mistress Atte Wood's cat. For the sake of protecting her kittens, the cat jumped from the loft onto the murderer's head with flying claws. Therefore it logically follows that the man who attacked me would have a head full of cat scratches." Slowly, dramatically, Chaucer descended the staircase, then turned to face the physician.

"Why, Master Richemont," said Chaucer as he walked closer to the man. "You're wearing your coif far lower on your face than usual. I don't like it—it is rather unbecoming. Master Canty, would you please remove Master Richemont's coif?"

"Gladly," said Canty. He snatched both hat and coif off the physician's head, causing the prisoner to wince from pulled hair.

"Ha!" cried Chaucer gleefully. The physician's upper forehead was crisscrossed all over with long, angry scratches. "So it was you that my feline friend mauled in her valiant efforts to save me and defend her kittens!"

Gaunt pushed his way forward to stare at the physician as if he couldn't believe it. "So it was you!" he echoed Chaucer's words. The reality of the situation finally struck him. "Good God, I can go home now!"

The physician stared angrily at the floor, saying nothing. The room was silent; all were waiting to hear more.

"But how do you explain all this?" Harry Bailey finally asked.

"Ah! How do I explain it? Harry, my old friend, you thought my other two stories were boring. Well, I am going to tell you a tale that will chill your soul—and keep everyone in this room entertained for quite a while."

He took a deep breath. "Master Richemont, as we have already established, is from the north. It was undoubtedly up there that he met Don John and Brother Nicholas. Possibly he went to Kirksdell when monks suffered injuries that their infirmarian felt inadequate to treat. He may have once aspired to be a monk; he has admitted still wanting to be a priest, hoping to join an order of hospitallers. It is quite possible that, in his pursuit of his aspirations, some wise, astute churchman denied him entrance to the seminary. Everyone has observed how cold he is, with apparent disinterest in human contact, though he was fascinated with disease. Such an uncaring man would not have made a good priest. Men like him occasionally do slip by into the priesthood, but sometimes they are stopped before they can be ordained, and Master Richemont probably was. How fortunate for the Church! Yet he still hoped to take holy orders, and for that reason he didn't want the Church's power broken.

"Master Richemont is a cold man, probably choosing the priesthood at least partly because he has nothing to give a wife or family. Yet it is my firm belief that at some point in his life he became infatuated with the free-spirited pagan charms of a young gypsy girl. There was one thing that bothered me about him ever since the night he told his tale. There were certain gestures, certain expressions that he affected that reminded me of someone, but I couldn't recall who. It was only this afternoon that I realized who it was. Sophia. Sophia had the same way of lifting her chin when she turned her head, the same way of using her hands to talk while she was telling her tale. It all seemed too fantastic to be true—but it was certainly not impossible. There were a number of people on this pilgrimage who had known each other before—and all were from Yorkshire."

"But what are you trying to tell us?" demanded Alisoun of Bath.

"That Sophia was Master Richemont's natural daughter." A gasp spread through the room.

"Of course, you would never have married the mother, Master Richemont," said Chaucer. "She probably didn't want you for a husband anyway—if she'd had any sense she preferred her own kind. But you knew who Sophia was. The gypsies may have come and gone with the seasons, but in the spring they always returned to Yorkshire. You watched the child grow, with interest if not with love."

Master Richemont raised his eyes to Chaucer and opened his mouth to speak. But he sighed and closed it; better to say nothing. Still, the expression in his eyes was enough to tell everyone that Geoffrey had guessed the truth.

"You had other things on your mind besides your bastard daughter by a gypsy. You were concerned about the spread of Lollardy, and the growing anticlericalism. I don't think you cared that much about the doctrine or teachings of the True Church—only about its power. You still aspired to and passionately craved that power; now you wanted to defend it. Your political leanings were certainly more in favor of the Bishop of Norwich than John of Gaunt. Perhaps you hoped that your nefarious activities with the Brotherhood of the Sacred Silver would impress the church authorities so much they would confess their mistakes and finally admit you to the priesthood."

Chaucer then turned back to the widening eyes of his audience. He was enjoying this hugely. "Master Richemont either learned about the Brotherhood of the Sacred Silver from his contacts at Kirksdell, or from someone else who knew of his political leanings. It doesn't really matter; however, it does seem logical that at one time he had traveled to Oxford to be initiated into that Brotherhood."

"Geoffrey," John of Gaunt said darkly, "how did he come to kill Sophia?"

"Yes," said Agatha. "How could even the coldest of men slay his own daughter?"

"How could Virginius slay his own daughter?" asked Chaucer dramatically.

A hush once more descended over the people in the room. All were remembering how moved they had been by the physician's tale.

"Master Richemont probably didn't know that Sophia would come on this pilgrimage," said Chaucer. "But Sophia knew he was going, and when she met Sir Richard and Simon and decided to join them, she probably thought it a merry lark that she would be following her natural father, who had heretofore avoided her. At one time she may have threatened to tell the other pilgrims who she was, but whether or not she actually did was of no consequence. Master Richemont could have seen her very presence as an embarrassment, even if no one knew who she was. Certainly Sophia enjoyed needling the representatives of the True Church—Don John the monk, whom she knew to be the thief; Friar Hubert, who lusted after her and whom she enjoyed humiliating in front of the rest of the company; the nuns, who were annoyed by her very existence; Jack the summoner; and even the young priest whose cross Don John stole and to whom Sophia unwittingly restored it. And furthermore, there was the increasingly intense relationship between Sophia and Simon—which appeared to be going very rapidly in only one direction."

He paused for effect. Then Alisoun of Bath spoke up. "But wasn't Sophia at one time a nun?"

Immediately there flashed into Chaucer's mind a picture of the Tarot cards. The Popess, placed next to The Devil. The King of Lies. A monstrous lie about a nun.

"Sophia was never a nun!" Chaucer thundered. "Who fed us that outrageous lie? Master Richemont! I am sure that he only told us that to draw attention away from him. Looking back, I am quite surprised that any of us believed that bit of nonsense at all. How could a free-spirited, passionate, lustful girl like Sophia ever consider entering the quiet and disciplined life of a cloister? I think that Master Richemont would have liked for a daughter of his to be a nun. Look at how he admired Sister Cecily—I believe she was the only person on this pilgrimage for whom he ever smiled."

Chaucer advanced upon the prisoner. "After you'd had your way with Sophia's mother, what did you think of her? As a whore, a temptress, a succubus who had lured you away from the path of righteousness? How easy some men find it to shift responsibility for their own lusts and lack of self-control! And now you imagined that you saw your own daughter developing into the same sort of harlot!"

He turned away from the physician and back towards the company. "I believe that Master Richemont saw Sophia as a threat on three levels. First of all, she was a threat to his continuing ambitions to join the priesthood. What would the church authorities say if they knew he had once sired a child on a pagan gypsy? They would never admit him into their ranks, no matter what he accomplished with the Brotherhood of the Sacred Silver! Sophia may have made uneasy him by her flirting with churchmen. Suppose she told one of them who her father was?

"Secondly, she probably did know Brother Nicholas. We probably will never know how a gypsy girl and an illuminator could ever meet. Perhaps it was by chance, when the gypsies visited the monastery for shelter or alms. But Sophia knew Brother Nicholas, and probably sympathized with his Lollardist inclinations. She was, after all, a Christian, if an unorthodox one. She may have known something of Master Wyclif, of the Lollards, and possibly even of the Brotherhood. Therefore, to Master Richemont's way of thinking, she knew too much.

"Finally, there was Master Richemont's powerful belief in the wickedness of the relations between man and woman, and his adherence to the words of St. Paul, that chastity was preferable even to holy consecrated marriage." Geoffrey took a deep breath, then glanced around the room "Virginius slew his daughter rather than have her suffer shame at the hands of Appius. It is my firm contention that people often choose tales that reveal their own beliefs, and their own way of thinking. I believe that Master Richemont, on some twisted plane of his fanatical mind, feared for his daughter's immortal soul, and he watched every day as she continued her relationship with Simon, which would never have ended in marriage, but seemed destined to become lustfully carnal at any moment." He breathed deeply as he recalled the shadowy figure he had seen in the woods the day he had witnessed the passionate scene between Sophia and Simon. Of course, it had been Master Richemont…"He even spied on them in their most intimate moments."

Sitting at a table near the fireplace, Simon blushed hotly, and covered his face with his hands to hide it. Sir Richard placed a sympathetic hand on his son's shoulder.

Chaucer continued."Master Richemont saw Sophia primarily as a threat to his ambitions. And so he killed her. But he rationalized her murder by telling himself he had sent her straight to heaven, rather than allow her to consign herself to the fires of Hell because of her illicit love for Simon. Why, he even examined her private parts after he killed her to make sure she died a virgin!" He pressed his lips together in a thin line, cast a contemptuous look at the physician, and then went on.

"Secretly, while the two nuns and Mistress Alisoun were not looking—probably while they were praying for Sophia's soul—he sliced off a lock of her hair, in order to convince me and everyone else that Sophia was a failed nun, even going to the trouble to show me how one could tell if hair had ever been cut or not. Luckily I found it where he had discarded it," He took the hair, still wavy and shining, from his pocket, and walked over to Simon."Here," he said, placing the curl on the table in front of the squire."If you should wish to keep this, my lad, as a souvenir of the first passionate love you ever held for a woman, make certain you hide it well from your future wife and daughters. Women have a way of holding grudges and being jealous of previous lovers, even when they are long dead."

Simon looked gratefully up at Chaucer, then tenderly placed the lock of hair in his pocket.

"Master Richemont knew Don John. Perhaps they had consulted in York with each other on the monk's mission, discussing how important it was that Nicholas not reach Canterbury, that the intended recipient not receive word of the Duke of Lancaster's new funding. Whether or not they did, there is no doubt that at some point during the pilgrimage, they spoke, and Don John told Master Richemont what had happened to Brother Nicholas on the road to Canterbury. Oh, I know that the monk denied telling anyone. But either he lied, or he was too drunk that night to remember that he had told anyone anything. The night Sophia told her tale, Don John and Master Richemont were sitting near me. I had my Tarot cards out, showing them to Father Matthew."

In a highly theatrical manner Chaucer turned to the physician."You have the hands and skills of a surgeon. The King of Swords," he said more softly, recalling that physicians often used finely honed blades to perform surgical tasks."Don John has told us that he had carried Master Dyer's stolen dagger in the pocket of his cloak, which he had with him that night but had taken off because the room was rather warm. I am certain that those agile and slender fingers can just as easily remove a dagger from an unguarded pocket, or a card from a box, as a growth from a human body. Probably while Don John, Father Matthew and I were engrossed in Sophia's tale, you saw your chance and stole the dagger from Don John's cloak, and a card—any card—from my box." So much for my confusion about why the killer chose The Sun, Chaucer suddenly reflected. It didn't matter which card he took—he only needed a Tarot card. Any Tarot card would have done the trick.

"You figured that in spite of Don John's efforts to hide the body, Brother Nicholas would be found, and eventually his murder would be traced to Don John. You wanted to make it look as if Don John had killed Sophia as well, and so you used a dagger which he had stolen, and his signature of the Tarot card, trying to convince us all that Sophia was once a nun to give the impression she had been more closely involved with Don John and the others.

"And then there was Walter," Chaucer went on. "Walter's knowledge of the Brotherhood frightened you perhaps more than Sophia's flirting with the churchmen. Walter said that according to his knowledge, all members of the Brotherhood had to spend some time in Oxford, shadowing Master Wyclif and his followers, so as to learn who they were and what they looked like. Walter was probably only repeating gossip, but you jumped to the conclusion that he knew quite a bit about the Brotherhood and its membership, and perhaps had made the acquaintance of some of them. You wondered if he, at some time, might have seen you in their company. And so he had to go, too. You tried to kill him, not once, but twice. Thanks to the vigilance and the healing skills of Mistress Willard, the first try failed. The second would have succeeded if I had not found Sophia's hair in the rubbish heap."

He sighed, somewhat in disbelief. "I have killed, Master Richemont. I have cut down healthy young men in the flower of their lives, and left their wives widows and their babes orphans. Their faces will haunt me until the end of my days. But that was war. I was under the orders of my king, as were they. And they were as heavily armed and as skillfully trained as I, and had every chance to defend themselves and trade their lives for mine.

"But you, Master Richemont. You killed for selfish reasons, for your own gain and ambitions. You murdered your own daughter, in her sleep, while she was helpless. I am not sure exactly why Jack the summoner was a threat to you, except it appears he had some idea of what was going on with you and the other churchmen. But I doubt very much if he died of a pierced lung. I think that some of the hemlock which almost killed Walter found its way into the cordial you made for Jack—Jack, a sick, badly injured man whose well-being and whose very life we had all entrusted to you. Agatha! What of that hemlock patch?"

"I uprooted it, lest an animal eat it, or someone mistake it for parsley. I saw no more. Let us pray to God that was all of it."

"Good." Geoffrey turned back to Master Richemont. "Two victims—two human beings, who died before their time because of you. As Mistress Willard has so astutely pointed out, you used your knowledge of herbs and healing not to cure, but to kill. And it was only due to the timely intervention of one of God's humblest handmaidens—my friend the white cat—that two more victims will not be credited to your ledger in Hell. I don't like hangings, I don't like any kind of violence—my years as a soldier were enough to cure me of that—but I think in your case, Master Richemont, I will gladly stifle my prejudices and turn you over to the hangman!"

The physician finally spoke. "How can you possibly prove any of this?"

"Ha! I don't need to—I am certain everyone here, including Master Canty and the Duke of Lancaster, sees the logic of my arguments, which you haven't bothered to deny. But even though I have no proof that you killed Sophia and Jack, under the law, attempted murder is as much a hanging offense as a successful one. Is that not so, Master de Coverly?"

The man of law, who had been listening intently and reflecting carefully on everything that was said, was startled out of his reverie. "Yes!" he confirmed. "Yes, of course it is!"

Chaucer nodded with satisfaction and went on. "It should be enough for any magistrate, Master Richemont, that your head is covered with the scratches inflicted by my rescuer upon my would-be murderer—or that Master and Mistress Willard, as well as myself, and probably Sister Cecily, have been witness to the distinctive smell of hemlock in the contents of Walter's stomach, of which, thanks to Mistress Willard's ministrations, he so fortunately was able to rid himself! Master Canty! Send the man with the fastest horse to fetch the magistrate," he said. "The Duke of Lancaster is coming into town with me now."

Canty stepped forward. "You'll be coming too? All of you?"

"Of course," said Chaucer. "But make it fast, Master Canty. We need to have it all done by this afternoon. Tomorrow we're going on pilgrimage, and tonight—" Here he smiled at Jeni, who emerged from the kitchen carrying a tray full of tankards. "—tonight, we're going to a wedding!"

"Master Richemont!" Agatha cried out impulsively.

The shackled physician stopped in his tracks, causing Wulfstan Canty to crash into him. Richemont stared at Agatha quizzically.

"Master Richemont, why did Sophia limp?" Agatha asked curiously.

The prisoner evaded her eyes, then breathed deeply. "I don't know," he finally replied, "but her mother suffered from weak ankles. Often she would limp when she had danced too hard and too long. Perhaps Sophia had the same problem."

"Perhaps she did," said Agatha.

With that, Master Canty shoved the physician out of the door and away from the rest of the pilgrims.

Eighteen

Walter and Jeni were married in the little thirteenth-century church, by the same parish priest who had married Jeni's parents, and who had baptized her. Walter was weak, forced often to lean on the arm of his best man, Geoffrey Chaucer, but still he was happier than he had ever before been in his short life.

Simon stood next to his father in the first row, blinking back tears. He realized now he could never have married Sophia—but that did not take away the sweetness of the memory of her, nor alleviate the tragedy of a passionate young life over before it had even begun.

He wondered: if the Brotherhood of the Sacred Silver, committed to destroying the Lollards and quenching the ambitions of John of Gaunt, had not become involved with this pilgrimage, would Sophia still be alive? Would Master Richemont have felt the presence of his bastard daughter to be so severe a threat as to justify murder?

The Duke of Lancaster, deliberately underdressed so as not to detract from the attention due the bridegroom, stood alone in the back of the church, avoiding the company of everyone, including Sir Oliver Radley. He gazed at Walter, glowing with joy and tightly gripping the hand of his radiant love, and often wondered if being so high-born had deprived him of one of the few real pleasures of life: spending the rest of your life with your one and only love. He thought of Chaucer's sister-in-law, the beautiful Katherine, whom Gaunt loved with all his heart, but whom he had chosen not to marry because of his ambitions. He sighed when he thought of the woman who was his wife, whose position as a princess of Castile had beckoned him with her siren song of the promise of a crown. How different she was from Katherine—or from young Jeni.

From his place near the altar, Geoffrey Chaucer glanced back at the strange, motley congregation that stood watching Walter and Jeni take their deathless vows. A few came from the village of St. Mary Cray, but most were pilgrims. A wave of affection for his fellow travelers passed through Chaucer, followed almost immediately by sadness. A few hopeful faces had set off with them, that day less than a week before, but now seemingly a thousand years ago, when they had left the Tabard Inn in Southwark. Those faces were now gone—gone from the ranks of all pilgrims, forever. Sophia. Jack. Master Richemont.

Don John, oddly enough, was to continue with them to Canterbury. Word had come from the local bishop that the monk was to be escorted to the Archbishop, in whose custody he would remain until it was determined what to do with him. He would ride with the pilgrims, in the charge of the intimidating Father Matthew. He was not present at the wedding, however. He would celebrate on his own, still locked up in Aleyn Atte Wood's wine cellar.

The ceremony ended; eagerly Walter kissed Jeni, then the two of them walked—slowly, so as to make it easy on Walter—down the aisle, where everyone waited to shower them with flowers. As friends and relatives descended upon the young couple, all with their congratulations, Chaucer pulled away from the crowd, joining John of Gaunt at the church door.

"If they celebrate on into the night, they won't be in any condition to travel tomorrow morning," said Gaunt.

"They won't be celebrating very late," Chaucer replied. "Mistress Atte Wood was only able to prepare a small wedding feast, and Walter is still weak. I think everyone will be up at dawn as expected, and eager to be on their way." He watched as Jeni, her hair streaming with flowers and ribbons, threw her bouquet to the giggling young girls who had come from the village. "And what of you, my lord Duke? When do you return to Westminster?"

"As soon as I can, assuming that Oliver has been able to get everything packed properly. I always have my doubts about that!"

They wandered out towards the graveyard, away from the revelers. "Will you be seeing Katherine?" Chaucer asked tentatively.

John of Gaunt sighed. "I suppose. I don't really have time, but women put so much emphasis on attention, and I don't want to lose her. I'll have to force myself to make the time."

"Would you take a message to Philippa for me?"

The Duke's face softened. "Of course. What do you want me to tell her?"

"Tell her that I miss her, that I will ride for home as quickly as I can as soon as my pilgrimage is completed, and that I want—no, I hope to find her at home when I arrive."

Gaunt sighed again. "It seems a never-ending cycle. I neglect Katherine, so Philippa neglects you. Yes, I will tell her. I trust that she misses you enough to be there for you."

They had reached the cemetery; the pause in their conversation caused them to notice that they were not alone. Simon knelt by Sophia's grave, weeping unashamedly.

The sounds of footsteps caused the squire to look up. His expression grew dark when he saw who his visitors were; without warning he sprang to his feet, ran to John of Gaunt and started pummeling his chest.

The Duke of Lancaster drew back; Chaucer grabbed Simon from behind and dragged him away. But he could not silence him.

"You!" Simon cried in anguish. "This is all your fault! If it were not for your ambitions and your manipulations, Sophia would still be alive!" He spat, the product thankfully falling in the space between him and the Duke.

"Simon, calm down!" Chaucer urged, a touch of desperation in his voice.

In the distance he could see that they had attracted attention. Sir Richard, followed by Robert, Agatha and several others, was hurrying toward the scene.

Chaucer looked pleadingly up at Gaunt. "My lord Duke, the boy is distraught!"

"No need to plead for him, Geoffrey," said Gaunt acidly, more than a touch of bitterness showing in his tone. He stepped back, as if to put as much distance as possible between Simon and himself. "Despite what some people say, I am not a monster. I am not going to throw the lad in the dungeon. I too have lost a woman I loved. When Blanche died of plague, I wanted to blame everyone—from the seamen who brought it to my father the King all the way up to God. I would have spit on the face of Christ himself had I had the chance. I understand. But keep him away from me until he calms down!"

He turned; Sir Oliver Radley had seen to the saddling of Gaunt's horse, and stood beside it waiting, while a groom held the reins. "It is time for me to go," Gaunt finally said. "If I ride hard now, I should reach Westminster by midnight." He turned, deliberately showing his back to Chaucer and Simon, just as Sir Richard approached. "Sir Richard, see to your son. And Geoffrey," he threw over his shoulder, "I will take your message to Philippa!"

"Simon, that was a very unwise move!" Chaucer hissed as John of Gaunt's massive figure grew smaller. "Thank God he was in one of his more charitable moods!"

Simon only scowled and pulled out of Chaucer's grasp. He caught Sir Richard's concerned eye. "Don't worry, father. I have every intention of obeying the Duke's orders. I will stay away from him until I calm down—and for as long thereafter as I possibly can!"

The wedding guests were carrying Walter and Jeni back to the inn, where the wedding supper was already laid out. John of Gaunt had thrown the young couple a purse of gold, then kicked up his horse. He was now disappearing from the yard, followed by Radley, Peter Adams, and the rest of the guardsmen. Before he passed behind the barn, Gaunt raised his arm and waved a farewell to Chaucer.

Simon watched him go, not without satisfaction. He then turned to his father. "I am going to the inn, to help Walter and Jeni celebrate," he said. "I trust you two will follow me." With that he strode off.

"You have a fine son there," Chaucer finally told Sir Richard. "Few men in this country would have the courage to spit on the Duke of Lancaster."

"Courage—or foolhardiness?" said Sir Richard, still wallowing in relief from his son's narrow escape.

"Aren't we all foolhardy when we are young?" asked Chaucer.

Sir Richard answered only with a shake of his head, then followed Simon. Chaucer lingered a little, wandering over to the graves.

Sophia. Jack. Brother Nicholas. All dead before their times. All victims, to some degree, of the ambitions of John of Gaunt.

Johnny. His friend. Whom, God help him, Chaucer still loved like a brother.

Tears began to fill Chaucer's eyes, both in grief for the three whose graves lay before him, and for the man John of Gaunt might have been had he not been born a Plantagenet.

How complex an animal is the human, Chaucer reflected. He stood quietly for a moment, allowing a sea of churning emotions to wash over him.

"Geoffrey—" said a familiar voice.

Chaucer started. He had totally forgotten that Agatha and Robert had followed Sir Richard to the graveyard. Agatha stood before him, gazing at him with compassion, but still impatient.

"Geoffrey, Walter will be very upset if you don't go to his wedding feast," she continued. "Hadn't you better come with us?"

Chaucer nodded, trying to blink back the tears that continued to well up. "Yes, I should come," he finally said. "We must make it an early night. We have a long ride ahead of us tomorrow."

"And not all of the tales are told," said Robert.

Arm in arm, the three friends left the graveyard and headed back toward the inn.

THE END

Epilogue

We don't know for sure if Geoffrey Chaucer ever really solved mysteries, but his experience as a spy in the days of King Edward III certainly would qualify him. It is well known that Chaucer was conversant with astrology, as a number of references in the *Canterbury Tales* are astrological in nature. He also wrote *A Treatise on the Astrolabe*, which was a tool for astrologers of the time. We don't know if Chaucer was familiar with Tarot cards, either—in fact, we don't know for sure if Tarot cards actually existed in his time. However, there was at the French court, where Chaucer often visited, an artist named Jacquemin Gringonneur, who was known to have designed playing cards of some kind for the French king. Chaucer could well have met him—and if the cards designed for the king were Tarot cards, Chaucer probably at least knew about them.

Chaucer may have actually gone on a pilgrimage like the one outlined in the *Canterbury Tales,* and in this book. If he did, he undoubtedly met characters like the ones here. Where Chaucer gave them names in the *Tales,* I have kept those names. Where no names were given, I gave the characters names out of my own imagination.

John of Gaunt is a very real character. He was the Regent for the young King Richard II at the time, and he and Chaucer were close friends. Robert and Agatha Willard, however, are figments of my imagination.

About the Author

Author/singer MARY DEVLIN is quite well known in the fields of astrology and New Age thought. She is a certified Professional Member of the American Federation of Astrologers, and was trained by Marcia Moore in karmic astrology and past-life regression. Mary's many published works include books such as I AM MARY SHELLEY, ASTROLOGY AND PAST LIVES and ASTROLOGY AND RELATIONSHIPS, and YOUR FUTURE LIVES, as well as a significant number of magazine articles. She has had a passion for medieval studies almost since she learned to read. A BA in English, she specialized in the heroic and medieval ages, including study of Chaucer and other medieval poets. Her current works in progress include *Medieval Music, Magical Minds,* a study of medieval music and its pagan metaphysical background, and *Tarot of the Rishis,* a combination book and Tarot card deck based on Hindu mythology, in conjunction with noted San Francisco artist Steven Johnson Leyba.

Ms. Devlin is also an accomplished vocalist. An Anglophile who divides her time between London and the San Francisco Bay Area, she performed for several years with a London-based medieval ensemble called The Lion Tree, and at the same time maintained a solo career concentrating on songs of the Elizabethan period. Presently she directs the Sherwood Consort, a medieval ensemble dedicated to medieval and Renaissance music of the British Isles, and of northern France. Ms. Devlin also sings with the Women's Antique Vocal Ensemble (WAVE), directed by Cindy Beitman, a group specializing in medieval and Renaissance sacred music.

Ms. Devlin has traveled all over the world, from Mexico to Australia to Kenya to all parts of Europe, and has spent a considerable amount of time in Paris, France. She is the mother of two sons, Thomas and Allan Dye, both award-winning cartoonists, and a daughter, Laura Meador, a real estate management specialist. Ms. Devlin currently lives in Richmond, California, with her son Thomas, their housemate and colleague Tim Rayborn, and two cats, Cricket and Draupadi.

Printed in the United States
1581